The Ca_ _ _ _ _ _ _
Cantankerous
Carcass

The Case of the Cantankerous Carcass

Yet More

Chronicles of Brother Hermitage

by

Howard of Warwick

From the Scriptorium of
The Funny Book Company

The Funny Book Company

Published by The Funny Book Company
Crown House 27 Old Gloucester Street
London WC1N 3AX
www.funnybookcompany.com

Cover design by Double Dagger.

ISBN 978-1-913383-20-6

Also by Howard of Warwick.

The First Chronicles of Brother Hermitage
The Heretics of De'Ath
The Garderobe of Death
The Tapestry of Death

Continuing Chronicles of Brother Hermitage
Hermitage, Wat and Some Murder or Other
Hermitage, Wat and Some Druids
Hermitage, Wat and Some Nuns

Yet More Chronicles of Brother Hermitage
The Case of the Clerical Cadaver
The Case of the Curious Corpse
The Case of the Cantankerous Carcass

Interminable Chronicles of Brother Hermitage
A Murder for Mistress Cwen
A Murder for Master Wat
A Murder for Brother Hermitage

The Umpteenth Chronicles of Brother Hermitage
The Bayeux Embroidery
The Chester Chasuble
The Hermes Parchment

The Superfluous Chronicles of Brother Hermitage
The 1066 from Normandy
The 1066 to Hastings
The 1066 via Derby

The Unnecessary Chronicles of Brother Hermitage
The King's Investigator
The King's Investigator Part II

The Meandering Chronicles of Brother Hermitage
A Mayhem of Murderous Monks
A Murder of Convenience

Brother Hermitage Diversions
Brother Hermitage in Shorts (Free!)
Brother Hermitage's Christmas Gift

Audio
Hermitage and the Hostelry

Howard of Warwick's Middle Ages crisis: History-ish.
The Domesday Book (No, Not That One.)
The Domesday Book (Still Not That One.)
The Magna Carta (Or Is It?)

Explore the whole sorry business and join the mailing list
at
Howardofwarwick.com

Another funny book from The Funny Book Company
Greedy *by Ainsworth Pennington*

The Case of The Cantankerous Carcass

Caput I: A Happy Wanderer

'Run away and hide, you mean.' Cwen scowled as they sat around the table in Wat the Weaver's kitchen.

'Not at all,' Brother Hermitage replied. It was no surprise that they didn't understand detailed theological issues like this. Cwen, while being an excellent young tapestrier, was not imbued with a cautious, careful and thoughtful approach to the world. If she could approach it, there was a good chance she would try to hit it, despite her diminutive stature and only seventeen years of age behind her. She'd even try to hit a well-armed Norman soldier. They seemed to be her favourite.

Wat himself was a worldly wise weaver, far too worldly wise in Hermitage's opinion. There was something in his eyes and in the nonchalant tousle of black hair sitting comfortably on his head that said he knew things. All sorts of things. Mainly the wrong sorts of things. He was only a few years older than Hermitage's twenty-something, so by rights should not know much more at all. Hermitage's knowledge was wide, but it was of an entirely different nature. A much better one.

Wat put far too much of his worldly knowledge into the images he made. They included fine detail of things no decent person ought to have heard of, let alone seen. Lots of knowledge but very little wisdom.

It was a good job Wat was a naturally persuasive fellow. His skill at persuading people to part with large sums of money in exchange for disgraceful tapestries came in useful when he persuaded well-armed Norman soldiers not to chop

1

Cwen to bits for her impudence, or Hermitage just for being a monk.

'Becoming a hermit is not hiding at all,' Hermitage explained. 'It is simply removing oneself from the world and living in solitude as a religious discipline. After all, my given name indicates that this should be my calling.'

'It would also mean removing oneself from the Normans and any of your duties as the King's Investigator,' Wat observed. 'And I'm not sure King William will be very supportive of that.'

'Or actually take any notice at all,' Cwen added.

'Oh, he's a hermit now is he?' Wat did a rather good impression of King William's gruff accent. 'Good, he won't put up a fight when you go and get him.'

Hermitage had to admit to himself that the life of the hermit was attractive for that very reason. It was pure chance that he happened to have worked out one or two murders and for that he was expected to do it all the time. He had never asked to be King's Investigator. In fact, on a few occasions he'd specifically asked not to be. It didn't seem to make any difference to the king.

He countered his own argument by considering that if the life of the hermit was attractive then he shouldn't be doing it. Surely no hermit should actually enjoy being a hermit, what was the point in that?

He looked at the pair of young faces opposite and appreciated their argument. He also appreciated that all three of them were still in their early years and had long, productive lives ahead of them. The thought of spending them all as King's Investigator really did make him want to hide at the back of a cave.

He stared at the kitchen table as if it would supply his

inspiration. He sat back from its surface as he thought it would more likely give him something rather nasty.

Mrs Grod, Wat's cook, had disappeared for the evening, making the kitchen a safe place to be. She prepared meals on this surface and had just fed the apprentices, several of whom were now forcing themselves through the labour of digestion. Hermitage knew that dirt and grime was good for you, but he wasn't so sure it should be used quite so copiously in cooking. While the structure in front of them was called a table, it most strongly resembled a rotten tree stump. The rot being one of Mrs Grod's most frequent ingredients.

In a reflective frame of mind, Hermitage speculated that if you could scrape the layers of the surface away one by one you could probably work out what the apprentices had eaten going back several years. He suspected the results would be quite horrific.

Needless to say, none of them had eaten from Mrs Grod's hand, although eating from her hands would probably be more healthy than eating from her plates. They had their meals delivered from the local inn, a place Hermitage was pleased to avoid with its reputation for drunkenness, violence and debauchery. The inn keeper was happy to take Wat's money and to bring their food up. He said that having Wat anywhere near his inn would lower the tone.

'And what good would being a hermit do anyway?' Wat pressed. 'You're better off with us two around. I dread to think what would happen if you ended up dragged away by William to investigate on your own.'

Cwen nodded sagely at this comment.

'How so?' Hermitage asked. He knew Wat and Cwen were always a great help, but they relied on him to resolve the mysteries at the end of the day. It usually was at the end. Just when everyone's patience was running out and before something horrible happened.

Wat sighed and smiled some encouragement. 'You usually end up accused of the murder you're investigating, you know.'

'And if we weren't there, you'd probably end up found guilty and executed.' Cwen gave a helpful shrug.

'Oh,' Hermitage said, 'I'm not sure it would come to that.'

Their looks said that they were quite confident that was exactly what it would come to. He had noted that when it came to murder and the like, the people involved could be really rather difficult. On occasion they did turn their ire on Hermitage but he'd never murdered anyone, or even come close, so it was surely nothing to worry about. Hermitage had long practise at worrying about things that were nothing to worry about.

He pondered some more and tried to think what he could do that would legitimately get him out of any more investigations. He knew that it might be his duty, a sign from God that investigation was to be his task in life. But if that was the case, God would make it unavoidable. If he could come up with a way of avoiding it, it couldn't be God's will. Even he thought that this reasoning was rather doubtful. He cast his mind around to try and come up with something that could explain the absence of a monk when you wanted one. An image of his old abbot leapt into his head.

'Pilgrimage!' he cried out.

'What?' Cwen frowned.

'Next time William sends for me to investigate, you could say I've gone on pilgrimage. He couldn't possibly object to that. Stopping a man doing pilgrimage is the most awful sin.'

'Tell him you're on a pilgrimage?' Wat checked.

'That's right.'

'Even if you're hiding under your cot?' Cwen asked.

'No, no.' Hermitage was shocked at the very idea of such dishonesty. 'I really will go on a pilgrimage.'

The frowns said that Wat and Cwen were as concerned about letting Hermitage go on a pilgrimage on his own, as they were about him dealing with murderers.

'Where to?' Wat asked.

Hermitage hadn't thought that far.

'Jerusalem?' Cwen suggested.

'Compostela?' Wat threw in.

They were all quite a long way away and probably quite dangerous. And he had met some pilgrims who claimed to have visited those places and they were most disreputable fellows. In fact their claim to be pilgrims just because they walked about a lot, was extremely questionable.[Perhaps unsurprisingly, this meeting is recounted in a Chronicle of Brother Hermitage: Hermitage, Wat and Some Druids is the volume you need.]

'I've heard very interesting things about Walsingham,' Hermitage said.

'The one near Norwich?' Wat asked, sounding unimpressed.

'That's the place,' Hermitage nodded. 'A vision of the Virgin Mary, apparently. They've built a replica of the very place Our Saviour was born and have a vial of the virgin's milk.'

'Yeuch.' Wat turned his nose up at that.

'Yeuch?' Hermitage was appalled at this reaction to a sacred relic. He knew that the common folk took their devotions very seriously - when they were doing them - but could be lax and positively sacrilegious when out of sight of the church. But Wat was an intelligent man. He should know better.

'It's not very, erm, what's the word?' Cwen moved the conversation on. 'Not very far away. That's it. For a pilgrimage, it's not very far away. Not very pilgrimmy, if you see what I mean.'

Hermitage shook his head. 'The people who live near Jerusalem or Compostela are not thought less of because they don't have far to go.'

'I bet they are,' Wat muttered. 'And in any case, if William's men turn up and we say you've gone to Walsingham they'll be after you like an arrow to a Saxon's eyeball.'

'And you're going to walk to Walsingham?' Cwen asked.

'That is normal for a pilgrimage,' Hermitage said, without a hint of sarcasm, which he couldn't do anyway.

'Through the open countryside full of Norman soldiers and robbers and worse.'

'They wouldn't attack a pilgrim.' Hermitage was confident.

'And you wonder why we think you'll come to harm.' Wat shook his head gently.

'When are you thinking of leaving?' Cwen asked.

'Oh,' Hermitage said. He hadn't really got as far as thinking about the details. Or about the implications of leaving at all, really. Pilgrimage sounded like a marvellous idea. He liked marvellous ideas and frequently had several in one week. Fundamental to the nature of their being marvellous was that you didn't have to actually do anything about them. As soon as one idea was fully rounded you could put it aside and wait for another one.

The marvellous element of this one was that he wouldn't be in when the king sent for him again. He could see straight away that just having the idea of not being in would be little use in dealing with a group of armed and angry Normans. He would actually have to leave. Such men were never willing to engage in intellectual speculation, no matter how fascinating. And they always seemed to be armed and angry. He sometimes wondered why they invaded the country at all; they didn't seem to be enjoying it much.

Perhaps he could just get ready for his pilgrimage and then be off as soon as he saw someone coming. That didn't sound terribly devout, somehow.

'Won't take long for you to pack,' Wat interrupted his thoughts. 'Only got that little book of yours and your sandals. You could be off first thing.'

'If not tonight,' Cwen put in. 'Must be very holy, setting off on pilgrimage in the dark.'

The idea wasn't sounding quite so marvellous any more.

'And if you keep up a good pace and don't get robbed or murdered or anything, you could be there in a week.'

'I expect there's lot of monasteries on the way that you can stop in.' Wat said.

Of course a monk on pilgrimage would be expected to take lodgings at monasteries along the way. Which was another drawback. Hermitage had never got on terribly well with other monks.

He always considered that staying at Wat's workshop with Cwen, the apprentices and Hartle, the old weaving teacher, was fulfilling his Godly duty; persuading the place away from creation of the extremely rude images Wat tended to produce if he were left alone. While it meant that he didn't have to go anywhere near a monastery, he reasoned that this was a sacrifice he was prepared to make.

The truth was that he didn't like monasteries very much, which was not a very positive trait for a monk. More accurately, it was that the monasteries didn't like him. Or rather the people inhabiting the monasteries didn't like him. The other monks. If he could find a monastery without any other monks he would be fine. He had never managed to put his finger on it exactly, but there was something about everything he said and everything he did that just rankled with his brothers.

And if the brothers were rankled, the more senior members of the community, priors and abbots and the like, could be downright difficult.

At one extreme sat the old abbot who had given Hermitage his name. He had been a very kindly fellow and recognised the impact Hermitage could have on his brothers. And the impacts they subsequently had on him. He suggested that if the young monk went and lived on his own in a cave it might be best for everyone.

At the other end of the scale sat Prior Athan.[Prior Athan appears in a number of the Chronicles and would probably get a series of his own, if he wasn't quite so revolting.] "Relatively kindly" could still cover the most appalling behaviour when weighed against Athan. If Hermitage could take a crumb of comfort from the fact that Athan was horrible to everyone, close examination would reveal that the crumb was mouldy.

A pilgrimage could be a real trial if it involved several nights in the company of other monks. Or even other pilgrims.

Once more he seemed faced with a choice between the lesser of two evils; a dilemma he was never able to satisfactorily resolve. It was only reasonable that a pilgrimage should not be thought of as an evil at all. Just because he didn't like the idea, didn't make it evil, as such. The Normans on the other hand, definitely evil. Pilgrimage it was then.

'There's no chance of sitting here and the king forgetting about me altogether,' he reasoned.

'I don't know,' Wat mused. 'He couldn't even remember your name last time we met.'[A meeting The Case of The Curious Corpse covers in considerable detail; some of it relevant.]

'That's true. But he always seems to recall that he has an investigator when he wants one. I don't think that remembering names bothers him much.'

'And as soon as some horrible murder turns up, he'll send for you anyway,' Cwen said.

'Yes, thank you. I think that summarises the problem neatly.' Hermitage returned to his fretful cogitation.

A silence joined them at the table as they considered the problem.

'Couldn't you invent something religious?' Wat asked.

Hermitage gave him the blankest look he possessed. 'Invent something religious?' Wat was spouting gibberish again.

'Yes, you know.'

'No, I most certainly do not know. What on earth are you talking about?'

'Well.' Wat pursed his lips as he worked through his argument. 'The Normans don't seem terribly church-minded.'

'Church-minded?'

'I know they have priests and bishops and what-not, and they go on about sanctity and supporting the church all the time. But William himself, and his man Le Pedvin, they're not very holy men.'

'Absolutely not.' Hermitage couldn't immediately bring to

mind anyone less holy. Yes, William had got blessing from the Pope for the invasion of England, but that was not the same as being a good Christian.

'So they won't know if you're having to do something religious. Something that would prevent you investigating.'

'Such as?'

'Well, pilgrimage would be one, but that seems a bit drastic. What about a festival?'

'Festival?'

'The church has lots of festivals. This could be the middle of the festival of something or other. The festival that quite categorically prohibits investigation.'

Cwen was nodding that this seemed to be a very good idea.

Hermitage checked what was being suggested. 'So I make something up and tell the Norman soldiers that I can't possibly investigate because it's the middle of the Festival of, I don't know, the Recumbent Postulant?'

'Is it? There you are then. Perfect.'

Hermitage just looked at them both. 'No it isn't. There's no such thing. Recumbent Postulant? It's nonsense.'

'Ah, but they don't know that,' Wat argued.

'But I do. You know my views on dishonesty.'

Wat and Cwen now took to rolling their eyes at one another. Something they did quite frequently.

'Pick a real one then,' Cwen suggested. 'It's always some saint's day or other. Just tell them that you're not allowed out because it's saint Oswald's day, or something.'

'Saint Oswald's day, or something,' Hermitage repeated slowly. 'You're suggesting I should use the holy saints to trick the Normans into not taking me away for investigation?' He hoped that the horror at such an idea was clear from his voice.

'It wouldn't be a trick, would it? Not if you used a real saint. What did Oswald do anyway?'

'The Blessed Oswald,' Hermitage emphasised the name. 'Was bishop of Worcester and died during Lent when he was washing the feet of the poor.'

'Perfect,' Cwen beamed. 'You can say that you can't go out because you're washing your feet.'

Hermitage shook his head in sorrow. 'I'm not sure which is worse. The Normans with all their death and destruction, or you two.'

'Us?' Wat sounded offended. 'What did we do?'

'Probably blasphemy.' Hermitage glared hard, which only got a shrug from the two weavers.

'I don't know how you two can kneel in church and then come up with ideas like this.'

'If you don't want our help, you'd better go and pack,' Cwen smiled. 'Pilgrimage or Normans. They'll both get you out of the house.'

Hermitage returned to staring at the table. He would just have to take his normal approach to the problem. Do nothing and just hope for the best.

It had been several weeks since his last encounter with the Normans. Perhaps they had forgotten about him. Or not had any murders. He thought that unlikely. They'd doubtless had lots of murders, just didn't want them investigating. Which suited him.

Such was the depth of his reflections that he failed to respond to a knock on the outer door. It was not the hammering of Norman, nor was the door simply thrown aside by someone who thought they were entitled to just walk in.

Cwen rose from her seat and went to answer. Hermitage

did now look up and felt a shiver of anticipation. It was only reasonable that this would be nothing to do with him, but that didn't help. Many people knocked at the weaver's door for a whole variety of reasons. Suppliers, other tradesmen, customers; there was a regular coming and going.

He did think that someone knocking after dark would most likely be a disreputable fellow at least. Probably after some of Wat's old works; few people wanted to be seen making those sorts of enquiries in daylight.

He leant back on his seat to look down the corridor to the front door to see if he could spot who the visitor was. All he could see was Cwen's back.

'It's all right,' she called back. 'It's only a monk.'

Hermitage felt the relief flood through him. It was probably a Brother seeking alms or a place to rest for the night. A Brother who clearly had no idea who Wat the Weaver was or the sorts of work the man produced. A fellow monk would be an interesting visitor. It was fine when monks were visitors, it was when he had to live with them that things started to go wrong.

'Monk?' A strong, mature voice queried the title with no little offence in its tone. Offence and overt criticism of the person who had used the word.

Hermitage frowned as that single word set off a distant reminiscence.

'I am no monk, girl.' The voice clearly thought little of Cwen if she couldn't spot this.

Not a monk? Hermitage thought. The visitor must be dressed as a monk or Cwen wouldn't have reached the conclusion. And that voice really was skittering around inside his head, trying to tell him something. The recollection sprang into instant clarity with the next words.

'I am looking for Brother Hermitage.'

'Hermitage?' Cwen sounded very puzzled. 'Funny name for a monk.'

'It's all right, it's all right,' Hermitage called out as he jumped from his chair and sprang towards the door. 'It's Abbot Abbo.'

'Abbot Abbo?' Wat smirked.

Hermitage was deaf to everything as he almost bowled Cwen aside to greet the arrival. He smiled and nearly skipped with joy as he took in the figure of the abbot.

It was a slight and old figure, the face creased by the years and the tonsure whitened by time. The habit dropping from neck to floor was neat and well presented, although it was little troubled by the narrow frame of the abbot, which was doubtless as thin and drawn as the face.

'Ah, Hermitage my boy,' the abbot held his arms wide and beamed as brightly as a summer's day, his scornful treatment of Cwen forgotten.

Hermitage happily entered the embrace and the two men exchanged enthusiastic slaps on the back. After a couple of these he realised that this was entirely inappropriate behaviour for a monk and his abbot and so he withdrew. Nevertheless, he felt a level of security and comfort that he had forgotten existed. If the Normans turned up now he would simply turn to his old abbot who would send them on their way with a massive flea in their ears.

He turned to see Wat and Cwen looking at them with wry amusement. 'It's Abbot Abbo.'

'So we gather,' Wat nodded.

The demeanour of the abbot dropped to mid-winter. 'This must be Wat the Weaver,' he noted with disapproval. Not the simple disapproval of a parent who doesn't like their child's choice of friend. No, this was the disapproval of a man who has years of experience disapproving of things; and knows how to do it very well.

Wat tried a smile, but it was like sending a mouse in to stop a cat fight.

'It will be interesting to hear about your connection with this man.' "Interesting" was clearly not a good thing.

'Come in, come in,' Hermitage stepped back and beckoned the abbot to enter. 'It is so good to see you.'

Abbot Abbo did step over the threshold, but not without crossing himself first. He looked around the place, which was comfortable, clean and expensive. Disapproval obviously extended to comfort, cleanliness and expense as he managed to turn his nose up while simultaneously smiling at Hermitage.

'We can go to the upper chamber,' Wat offered. 'I'll bring some wine.' He seemed quite keen to leave the abbot's company and beckoned Cwen to help him.

Still overcome by the sight of his abbot, Hermitage didn't notice that the atmosphere had enough frost to open a fair. He led the way up the rickety stairs to the large chamber Wat used for greeting customers and preparing his larger works. He gestured that the abbot should take the most comfortable chair by the window. The window with real glass.

The man did so with the sigh of someone who has had a long and tiresome journey. He closed his eyes for a moment but then opened them to gaze upon Hermitage once more. 'Brother Hermitage,' he nodded gently.

'Abbot Abbo,' Hermitage replied as part of this very informative conversation.

'You look well,' the abbot commented.

'Ah,' Hermitage said, feeling guilty about this. 'The weavers are kind to me.'

'Yes,' the abbot made it clear that this was not the sort of thing a decent monk would confess to.

Hermitage needed to get his explanation in early. 'And I believe that I have spent my time constructively, moving Wat away from his previous works. He and Cwen now produce tapestries of a much more wholesome nature.'

'Really?' At least this seemed to be news to the abbot.

'Oh, absolutely. They are currently working on a representation of Saint George slaughtering the dragon in a most pious manner.' He didn't mention that he had had to insist on a lot more clothing for the maiden chained to the rock.

'Hm.' The abbot looked like he might be willing to accept this. 'At least it's better for you than that ghastly De'Ath's Dingle place.'[It was ghastly, but the book's not so bad: The Heretics of De'Ath - where it all began.]

Wat and Cwen arrived bearing wine in the best cups and distributed it.

'We'll, erm, leave you to it then,' Wat was keen to get away.

'This may concern you, weaver,' the abbot raised a hand. 'If what I've heard is true.'

What you've heard? Hermitage thought. People tended to hear only bad things about Wat.

'You have news then?' Hermitage asked, without concern. Abbot Abbo was the only man in Hermitage's life who had ever given him any support, encouragement or even civility. It was he who had suggested the life of the hermit in the first place. He always seemed to have Hermitage's best interests at heart and if there were news, it was almost certain to be good.

Perhaps he was going to invite Hermitage to join him in some theological adventure.

'Much as it is a pleasure to see you again, young Hermitage, my visit is not purely social.'

'I see.' Perhaps a ticklish point had come up concerning the post-Exodus prophets, and only Hermitage could resolve it.

'I have always followed your progress with great interest and am pleased to note that you continue to prosper.'

Hermitage wouldn't have called the few years of his life before meeting Wat as prospering. He had survived, but then he supposed that was as much as some can hope for.

'And I hear that you have come to the notice of the king?'

'Ah, yes.' Hermitage was modest. 'I did meet King Harold, just before the events of Hastings, and then William.'

'They gave you an official appointment?'

'King's Investigator, yes. It is an appointment but is more burden than benefit.'

'You investigate deaths I understand.'

'I do. And most disturbing it is. The things I have had to look into do not bear repetition. Why do you ask?'

The abbot looked thoughtful and took a breath. 'I ask because I need you to investigate a death.'

Once he had managed to take the words in, Hermitage felt thoroughly conflicted. Of course he wanted to help his abbot in any way he could. And of course he hated investigating deaths. Perhaps without King William breathing down his neck it wouldn't be so bad. And being for the abbot it was bound to be a straightforward matter. Perhaps something about a bequest that was in dispute.

'I see,' Hermitage was cautious. 'Erm, whose death would you like me to investigate?'

'Mine,' the abbot said.

Caput II: Death For One

'Yours?' Hermitage was now completely lost. And he hadn't even started investigating anything yet. Confusion usually reigned once he got into the meat of a problem. It shouldn't start this early. 'But,' he said, his mouth open.

Wat took a sip of his wine. 'You don't seem very dead.'

'Well I'm not. Obviously,' the abbot's reply was heavy with contempt.

'Are you going to be?' Cwen asked.

'It will be an event of some note if I'm not.' He arched an eyebrow.

Cwen and Wat exchanged looks that said they couldn't understand why the man was being so rude to them.

'Is someone threatening you?' Hermitage asked. He thought it might be good to be able to stop a murder for once, instead of arriving after the event. He was regularly threatened with death himself so could appreciate the problem. The king threatened him with death to make him carry out an investigation and then those being investigated threatened him with death as well. It really wasn't fair at all. Still, at least no one had actually done anything about it yet.

'Not at all.' The abbot gave Hermitage a comforting smile.

'I'm not sure I understand then,' Hermitage sounded as confused as he felt.

'Putting it quite simply,' the abbot glanced at Wat and Cwen as if they needed the simplicity. 'People tell me that I am dead.'

'People tell you?' Hermitage asked. 'What people?' He

couldn't imagine what sort of people went around telling others that they were dead. There were some very strange heresies abroad these days, many that challenged the orthodox view of the separation of the spiritual from the physical world. He'd never come across any who said the living were actually dead though.

'Everyone.'

'People you talk to?' Wat asked.

'Of course. They could hardly tell me I was dead if they didn't say something.'

'But surely they see you talking to them?' Hermitage said. 'They can see you're not dead.'

'You would think so.'

Hermitage gave it some thought. 'I can imagine people meeting you and saying, "Oh, I heard you were dead." False rumours can spread quite easily. Particularly if you've had an illness or something.'

'I am perfectly well, and have been for years.'

'Then surely they would be glad to see that they were wrong and that you are, in fact, alive.'

'That would be a reasonable conclusion.'

'But they don't?' Hermitage couldn't understand how anyone, faced with a living person, would insist that they were dead.

'They don't. Instead they say that I am not alive at all. They tell me that I am not Abbot Abbo, or that if I am, I am a spirit of some sort.'

'That's ridiculous.'

'Why do they think you're dead?' Wat asked.

'That's why I've come looking for the Investigator. All I can get out of any of them is that they have heard from authoritative sources that I am dead and that's that. Everyone says that I am dead, so I must be. I insist that I am alive and well and they say that that's only my opinion.'

'This is most peculiar.' Hermitage took a much larger drink of wine than he was used to.

'And does it worry you?' Cwen asked, 'being dead?'

'Not personally,' the abbot replied. 'But it is most inconvenient. I have been expelled from my monastery, no one will give me alms and a lot of the people I approach have now taken to running away in fear.'

'Surely the brothers and your prior and such will testify that you are not dead?' Hermitage couldn't even imagine what it would be like to be told he was already dead. King William promising him that he would be dead very soon was different.

'They seem helpless.' The abbot took a drink from his own cup. 'My prior says that he has had it from the bishop that I died. Apparently all the necessary work has been done and it's official. Far too difficult to undo it all again. Unless I'm claiming to have come back from the dead. Which I'm not, because I haven't been there in the first place.'

'He could tell the bishop that you didn't die at all and have been found.'

'Contradict the bishop?' the abbot sounded alarmed.

'I see your point.' Hermitage knew that when bishops spoke, they didn't expect replies. 'My goodness!' he burst out.

'What?' Cwen asked. 'Have you thought of something already.'

'Indeed I have. Poor Abbot Abbo must be starving. If no one would give him alms. We must get food.'

The abbot did not protest at this suggestion and so the group trooped back down the stairs to see what could be found in the kitchen. Anything that had not been prepared by the cook would do.

Cwen found a leg of something that looked too small for a cow and too big for a lamb and tried a tiny taste before putting it on the table. It had a very peculiar texture but hadn't actually gone off so it would have to do. As she put it down she momentarily considered that old farmer who had come knocking on doors looking for his missing wolfhound. She shook the thought from her head.

Wat discovered some bread and soaked it in milk to try and take the edges off its granite-like hardness. The edges of the loaf itself would have to be removed. Mrs Grod's crust could cut through the table if you weren't careful.

The abbot blessed his meal and nibbled away with commendable resilience.

'Breakfast will be better,' Wat promised. 'We have that delivered.'

Once Hermitage, Wat and Cwen had finished watching the abbot eat, never for one moment thinking of joining him, they relaxed again with their wine.

'It's probably just a mistake,' Cwen said. 'You're obviously not dead so perhaps someone else is. Another abbot has died, the two of you have been mixed up and now it's too late to put everything straight.'

The abbot gave a long sigh and ended with a world weary "tut". 'Of course I had considered that. But if it were the case there would be a dead abbot somewhere, still running his monastery. If you can locate such a place and persuade the brothers that they are taking instruction from a corpse, I think that would resolve things.'

'Only trying to help,' Cwen muttered under her breath.

'Could you not go to the bishop?' Hermitage suggested. 'Even an apparently chance meeting might cause him to remark that you seem to be more alive than he had been led to believe.'

'Unfortunately, the bishop has left for Rome to be given his pallium.'

'Nasty,' Cwen commented.

'It's a cloak,' Hermitage explained, with a slight tut of his own. 'It is bestowed by the Pope to indicate the bishop's authority.'

'He's gone all the way to Rome to get a cloak?' Cwen asked. 'It'll take months to get there and back; if he doesn't drown during the voyage.'

'It is a sacred task,' Hermitage pointed out, quite pointedly for him.

He used the silence that now descended to give the whole problem some thought. Wat and Cwen looked bemused by the idea of going to Rome for an article of clothing and didn't have any more comments to offer. The abbot was watching him, clearly waiting for some positive suggestion to emerge. But he didn't really have one. What could he do?

His role as King's Investigator didn't seem to cover people who weren't dead at all. Investigating the living must be someone else's job. You couldn't resolve a death if there wasn't one. And who would you report to? It was bad enough going to King William and explaining when he had solved something. He didn't think the man would be at all interested in the news that an old abbot was still alive.

But he was King's Investigator, after all.

'I can go to the bishop, on his return,' he announced.

'And what good will that do?' Wat asked. 'If the man is convinced the abbot is dead, how will you change his mind?'

'I am King's Investigator.' He felt his chest swell slightly.

'You spent most of the evening saying you didn't want to

be,' Cwen pointed out. The abbot frowned.

Hermitage smiled apologetically. 'It is the people I have to deal with,' he explained to Abbo. 'The sinfulness you know. Most of it deliberate. And it does necessitate getting closely involved with the whole sorry business, frequently at risk of our own lives.'

'You always were a cautious fellow, Hermitage.' The abbot laughed, lightly.

'But,' Hermitage went on. 'If I go to the bishop with the authority of the king, he will have to believe me.'

'Which we know will be months away,' Wat said.

Hermitage thought about this, but only for a moment. 'Then the abbot must stay here until then.'

'Absolutely not.' The abbot and Wat were in perfect harmony.

Abbo got in first. 'I cannot be seen to lay my head in a place such as this. With Wat the Weaver? Unthinkable.'

'Just what I was going to say,' Wat agreed. 'And it sounds like the poor abbot has been dead for a while now. Not sure another couple of months is fair.'

Hermitage could see that the abbot might not want to be seen with Wat. Despite the improvement in his products his reputation still went before him, usually generating sniggers on its way.

Quite why Wat would not want such a charming guest as Abbo, he could not understand.

'What then?' he was lost again. He did have one awful thought, but surely his old abbot would not ask such a thing of him. Their past together and the love the old man clearly held for Hermitage would stop him making such a terrible demand. Being the honest monk he was, he had to offer though. He tried to make it sound like it was already a very bad idea.

'Do you, er, want me to go to the, erm, king then?' he said.

'Oh, heavens no,' Abbo responded, much to Hermitage's relief. 'The king would not care about such matters as this.'

'He would probably solve the problem by making you dead for real,' Wat offered, with a shrug. 'Tidy things up nicely.'

Abbot Abbo ignored him. 'No, Hermitage. I have already considered my situation, as you can imagine.'

Hermitage nodded.

'The bishop is away and so there is no one who can put the record straight, despite your new-found authority.'

'So?'

'What I would like you to do is find out how it came to pass. How did word of my death start in the first place and how has it continued? Continued despite the fact of my being here and going to tell people that I am not dead.'

Well, that sounded pretty harmless. Chasing a few rumours and bits of gossip. He would just need to speak to some well-chosen individuals and he was sure he could get to the bottom of it pretty quickly. It would be quite a bit of trouble and he couldn't really see the benefit, but it was for his old abbot and so it was the least he could do. It might even be enjoyable. Investigating something where no one was threatening to kill him, or worse. And where no one was even dead. That would be a very nice change.

'Yes.' The abbot was nodding to himself. 'There is devilment at work here and it must be uprooted.'

Uprooting devilment? Where had that come from? 'Erm,' Hermitage said.

'It is as you say. A simple rumour of death is easily put to rest. I demonstrate that I am not dead and that's that. There is more at work here. My suspicion is that someone is going to a lot of trouble to make sure I stay dead.'

'Really?' Hermitage hoped he didn't sound too worried at this development.

'Of course. At first word of my death I tried to make correction, only to find all the records have been updated and everyone from the bishop to the dung collector thinks I am dead. Not only do they think it, they know it. And even being faced with the deceased walking up and down in front of them, they refuse to believe otherwise.'

'It is a puzzle.' Hermitage was thinking it was one that could quite easily be left alone. 'But who would do such a thing?'

'That's what I want you to find out.'

'Maybe it's a joke.' Cwen got a very firm stare from the abbot.

'A joke?' he was disbelieving.

'Gone wrong, probably,' Cwen explained. 'Someone starts a joke that you're dead and before they know, it's got out of hand.'

'Then it would be easily corrected.' The abbot turned away from her and back to Hermitage.

With his back turned she stuck her tongue out at him and made a very rude gesture. Wat contained a snigger.

'Who is behind this, and why?' the abbot went on. 'That's what we need to discover.'

Hermitage thought that the abbot might be reading an awful lot into a simple mistake. It could even be as Cwen had said. Someone started a joke about the abbot, only to find it had a life of its own. Or another abbot had died and they had been mixed up. Or another fellow called Abbo was dead and everyone just assumed it was the abbot. There were a lot of possibilities before one needed to consider devilment.

He had to admit that it was unlike the church authorities to leap into action like this. It often took a very long time before news was acted upon. His own request to be moved from the monastery at De'Ath's Dingle had been submitted almost as soon as he arrived in that dread place. That was years ago and he still hadn't had a reply. Strange that the office of the bishop would act so rapidly on news of a death. Which raised another thought.

'What about the funeral?' he enquired.

'What funeral?' the abbot asked.

'Yours. Being an abbot there must have been a suitable ceremony. Great piety and devotion at your passing?'

'They're hardly likely to send an invitation to the deceased, are they?' Wat said. 'He's usually the one in the box.'

'I'm told that there was an internment. A modest affair, in keeping with my humble position.'

Hermitage nodded to himself at that. The abbot had always been an example to him. He had never been one of those who heaped comfort upon himself. He gave to the poor, he went on pilgrimage, proper pilgrimage, and he prayed with devout dedication. It was no wonder he had not risen in the church hierarchy.

'And where are you buried?' Hermitage asked. Momentarily, he thought that digging up the body would prove things one way or another. The monumental nature of such a sin soon put that idea in its place.

'In the family tomb,' the abbot explained, with a rather wistful look. 'I imagine they've already engraved my name.'

'Family tomb?' Wat asked, sounding puzzled that a humble abbot had a tomb of his own.

'The abbot's family is a significant one,' Hermitage explained. 'The abbot himself took the cloth, but other members are in positions of authority. Or, they were.' He posed this last as a question, not knowing how the family would have fared under the Normans.

'As you know, Hermitage, I have little to do with any of them,' the abbot said. 'I put all worldly matters away when I entered the cloister. Some of them still hold their lands, but how long that will last, who can tell? King William distributes the country to his favourites. An old Saxon family is not going to be high on that list.'

'Well connected family eh?' Wat was thoughtful.

'Not any more, I suspect,' the abbot noted.

'Even so.' Wat sounded as if he was making up his own scheme. 'Well connected family, one member of it suddenly appears to be dead when he isn't? I could understand if the common man was told he's dead by mistake. Everyone would tell him to stop making a fuss. Doing it to an abbot is suspicious enough. Picking an abbot from a good family sounds deliberate.'

This brought another silence to the room, and to Hermitage's thoughts. What had seemed like a harmless matter of mistake was starting to sound serious. Serious always made the thoughts in his head run for cover.

'No, no, no,' the abbot dismissed this out of hand. Seemingly offended by the suggestion and the idea that Wat might have said something useful. 'The cause will be the usual. All that Hermitage needs to do is uncover the details and things can be put straight again.'

'The usual?' Wat asked.

'Incompetence,' the abbot said bleakly. 'That's the reason most things go wrong in my experience. The people doing them aren't up to the job. Or they can't be bothered to do it right.'

'Oh, I'm not sure about that..,' Hermitage began.

'You haven't been an abbot for as long as I have. Or alive for as long come to that. What I have seen in all my years is that there are three approaches to any task that people are given.

'The first is when they don't want to do it at all and so they simply don't bother. In this situation they will wait long enough until someone else does it for them. Hardly likely to get the best results in that situation.

'The second is that they will take it on with bad grace. These are the ones who have to complete the task that the first person has not bothered with. They may be capable but they won't give it their best attention and at best do a poor job.

'Finally there are the enthusiasts. These people willingly take on anything given them, in the almost certain knowledge that they aren't actually competent to do it in the first place.'

'What about craftsmen?' Wat asked.

'And women,' Cwen added.

'Yes. How do we fit in? The ones who take pride in their work, who enjoy it and do their very best every time?'

'Not many of them come across an abbot's table.' Abbo grunted.

'It's a rather miserable view of the world,' Wat said.

'And that's why old people are so miserable.'

'Well, old abbots might be,' Cwen muttered. 'So which one was your death?' she asked, with a strong hint of irritation at the abbot in her voice.

'I thought number three. Someone had been told to deal with my death and so they got straight on with it without ever knowing what they were doing. Never checked anything, never thought to ask me. Incompetent. The devilment is in the fact that they are now trying to cover up their error. They don't want to be held responsible for something going wrong and so they deny it's gone wrong at all. In the face of all the evidence to the contrary they'll say what a marvellous job they've done.

'If I demonstrate that I'm alive it would show up their failure. Instead they'll probably boast about how well they dealt with the death of old Abbot Abbo, despite Abbot Abbo still wandering around telling everyone that he's not dead.

'If people put as much effort into doing things right in the first place as they do into covering up mistakes, the world would be a better place.'

'And you'd be less dead,' Cwen said.

'Exactly. All Brother Hermitage has to do is unravel the trail of mistakes. He should be very good at that.'

'But if it was deliberate?' Wat said. 'There's a number four. Those who do want a job done and do it very well. But it's a job that should never have been done in the first place. Self interest, deceit, dishonesty. They're probably extremely competent at those.'

'I can't imagine what anyone would gain from my death.' The abbot's disappointment with human endeavour expanded to incorporate this whole new category.

'You'd be surprised what we've uncovered in our time,' Hermitage shrugged.

He cast his mind back to all the investigations he had done. As he pondered each occasion he came to the conclusion the abbot may be right. There was an awful lot of mistake making and incompetence when you thought about it. And as he'd managed to resolve the issues in each case, the killers involved can't have been very good. Surely any half-decent murderer would be able to do the deed and get away with it.

Particularly in these trying times. And particularly with Hermitage after him. He would certainly not count himself among the competent when it came to investigators.

'I am a humble abbot. I have no possessions, no land. I have renounced my family.' He shook his head. 'No, it is simple mistake. The incompetent, blundering mistake of an idiot. All we have to do is find that idiot and put things straight. If no one will believe me when I tell them I'm not dead, perhaps they'll believe the person who started the story in the first place.'

Hermitage thought that this should be pretty straightforward. He would just go to someone who believed the abbot to be dead and ask who they heard it from. He would then ask the same question of the next person. Enough questions, and enough people and he would have the answer. He would arrive at one person who hadn't heard it from anyone. And that would be the source of the apparent death.

It might even be possible to correct the whole situation by starting the rumour that the abbot was alive in the same place, with the same person. He would be able to tell this final individual that Abbo was alive. Word would spread by the same route and everything would be sorted out. In fact, as King's Investigator, his rumour would surely carry more weight. Come to think of it, why start a rumour at all?

'A letter,' he said. The word at the end of his train of thought clearly having no meaning for the others.

'What letter?' the abbot asked.

'I could give you a letter. From the King's Investigator, signed and with a seal and everything. It would be official confirmation that you are alive. You can simply show it to anyone who doubts, including the bishop. You could even keep it by your side in case it ever happened again.'

'Twice would be a bit more than a coincidence,' Wat said.

'Do you have a seal?' Abbo enquired. 'The seal of the King's Investigator?'

'Well, no,' Hermitage admitted. 'But I'm sure we could make one. I must be entitled.'

'And when you really die,' Cwen put in, 'you can hang on to the letter and no one will believe you're dead. That'd be a nice twist.'

The abbot gave her a fully dark scowl. 'I fear brother,' he said to Hermitage, 'that if the presence of the real person doesn't convince, I'm not sure that a letter will work.'

'You may be right,' Hermitage acknowledged with some disappointment. Resolving a whole investigation with a simple letter had been a very attractive prospect.

'Excellent.' Abbot Abbo rubbed his hands together, satisfied that it was all agreed. 'I am confident that with the presence of the most excellent King's Investigator on the matter, the problems will fall away.'

Looks on Hermitage, Wat and Cwen's faces said that they weren't quite so confident.

The abbot yawned and stretched his arms out in front of him. 'We can set off back to the monastery at first light and have everything sorted out in a day or two. Now,' he turned to Wat with a far more demanding tone. 'If I must spend the night in this place, perhaps there is somewhere suitable for me to rest?'

Wat raised his eyebrows at the explicit demand. 'I'm sure I can think of an appropriate spot,' he said, rising to to his feet and inviting the abbot to lead the way from the kitchen.

Abbo nodded with a smile for Hermitage and a curt frown for Cwen.

Once they had gone, Cwen turned to Hermitage. 'Well,'

she said, in that manner that clearly indicates she has a lot more to say on a particular topic.

'Well?' said Hermitage, missing the indicators, as usual.

'He's a bit cantankerous for a carcass, isn't he?'

Caput III: Reports Are Exaggerated

Wat rejoined them in the kitchen, having deposited the abbot somewhere or other. He took a long swig from his wine. 'What a handful.'

'I wouldn't like to meet him in his monastery,' Cwen said, 'if this is what he's like when he's dead.'

Hermitage looked at them both with a very puzzled expression.

'He's awful, Hermitage,' Cwen explained. 'Rude, objectionable and demanding. And believe me, I should know.'

Hermitage looked like they were talking to him in Welsh.

'Not to you, obviously,' Wat complained. 'He seems to think you're the best thing since shaved heads.'

'Has he always been like that?' Cwen turned up her nose.

Hermitage found his voice. 'He has always been most supportive and kind. He encouraged my studies and ensured that the other brothers left me alone and stopped setting light to the parchment I was working on. He said I could always turn to him in times of trouble.'

'Including De'Ath's Dingle?' Wat asked, pointedly.

'Ah, well,' Hermitage said. 'That happened while he was away on pilgrimage. His prior, Brother Grim was left in charge and thought that I should broaden my experiences by moving to another monastery.'

'Brother Grim?' Cwen asked.

'Oh,' Hermitage clapped a hand to his mouth. 'Did I say that? His real name was Godric, that's just what the other brothers called him. Most disrespectful. He said the move would be a good thing, but of course it didn't turn out that way.'

'But you were the abbot's favourite, and when he was out of sight you were moved on?' Wat asked.

'Oh, I'm sure Abbot Abbo has no favourites.'

'Of course not.' Cwen had a very odd tone and her well-practised eyes rolled once more.

'Maybe he sees you as the son he never had,' Wat said.

'Didn't you notice how horrible he was being to us?' Cwen asked.

'Not at all,' Hermitage protested. 'He probably has strong views about Wat's old works. He doesn't know how much you've moved on.'

'I think he comes ready-made horrible if you ask me. I'm not surprised he's dead.'

Hermitage really could not make head or tail of this conversation. It was as if Wat and Cwen had been talking to an altogether different abbot. The comforting presence of Abbo was surely a pleasure to all.

'There's a thought.' Wat rubbed his chin and looked at Hermitage. 'He was very interested in what you had to say and was pretty short with us. I imagine he was the same at his monastery.'

Hermitage gave this some consideration. He was used to receiving the smiles and encouragements of the abbot but was aware that the man could turn a sharp tongue when he had to. He had never been on the receiving end himself but, now that Wat and Cwen mentioned it, some recollections did come back. 'I suppose he did keep the other brothers in order with some vigour. Only right and fair though.'

'The ones who were setting light to your parchments?'

'I suppose so.' Hermitage never knew what actually happened to the brothers who were disciplined for their actions. They did tend to give him some rather harsh looks when they next saw him though.

'So,' Wat said, 'if our dear Abbot Abbo can be a touch sharp now and again?'

Hermitage reluctantly accepted this with a shrug.

'Then there might be those who would very much like it if he were dead.'

Hermitage couldn't go that far. 'It is one thing to wish that your abbot would be less harsh, it is another to wish death upon him.'

'You never wished Prior Athan was dead?' Wat asked.

'Of course not.' Hermitage was horrified at the suggestion. 'I might have wished that he wasn't quite so close most of the time, but I would never wish the man harm.'

'Well, your abbot hasn't come to harm, has he? He's dead without being dead. Quite a happy outcome for the whole monastery I should think.'

'Very neat.' Cwen's smile was rather disturbing.

'I don't understand,' Hermitage said. 'Are you suggesting that his own monastery has reported him dead?'

'It would take some organisation,' Wat accepted. 'But if your lovely abbot is actually a pain in everyone else's habit, what better way to go? Good of them not to actually get rid of him when no one was looking, but this works just as well. In fact, we've only got this report that the bishop thinks our man is dead at all. If he has gone to Rome for this palladium of his, he may not have a clue what's going on.'

'I bet he's a stickler for devotions and the hours and the like?' Cwen painted a picture of the whole man.

'Oh yes,' Hermitage's reminiscence was a happy one. 'The abbot always made sure that we were all present at every order of the day. Even the sick would be brought to chapel at the appointed hours. It was frequently my task to go and wake the brothers for the night time and early morning devotions.'

'I can see it was a very happy place.' Cwen made the word "very" come out in quite a peculiar way.

'He went off on pilgrimage, you say?' Wat asked. 'Before you were despatched to De'Ath's Dingle.'

'That's right. He would make frequent trips to holy sites. Usually, they were close by but occasionally further afield. It was a recollection of Abbot Abbo that gave me the idea for a pilgrimage.'

'How nice.' Wat moved on quickly. 'So, what if, when he's away on one of his visits, some of the brothers got together and started speculating about how nice life would be if the abbot never came back. Of course, being monks they'd draw the line at actually doing anything about it, but perhaps one of them suggested a little game. "Pretend the abbot is dead"?'

'I hardly think so.'

'I think if you'd still been there, you wouldn't have been invited, Hermitage,' Cwen noted.

Hermitage had to accept that. He was seldom involved in any of the other brothers' activities, which suited him down to the ground, most of the time.

'And then they discover that they like this game,' Cwen continued the explanation. 'Maybe one of them jokes that when the abbot gets back they could tell him that he's dead. Just to see the look on his face.

'Except one of them goes a bit further. One with a bit more about him than the others, perhaps one involved in the running of the monastery. A prior maybe?' Cwen sounded like she'd just plucked the title out of the air.

'The prior?' Hermitage knew that the old prior had been a

contradictory fellow, always picking Hermitage up for something or other, and quite openly questioning the abbot on occasion.

'The prior doubtless knows the process for dealing with the death of a monk.'

'Of course,' Hermitage confirmed.

'And an abbot? If the abbot was to really die, I imagine the prior would make all the necessary arrangements?'

'That's right.' Hermitage started to get a little sinking feeling about how this was all adding up.

'So the prior suggests that he could quite easily make the abbot officially dead. Just send word here and there, do it quick while the abbot's away and there you are. One dead abbot. Of course, he'd have to get the rest of the brothers to play along. Couldn't have anyone who would stand up for the abbot.'

'Good job you left,' Wat said.

'But the abbot would come back,' Hermitage protested.

'He would. But it's no good him protesting he's still alive, is it? The prior has official word that he's dead. He doesn't mention the fact that he's the one who sent the word.'

'The abbot's perfectly alive and well,' Wat summed it all up. 'And the monks have just made their lives a whole lot easier.'

Cwen held her hands out to demonstrate that that was that. Hermitage gave this all the most careful thought. A lot of this thought involved looking from Wat to Cwen with a wide variety of expressions on his face. At first, he couldn't believe such a long-winded and complicated scheme could even be considered, let alone be given life. And by a prior? And monks? A prior and monks of the abbot's own establishment? If he wasn't thinking about it right now, he'd say it was unthinkable.

He weighed the idea in his head, balanced the contradictory factors and considered the various behaviours of this particular religious community as he remembered them and as they pertained to the proposal before him.

He reached his carefully considered conclusion. 'They wouldn't.' Although as he said it he thought that yes, they would. Particularly if Brother Barble was involved; the young monk who always played the most inappropriate tricks. On Hermitage, mainly.

'The prior probably expressed surprise when the abbot returned, saying that they'd had word that he died on his journey,' Cwen said.

'It's just the same as all the other investigations we've done,' Wat said. 'We look into it and see who has most to gain. In this case, it's a whole monastery full of monks and a rather doubtful prior.'

'But,' Hermitage put in, thinking that this couldn't possibly be the case. 'The abbot is so well-liked.'

'He's well-liked by you,' Cwen retorted. 'He's only met three people this evening and two of them don't like him already.'

'If he went and died for real tonight it wouldn't even put me off my breakfast,' Wat said, quite outrageously.

Hermitage dropped his head and shook it slowly from side to side in sadness. The abbot had been such a friendly foundation for him that he found it hard to believe other brothers would not share his opinion; apart, obviously, from Brother Mark who'd been put on permanent privy duty for coughing during vespers. And Brother Simeon who had to go without sandals because, after walking five miles to the village and back, he complained that his feet hurt. And of course the cook, Brother Lemuel, who'd accidentally given the abbot a piece of uncooked chicken. It still wasn't nice to think about what that had led to.

Perhaps he could see that the abbot might get tetchy now and then, but surely that was not sufficient to drive a religious community to commit such an outrage?

'We have no evidence for this,' he protested. 'Just speculation from a distance about a proposal that no decent brother would think of in the first place.'

'Only the evidence of being with the man for a couple of hours,' Cwen snorted. 'I can already tell that if I had to live with him I'd be considering something pretty drastic.'

'And you have to admit it is bizarre,' Wat said. 'You're a prior and a perfectly living abbot walks up to you and explains, to your face, that he is a lot less dead than rumour would have it, and still you protest that you don't believe him? And you're his prior? And you can't do anything about it because all the parchment work has been properly completed?'

'It's a problem isn't it?' Cwen did a very good impression of a tradesman sucking breath through his teeth while he explains to the customer how much this is going to cost him. 'I mean you say you're alive but I've got the notice here that you're not. More than my life to go against the notice.'

Hermitage gazed at them both. It all sounded perfectly reasonable while being completely unreasonable. 'There's only one thing for it,' he said. 'We shall have to return with the abbot to his monastery and see what the truth of it is.'

'I liked the idea of a letter,' said Cwen, sounding quite keen.

'But as the abbot said, if no one believes him when he's there in person, what good is him carrying a letter going to be? And he is my abbot,' Hermitage thought wistfully of happier times. Not so happy for most other people, he was now concluding. 'I have to help him and it won't be like a king's Investigation. At least the Normans aren't involved and the dead body is a lot less dead than most of them are.'

'So perhaps you and the abbot could manage on your own,' Cwen suggested. 'You know, no Normans, no death?'

'Only a monastery full of monks and priors who could be behind it all,' Wat said. 'A full monastery that Hermitage would have to deal with alone?' He left the question hanging and Cwen's shoulders sagged.

'More time with the abbot,' she sighed. 'How lovely.'

'So, Hermitage. Now you've had a chance to think about all this, what if the truth is that his community would much rather he stay dead? What do we do then?' Wat asked.

'Erm,' said Hermitage, not having the first idea what he would do.

. . .

The next morning broke bright and early. In fact, it broke a lot earlier than was welcome as the abbot roused them all for prayer just before dawn. Even Hermitage, who should be used to this sort of thing, felt a pang of anguish. He also had several pangs of guilt to go with them as he realised how lax he had become.

Wat and Cwen, whose devotions were normally directed to avoiding the ministrations of the church, despite the peril to their souls Hermitage regularly reminded them about, found themselves on their knees before a makeshift altar.

'I hope this monastery is close,' Cwen said when the three of them were eventually released to prepare for the journey and had gathered in the kitchen once more. 'I don't want to go through that every morning.'

They had tried to persuade the abbot that setting off as soon as possible would be best, in which case they had best forego prayers. The response to this was that the prayers should be doubled, just to cover the journey.

It was still too early for Mrs Grod's arrival, and with any luck, they would be out of the way before her knives started the day's work.

'It is beyond De'Ath's Dingle, to the east,' Hermitage explained.

'East of De'Ath's Dingle?' Wat asked, sounding lost already. 'There isn't much at all to the east of De'Ath's Dingle.'

As that dread monastery was located close to the south bank of the great River Humber as it joined the sea, very few people had much idea of what lay to the east of it. Or much interest. Certainly, there was the sea, but land and sea tended to merge into one another in that part of the world. So much so that a traveller would be hard-pressed to chose between boots and a boat.

There was certainly nothing worth visiting. The roads led nowhere and even the Romans had headed on north and not bothered to look to the right. Most of the old Manors in that part of the world had probably not been touched for years. A popular landing place for the Vikings, but then they landed wherever they wanted anyway.

'Well, when I say east, it's sort of over the river,' said Hermitage. 'Probably a bit north and east, to be honest.'

'Over the river?' Wat sounded more worried now. 'Exactly where, over the river, Hermitage?'

Hermitage couldn't see that the specific location was an issue. You either crossed the river on a ferry or you walked all the way around and crossed the bridge at York. That was absolutely miles away and no sensible person would walk all that way when there were perfectly serviceable ferries at various points along the river's course. Perfectly serviceable to people who were prepared to set foot on a boat in the first place. Brother Hermitage had crossed on the bridge at York.

The realisation dawned that he was probably going to have to go on a boat to get back to the abbot's monastery. It made his voice shake. 'It's down the coast from Kilnsea,' he explained.

'Means nothing to me,' Cwen shrugged. 'Do you know it?' she asked Wat.

Wat was frowning and thinking hard. 'I've been that way a couple of times, sailors can be good business but they tend to buy just the once and then ask for their money back. Pays not to hang around. So this place is in Northumbria?' he checked, with a warning tone.

'Well, yes, I suppose so,' Hermitage acknowledged. 'But the Vikings will be long gone after Harold dealt with them. And I'm sure the Normans will be there soon if they aren't already.'

'And down the coast from Kilnsea?' Wat was looking positively befuddled. 'There isn't any coast south of Kilnsea, it's already at the edge of the world. Unless you count that long stretch of watery wilderness that stretches out into the sea and vanishes underneath it quite regularly.'

Hermitage swallowed his reminiscence. 'That's the place.' He tried a smile.

'Good God,' Wat breathed. 'There's a monastery out there?'

'A challenging place for the worship of the Lord.' Hermitage quoted the abbot.

'I'll say,' Wat agreed. 'Didn't you get washed away?'

'Not completely.'

'I'm not surprised you've got a thing about going on water.' Wat gave a low whistle. 'You must have had quite a lot of it trying to get into your cell.'

'Sounds bad,' Cwen said.

'It's not the sort of the place I'd keep a fish,' Wat replied. 'It was a rough old day when I was there and no one in their right mind would venture down there. How did you ever get out?' he asked Hermitage.

'Quickly. Wait for low water and then run.'

'And you liked it?' Cwen was surprised.

'Well,' Hermitage had to admit the place itself was pretty uncomfortable, but then monasteries weren't supposed to be comfortable. 'We did spend quite a bit of time mopping up. But the scriptorium was upstairs, so that was alright.'

'And it's still there?' Wat was incredulous. 'I thought that land went back into the sea quite regularly.'

'It was there when I left,' was all Hermitage could offer.

'I'm not surprised the monks wanted their abbot out of the way,' Cwen said. 'Keeping them in a place like that. I wonder why they didn't all disappear themselves.'

'Perhaps they have, now that he's dead,' Wat said. 'Could be they cleared out of the place as soon as they saw the back of him.'

Hermitage recalled that a lot of the idle conversation in the place, whenever he caught wind of it, concerned monasteries where discussion focussed a lot less on sea conditions. The monks frequently speculated about how nice it would be to take a walk about a monastery garden, instead of having to be secured by a rope to something solid if you had to step outside the door at the wrong time of day.

They got used to the battering of the wind and the waves

but when passing fishermen, hardened from their life of trial upon the waters, pointed and laughed at the brothers from the safety of their vessels, mutterings of dissent grew louder.

He recalled that time when poor Brother Wilfrid decided he had had enough and simply walked into the boiling waters. He was carried away at great speed, faster than the brothers could follow, and was soon given up for lost. That was before the waters spun him hither and thither and then, as if content that they had had their fill, disgorged him once more, right below the monastery gate.

"Oh, bloody hell", had been his most unchristian comment as he plodded soggily back to his cell.

All these memories disturbed what had been happy recollections of his time with the abbot. Perhaps he could see, in the light of all the revolting experiences he had had since then, that it might not have been such a happy time for his fellows.

His period in De'Ath's Dingle made him see what life in an awful monastery could be. And his time as King's Investigator had revealed how awful things could be if you weren't in a monastery at all. And awful times drove people to awful measures. But even so. Monks pretending their abbot was dead was going too far.

'Ready then?' the abbot called as he joined them in the kitchen. A simple pack was thrown across his back and a stout staff clattered on the flagstones. He smiled at Hermitage and cast his usual glance of disdain, topped with annoyance at the others.

'Indeed we are, father,' Hermitage smiled a welcome. 'Once we return to the monastery we can see what the prior can tell us and move on from there.'

The abbot nodded at this, but he was frowning at Wat and

Cwen.

'We can break our fast as we go,' Wat said. 'We might catch the Inn Keeper on his way up. Certainly don't want to be here in case Mrs Grod tries to feed us.'

The abbot gazed at them all with fierce intensity. 'You keep saying 'We',' he noted. 'What's this about we? Brother Hermitage is the King's Investigator.'

'He is,' Wat confirmed, in a rather stiff tone.

'I am,' Hermitage confirmed the confirmation.

'But we work together.' Wat said no more and even went so far as to fold his arms.

The abbot stared at Cwen now.

'And me.' Her arms were even more folded.

'This is not what I expected at all.' The abbot's look bounced around the three of them now. 'I only included these two,' he waved a dismissive hand in the direction of Wat and Cwen, 'so that they would know why Hermitage needed to leave. I'm not sure that looking into this with Wat the Weaver and, erm, someone else in tow is good at all.'

'And why would that be?' Wat demanded.

The abbot didn't hesitate. 'We're very likely to speak to people of importance and influence. We can hardly do that while they're sniggering about your tapestries behind their hands.'

'Ha.' Wat smiled broadly. 'I think you'll find that quite a lot of the important and influential people are also my customers. A few careful reminders about past purchases does wonders to get people talking.'

'Now I doubt that.' Abbo shook his head sadly at Wat's illusions.

'Bishop of Dorchester a friend of yours?' Cwen asked.

'Of course not,' the abbot snapped. 'Such a high servant of

God would not stoop to engage with a humble abbot.'

'Well we've seen him stooping to engage with an awful lot more than that,' Cwen smiled, horribly. 'Haven't we, Hermitage?'

Hermitage recalled the image in question and blanched. All he could do was nod in a very reluctant sort of way.[The Tapestry of Death goes into all this in unnecessary detail.]

Wat was looking very smug when it became clear that the abbot was lost for words. 'I don't believe it,' he eventually came up with. But it was said in the way people do when they believe it perfectly well, but just don't want to.

'Wat and Cwen are a great boon in my investigations.' Hermitage spoke quickly, hoping to move the conversation on and warm up what even he could tell was a frosty encounter.

The abbot gave this thought. Painful and uncomfortable thought, by the look on his face. 'Do they have to say who they are?'

'People tend to know Wat when they see him,' Hermitage shrugged.

'At least those with something to hide do,' Wat added with a grin.

'And Cwen has a great talent for, how can I put it?' Hermitage noticed that Cwen was staring at him intently. He had better get this right. 'Confronting wrong-doers with the facts.' He smiled as he saw that she seemed content with this.

The abbot spoke. 'This is your decision, Hermitage. It is not for me to judge the right and the wrong of it.' He sounded pretty judgemental. 'Perhaps they can stay outside the monastery when we get there.' He strode off towards the door, not giving them a second glance.

'Not likely.' Cwen made another very rude gesture.

Caput IV: Family, Eh?

Stepping out from Wat's workshop to start an investigation usually gave Hermitage the shakes. Mainly because it would be in the company of Norman soldiers, at the behest of someone truly horrible, or was to look into something completely ghastly.

Very likely it would lead to threats to his own life, peril for his friends and encounters with people who came straight from the worst pages of the Bible. All of his prayers to be relieved of the burden of being King's Investigator had gone unheeded and it was only yesterday he'd been seriously considering pilgrimage, just to get out of it.

All of the investigations he had carried out had been reluctant. So reluctant that it usually required the point of a sword to get him to do them at all. He had no idea what he was doing when he started, when he was in the middle of it, and even frequently at the end. Everyone would seem happy that he had resolved matters but he could never really put his finger on how he had done it. Or what he had done, sometimes.

He had seen the method of only one other investigator, the Saracen, Abdul. That had involved dealing with one of the more awful deaths, what with King William and the Normans in the thick of it. Nevertheless, Abdul had been terribly well organised. He was thorough, had excellent attention to detail and followed the evidence meticulously.[The Case of the Curious Corpse reports on this excellent organisation of an investigation - just not by Hermitage.] Hermitage had thought that he might try the same approach when the opportunity arose. Perhaps this was it.

It was either that or stand in the middle of the chaos and just hope something occurred to him, as usual.

He always felt that he just stumbled into hopeless situations, asked a few questions and found things out that he really didn't want to know. People and events swam about in front of him until, eventually, he managed to make some sense of them. Well, he had so far.

He was utterly convinced that he never had a clue what he was actually doing and that the day of his discovery was near. King William would tap him on the shoulder and say "I know you're useless, so you're dismissed." While that would be a huge relief, he knew that William tended to dismiss people in a rather permanent manner.

This was different, though. There was a clear problem, it didn't appear to be life-threatening and it actually intrigued him. If he had developed any investigative skills they would now be put to good use. He racked his brain to think what might constitute an investigative skill and whether he actually had any. He came up with nothing.

Still, he had Wat and Cwen to rely on. They'd make sure things progressed while his mind wandered around trying to make sense of any of it.

And at least he was in the company of Abbot Abbo and was striding along the path, happy to be spending time with the man again. If there was a tricky investigation at the end of their journey, it would be worth it. He would be helping the abbot in his time of need. So much of their time together up to now had been spent helping Hermitage in his times of need. And they had been pretty frequent. It would be good to pay something back.

'You really live with these people now?' the abbot asked as they walked along the path, Wat and Cwen following some distance behind.

'I do, father,' Hermitage felt it was a confession. 'Wat was most kind to me when things got very nasty at De'Ath's Dingle. He saved my life.'

'Hm.' The abbot clearly thought Wat had an ulterior motive.

'And then I just got sort of swept up into this King's Investigator business. I'm not sure I could have managed alone.'

'And the girl?'

'We encountered Cwen in one of the investigations. She and Wat are both weavers, and the last person she was working with was most disreputable.'

'Compared to Wat the Weaver?' The abbot clearly didn't believe that was possible.

'Even compared to him. I did consider going back to De'Ath's Dingle when things settled down but Wat pointed out that the prior there had actually sent me away.'

'Who was that?'

'Athan, was his name.'

'Ah.' The abbot looked like he'd just been told the secret name of the devil. 'I have heard all about Prior Athan. You are well out of that place.' He plodded on in silence. 'But Wat the Weaver?' He could not keep his disdain for that name out of his voice.

'I have done much to move Wat on from his old trade. He no longer makes any of the disreputable images. His focus is now entirely on sacred and decorative items.'

'Really.' The abbot was still not convinced.

'Oh, yes. As well as Saint George, his apprentices are

working on a very large hunting scene for a noble at the moment and every single person in the image has all their clothes on.'

'I see.'

'And they are all really hunting. There's no one getting up to anything improper in the background. Not even the animals.'

'I find it hard to believe that the man would change in this manner, and shall reserve my judgement. If it proves to be the case, however, I would have to say that you may have done well, young Hermitage.'

Hermitage smiled broadly. He'd forgotten what it was like to be told he had done well. Mainly because he hadn't seen Abbo for years and he was the only one who ever said it.

The abbot continued. 'If you have got him to change his ways, the next step might be to persuade him to change his name, perhaps? Then everyone will forget him and the world will be a more wholesome place.'

Hermitage said nothing to that, knowing how proud Wat was of his reputation. He hoped the idea would be quietly forgotten. He also made no mention of the stock of the old works that he strongly suspected Wat kept in a locked store at the back of the workshop.

'Once back at the monastery, I thought we might begin with the prior,' he said, hoping to get the conversation away from Wat and his weaving. 'After all, he must have had official word of your death. He can tell us where it came from.'

'Grim, you mean?'

'Oh, er.' Hermitage was embarrassed.

'I know what he's called,' the abbot smiled again. 'I am not so removed from the brothers that I don't know all that goes on.'

'Aha.' Hermitage hoped Abbo didn't know absolutely everything that went on.

'He says that he had it from the bishop's own hand.'

'Then we must see the actual document,' Hermitage said. 'I doubt that a bishop would write himself about such a mundane matter. It was probably some scribe or other. If we can find out which one, we can quiz him and see where he got his instruction.'

'My, my,' Abbo sounded very impressed. 'Is this sort of thing investigation, then?'

'Part of it.' Hermitage didn't bother to say that this was the part he'd learned from Abdul.

'But how will you know which scribe?'

'Oh, they are all different. Every scribe has their own style. Some even have small marks they use to indicate which works are theirs.'

'Remarkable.'

'And the master of the bishop's scriptorium will doubtless recognise the hand immediately.'

The abbot was nodding to himself as he took all this in. 'So, we don't just go to all the people who say I am dead and berate them until they change their minds?'

'Ah.' Hermitage saw that the abbot had much more direct action in mind. 'We could do that, obviously.' He thought quickly about why it might be a bad idea, apart from the fact it was not the sort of thing he wanted to do. He had always left berating people to those who had a natural talent. He could recognise a good berate when he saw one, having been on the receiving end of many. He wouldn't know where to begin when it came to doling them out.

'We might miss someone,' he said, and then he tried to

follow his own words. 'Rumours are terrible things. There will be dozens of people who believe you to be dead. Most of them we won't even be aware of. Brothers will have told shopkeepers. They will have told messengers and farmers and all sorts. We couldn't possibly go round everyone, putting them right.'

'What do you suggest then?'

'We start the process all over again. We find the origin of word of your death. We then send out word that you are alive. By that means all the records will be set straight and the news will spread once more.'

'Including to the farmers and messengers and so forth.'

'Exactly.'

The abbot nodded more extravagantly. 'What an excellent plan, Hermitage. I commend you.'

'And then we find out why it happened,' Wat spoke up.

Hermitage turned and realised that he and Abbo had been walking so slowly that Wat and Cwen had caught up.

'Pah, that again. ' The abbot's unfriendly tone was ready to hand. 'I told you. Plain incompetence. Someone has not done their job properly and is deceitfully covering up their error in the face of the bald facts.'

'Is one option,' Wat went on, his teeth now clenched slightly. 'But you are an abbot. And an abbot of good family. Things like that don't happen to abbots of good family by mistake.'

'You'd be an expert in this area would you, master weaver?'

'Only an expert in real life, really.'

The abbot sighed his sigh of dealing with idiots. 'My family is of no concern. I told you, I put all those matters behind me when I entered the cloister.'

'That's all well and good, but things you put behind you

are in the best place to bite you on the…,'

'Yes, Wat,' Hermitage leapt in. 'But dear Abbo has been an abbot for as long as I can remember and was doubtless a prior, brother and even a novice before that. Any connections to his family would be long in the past.'

'Very long,' Abbo emphasised.

Wat shrugged as if he had given the argument up. They strolled on several paces before he asked his next question. 'Were you a younger son then?'

'No,' Abbo replied, impatient that he thought this particular topic had been closed. 'I was, in fact, the eldest.'

'The eldest?' Wat was puzzled. 'Entering a monastery? From a good family? The eldest son?'

'I was called by God.' Abbo had to explain to Wat who this was. 'A true religious calling may be rare, but in my case it was genuine.'

Hermitage was nodding agreement at this.

Wat and Cwen both looked as if they didn't know such things existed.

'I was a small child at the turn of the millennium,' Abbo explained. 'It was a time of great upheaval and worry. One thousand years since the birth of our Lord and many prophesies of what was going to happen were being offered.'

'Yes,' Wat said, very knowingly, 'we heard about some of that.'[The Case of the Clerical Cadaver is a cracker for this sort of thing…]

'And I felt the call of God. As simple as that.'

'And as simple as that, the eldest child of the good family walked off and joined a monastery. And no one objected at all, or tried to stop you?'

'Of course they did,' Abbo waved all this away. 'But my will was strong and with the support of the Lord I prevailed.'

'The younger ones took over?'

'With my blessing. My younger brother became the head of the family. And he seemed very happy to do so.'

'I can imagine,' Wat said. 'Not very often that the one due to inherit most of everything decides to go into a monastery.'

They were walking along the stretch of road through Derby just now and the place was busy with the activities of the day. Most of the townsfolk knew Wat and the weaver's workshop and most of them scowled at him whenever he showed his face. The deepest scowls, accompanied by low comments of disappointment and disgust, usually came from those who found their way to the workshop after dark and suddenly seemed a lot less disgusted.

This morning though, the streets seemed not to notice his passing at all. Perhaps it was the presence of the abbot that kept them at bay. Hermitage imagined they would be wondering what on earth was going on. Was Wat taking to the cloister himself? Had all of his sinful ways finally become too much of a burden and he had determined to spend the rest of his life in repentance and prayer?

Or was this abbot trying to commission a new work from the weaver, something really rude?

They did see the innkeeper, who hadn't even left with their food yet, so they packed it up and took it with them. They also called in at the baker to get some loaves for the journey and then at the butcher for some salt meat. The abbot raised his eyebrows at such extravagance, particularly as the butcher greeted Wat as a valued customer.

'Meat?' Abbo asked, with dripping disapproval. 'On a weekday?'

'Every day,' Wat was not concerned. 'It's good for you. And I can afford it.' He made it clear that the wages of sin, in this case, were ready supplies of the best meat.

The abbot cast his heavy look of disapproval at the weaver and saved a lighter portion for Hermitage. The young monk knew what that meant. And he would not be able to protest that he had stuck to vegetables and bread through the week and not indulged in the fine food Wat provided. His pangs of hunger were too easily swayed. And his pangs of guilt at mealtime had lost their strength over the months; the months of chicken and beef and lamb and pork. As well as the wine, nuts, honey, cheese and fruit. The list was so long it weighed on his conscience and his stomach.

As they walked on out of town the abbot passed his next comment. 'You are too worldly, master Wat,' he said. 'You concern yourself with the comforts of this life, instead of the needs of the next.'

'Ah, well, this life is my favourite.'

'I can see that,' Abbo criticised the wrong answer. 'And while Brother Hermitage has done an excellent job in changing your ways to a degree, I fear that the influence may go in two directions. You will get no credit for strewing the path of a monk with pleasure and comfort.'

'Food and drink?' Wat said. 'Yes, I know what you mean. I saw De'Ath's Dingle.'

'That place is an aberration.' Abbo ignored the problem.

'You must have had your fair share of the better things, being from a good family and all.'

'Exactly why I left it all behind.'

Hermitage was wandering along listening to all of this, grateful that his friend and his abbot now seemed capable of a conversation that did not descend into insult and abuse. They still had a long way to go, however. He was fairly confident the insult and abuse would be back.

'And you have nothing at all do with your family any more?' Wat asked. 'Not even contact or discussion of family matters. No role at all.'

'None whatsoever. Obviously, I am in a better position to attend to their spiritual needs now, but the temporal, I leave to them.'

'And your brother continues to lead the family? No contact recently, no unexpected visits, no changes that might be relevant to your death?'

'If you must know, master weaver,' Abbo stopped walking to face Wat. 'My younger brother passed on a little while ago.'

Hermitage felt terrible about that. He hadn't been taking part in the discussion but was embarrassed, nonetheless. It would have been decent to ask how the abbot's family was and find out about the death that way, not plough along and then discover that the subject of the conversation had suffered a bereavement. Wat must be feeling awful.

'Really?' Wat didn't sound awful at all. 'So who is in charge of things now?'

Abbo resumed his steady pace. 'My nephews. My brother had two sons, fine boys. The eldest of them has now taken on the burden.'

'Along with the knowledge that he has an uncle still out there who would be the true inheritor if he chose to be.'

'We do not all think in the manner of weavers,' Abbo talked down his nose.

'You'd be surprised how many do.'

'Are you sure he's dead?' Cwen asked, having been following things as well as Hermitage.

'I beg your pardon?'

'Well,' Cwen went on. 'You've been declared dead when

you're not. Are you sure your brother is really dead? It might be something to do with the family, even if not you specifically.'

The abbot shook his head in what was clearly profound sadness at such a stupid question. 'My dear girl,' he said, which obviously annoyed Cwen no end. 'My brother was a talkative fellow.'

'Really?' Cwen didn't see what this had to do with anything.

'He was always telling people his plans and his hopes and his fears. He would while away the hours in pointless and frequently repetitive conversation. It was common knowledge that a stranger, having been in his company for half an hour, would know things in which even his nearest and dearest had absolutely no interest.'

'Aha.'

'He would even tell you how he was feeling about things, can you believe? How such-and-such had upset him. How he was excited by this or offended by that. And he would even ask you how you were feeling. He wanted to understand you so that he could offer better support or help.'

'I see. A very sympathetic fellow.'

'Indeed. And it was all absolutely ghastly,' the abbot concluded. 'Can you imagine? Who wants a complete stranger prying into your business like that?'

'But he wasn't a stranger, he was your brother.'

'Which only makes it worse, in my opinion. The man lacked all semblance of dignity. A bit of self-control and less prying, that's what he needed.'

'I'm not sure I understand what…' Cwen began, thinking that the abbot had wandered off into reminiscence, instead of answering the question.

'So,' Abbo continued. 'Being of such a talkative nature, never leaving quiet a moment when there were words available to fill it up.'

'Yes?'

'I think he would have mentioned something about not being dead when we buried him.' The abbot's contempt was oozing now.

Cwen's face turned from interested to offended. 'It was only a thought. Pardon me for trying to help.'

'The family tomb of course,' Wat made it sound very grand and expensive.

'Yes. Being in my position I was able to travel back from the monastery to officiate at the ceremony.'

'That must have been a very sad moment, father.' Hermitage thought this might bring some decorum back to the conversation.

'It was, it was. But then I know that my brother has gone to a better place and sits now with the saints.'

'Perhaps he's shut up, now he's really dead,' Cwen muttered to herself.

Hermitage upped the pace a little, hoping that if everyone was out of breath they wouldn't have a chance to talk about anything. Or maybe he could get the abbot ahead once more and they could discuss more comfortable matters. It was a long time since he had been able to have a decent conversation with anyone about the lexicography of the post-Exodus prophets.

He had tried to begin with the Exodus itself one evening, but he hadn't even got started on the sons of Israel before Wat and Cwen went to bed.

On the road behind him, they were engaged in their own deep conversation and he could only imagine what wild speculations they were coming up with. He had to confess that this business with the family did concern him. Such matters were a closed book while in the monastery, but perhaps becoming King's Investigator had made him suspicious. How awful.

Of course, it was perfectly possible that this whole business was just a horrible mix up and mistake as the abbot said. If that were the case it would be an intriguing matter to unravel and satisfying to resolve. If there was more to it. If the brothers in the monastery had conspired to bring about the apparent death of their leader that was a worry. Now there was the possibility that his family were somehow creating his death for their own ends, the worry was getting legs of its own.

What had been a simple task was now getting complicated. Hermitage didn't like complicated. It came with complications. Many of them in person. And the persons always seemed to take against him for some reason. Add to that, the fact that he was heading for a monastery where the brothers had taken against him years ago and he was not a happy investigator. He could feel in his bones that it would only be a matter of days before someone started threatening him with a death of his own.

Caput V: Route Planning

'Well, well,' Hermitage said to himself when they had walked for some time in relative peace. His discussion of the post-Exodus prophets had got as far as the significance of the three horses in Zechariah verse eight when the abbot said that he needed time to think and walked on alone.

The silence had given Hermitage a chance to consider his surroundings and a nagging doubt was swimming around his head like a leech in a bucket. He returned to Wat and Cwen. 'I erm, see we're heading sort of north-east? At a guess?'

He berated himself for not having taken any notice of their direction when they left. Wat knew the way, as usual, and Hermitage had just assumed that it would be due north. That direction was preferable because it required a lot of walking on land and very little sitting in a boat.

'Of course,' Wat said. 'We'll head for Nottingham, then Newark, Lincoln and on to Grimsby. If the monastery is where I think it is we can get a boat straight there.'

The leech now climbed out of Hermitage's bucket and bit his ear, saying "I told you so".

'That would be most direct,' Abbot Abbo confirmed over his shoulder as he slowed to allow them to catch up. 'I came the northerly route because I needed to visit York and see if there was anything I could do there to straighten this out. The people of that place seemed even more convinced I was dead than those I lived with.'

'York, aha,' Hermitage said with bright if rather strained enthusiasm. 'Might be a good idea for us to go there first eh? Follow the trail back?'

'I thought the idea was to go to the source of the problem,'

Cwen said. 'Set all things right from there.'

'But York may be the source. The bishop's scriptorium.'

'Don't worry, Hermitage,' Wat gave a little laugh. 'It won't be a long voyage, and the people of Grimsby are proper sailors. Vikings, most of them, probably. They'll get us across the water safely. And anyway, direct to Grimsby is going to be seventy miles. If we go to York first you can add another fifty at least. Walking for three days is going to be bad enough. I'm not adding two more for you.'

'Hermitage has a bit of a thing about boats and water,' Cwen explained to the abbot.

'Strange,' Abbo replied, with a frown. 'He was perfectly fine when he arrived at the monastery.'

'Quite. I suspect living in a monastery that regularly vanished underwater might have something to do with it.'

Hermitage gave Abbo a weak smile but got a frown of disappointment in return. 'Brother Hermitage, really,' the abbot shook his head at an obvious weakness. 'You know perfectly well that Brother Gad made regular trips across to Grimsby for supplies. They are not a very devout people, truth be told, but Gad had no trouble with the crossing.'

Hermitage tried to look apologetic. 'Well, yes,' he admitted. 'He did until he drowned that time.'

Abbot Abbo coughed sharply.

'And the body never even washed up, like they usually did.'

'Yes, well,' Abbo sounded rather evasive. He paused and took a deep breath before going on. 'To tell the truth,' he coughed again. 'Brother Gad didn't actually drown.'

Hermitage was alarmed to hear this. 'How did he die then?' he asked, images of the Vikings of Grimsby descending on a lone monk in a small boat flooded his mind. The forecast for this journey was getting worse and worse.

'And he didn't actually die, as such.'

'He's alive?' Hermitage was delighted to hear this. The tragedy of Gad's loss had played on his mind for many months. It even emerged still, on dark rainy nights.

He then felt very puzzled and not a little annoyed. Had all that worry about Gad and about the dangers of the waters been for nothing? He was quite capable of worrying about nothing on his own, he didn't need any help. 'You told us he'd been washed from the face of creation,' he reminded Abbo, as politely as he could.

'And indeed he was,' Abbo dismissed the whole matter.

'And where did he wash up?' Wat asked, a wry smile on his face. 'Exactly?'

Abbo huffed and strode back off along the road. 'With a baker's wife in Brough, I hear,' he called back.

Hermitage just gaped.

'He will be dealt with in the hereafter,' Abbo proclaimed, confidently. 'In the meantime, he is dead to us, as is right and proper.'

'But not dead to the baker's wife, I bet,' Cwen smirked.

'Naughty old Gad,' Wat added.

'Imagine it,' Cwen sounded amazed. 'Someone declared dead who isn't really. What a world we live in.'

'Anyone would think it happened all the time,' Wat was serious. 'So Father,' he called at the back of Abbo, which was striding along at quite a pace now. 'If you declared Gad dead when he wasn't, perhaps he returned the compliment.'

Hermitage was still trying to take all this in. Could it be that the abbot he had looked up to for so long had faults? When the other brothers had told long tales of Abbo's behaviour and his treatment of them, he had dismissed them as malicious gossip. After all, that was what monks did, gossip. Particularly about their abbot. Only now was he coming to realise that there may be a hint of truth about them.

Now it seemed that Abbo may have told an untruth about Gad; he still couldn't contemplate that the abbot may have lied. Not his abbot. But if Gad was indeed alive, what else had Hermitage taken as truths of the world, which were no such thing? That the reports of the abbot's death were the result of a mistake might have to join his queue of doubts.

'A busy chap, Abbot Abbo,' Wat said, as he and Cwen walked along with Hermitage.

'Getting quite a list of people who might like him dead,' Cwen said.

'A list?' Hermitage asked. While it sounded quite bad, he was good with lists. A list might help.

'Of course. First of all the monks in this monastery of yours. Sounds like they weren't having the best of times - if one of them ran away to live with the baker's wife.'

'Rowed away,' Wat corrected, with a smirk.

'Ha, ha,' Cwen laughed. 'Found somewhere new to moor his vessel.'

Now Wat laughed heartily, but Hermitage couldn't see what on earth was funny about Gad purloining the monastery rowing boat. Supplies would have to be brought along the coast from Kilnsea, which was always a treacherous journey.

He could only watch as they gradually calmed themselves from this mysterious behaviour, which included regular references to oars and wood and rising yeast. Sometimes the two weavers made no sense at all.

'Sorry, Hermitage,' Wat got his breath and tried not to look at Cwen. 'Where were we? Ah yes. Who wants the abbot dead? Well, we've got the monks in the monastery. Horrible damp existence with an overbearing abbot?'

Hermitage raised his hand to protest.

'Despite his kindness to you.' Wat answered before the question was asked.

'Maybe because of his kindness to you,' Cwen said.

'What would that have to do with anything?' Hermitage asked, thinking that this was certainly nothing to do with him.

'How would you feel?' Cwen asked. 'If one monk in the whole monastery was given preferential treatment. One monk who worked all day in the nice, dry scriptorium and got friendly words from the abbot while he was making everyone else's life hell?'

'Erm.' Hermitage suddenly got a glimpse of what may have been an awful truth all along.

'If the abbot was horrible to everyone all the time, it wouldn't be so bad,' Wat explained. 'When the others saw that the man was quite capable of being decent when he wanted, it would annoy them no end. They'd think they had good reason to sort him out. One way or another.'

Hermitage had been on the receiving end of poor treatment from abbots and priors for so long that he hadn't thought about his time with Abbo. That had been so comfortable he didn't consider what was going on around him.

'Then there's Brother Gad himself,' Cwen continued. 'The monk who actually got up the courage to run away. And he finds the abbot has declared him dead? Prime motivation for starting a rumour that Abbo himself is dead, I'd have thought.'

'Gad was such a fine fellow,' Hermitage said. 'He followed

the Order rigorously. I'm sure he would never have stooped to such behaviour.'

'Leaving the monastery to live with baker's wives is approved for monks then, is it? Somewhere in one of your books?'

'No, of course not.' Hermitage's world was spinning around. The things that he thought were solid and secure were starting to fall off.

'We haven't even got onto the family yet,' Wat said. 'Despite the abbot's assurances, young heads of families do not like errant uncles wandering around with half a hand on their inheritance.'

'Abbot Abbo is not interested in such things,' Hermitage protested.

'I'm sure Harold wasn't interested in examining the point of an arrow at close range. Didn't stop it dropping out of the sky and giving him no end of trouble.'

'The brother may have been all right,' Cwen said, with some sympathy for Hermitage's dilemma. 'But these nephews are new to authority. They may not even know Abbo at all, apart from meeting at the funeral. For all they're aware, the man is already plotting to reappear and take over the family. Better to have him dead. Even better have him dead without the guilt of killing him.'

'In fact,' Wat was thoughtful, 'if he wasn't an abbot he'd probably be dead for real.'

Hermitage could only look blankly at this suggestion.

'Normal family life would have had him disappear the day after his brother's death,' Wat explained. 'First act of the new head of the household? Reduce the size of the household. Particularly anyone higher up. But I imagine the church doesn't take kindly to having its abbots removed like that.

What would you think? Excommunication?'

'At the very least.' Hermitage was horrified at the very idea. 'It might even be Latae sententiae.'

Now it was Wat and Cwen's turn to look blank.

'Instant excommunication,' Hermitage explained. 'Sentence passed. It's certainly imposed on anyone who attacks the Pope, but I don't know about abbots. I'd have to look it up. It might be just an interdict.'

'Excellent,' Wat wasn't prepared to wait for this. 'So any nephew is going to think twice before actually getting rid of the abbot.'

'Must have had some help though,' Cwen speculated. 'All those records and parchments and so forth. Can't imagine any nephew getting all of that sorted out on his own.'

'Hm,' Wat pondered the suggestion.

They walked on, Hermitage in a whole new frame of mind. A frame that had holes in the bottom through which bits of his mind kept dropping. Was nothing sacred or even solid? He reasoned that he should be used to it by now, but reason was no help.

Simply being King's Investigator had presented him with so many opportunities to view the deceptions and deceits of human nature, but he had always thought of these as aberrations. They were the exceptions, surely. If the job didn't involve dealing with deeply unpleasant people all the time, he wouldn't keep meeting so many of them.

He had thought that if he could get back to the life of the humble monk, he would return to a more ordered and decent way of life. Even that was looking doubtful now. Of course, he knew that De'Ath's Dingle and Prior Athan had been aberrations in their own way, but he had always used Abbot Abbo as the mark against which to measure things. That measure was sinking fast.

'Could be the bishop is in on it as well,' Wat plunged Hermitage into new depths.

'Or someone in his pay, if he really has gone to Rome,' Cwen said.

'Now, really,' Hermitage had heard enough. 'This is all getting completely out of hand. We know nothing at all, other than what the abbot has told us. He says people think he's dead. We don't even know that for sure. We could get there and find it's nothing of the sort. He is an old man now, it could all be his own mistake.

'And what if his monastery really did believe he'd died on his most recent journey? If he was gone longer than expected, it might be a reasonable assumption. Once he turned up again that would be the end of it. To leap to the conclusion that his family, his monastery, his monks and now his bishop are involved in some devious plan is ridiculous. We have no evidence.'

'Apart from Brother Gad the baker,' Cwen said.

'Which, again, we only have the abbot's word about.'

'Does he lie often?' Wat asked.

'Never,' Hermitage was confident. 'But he could be confused. Or he has told himself that Gad is alive and well rather than face the truth that his last boat trip took him to the bottom of the river.'

'I wish I could do that,' Wat said. 'It's one thing I admire about you, Hermitage.'

'What is, exactly?' Hermitage asked, knowing that it was going to be something very doubtful indeed.

'Always seeing the best in people.'

Well, that wasn't so bad.

'Yes. Even when they haven't got a best at all. Or their best is really quite horrible.'

'Don't lose it, Hermitage,' Cwen patted him on the back. 'If you did, you'd be accusing everyone of murder most of the time.'

They walked on again, at least the collection of worries he was now building took Hermitage's mind off the trials of their journey. Nottingham to Newark to Lincoln to Grimsby would be a long trek, although the towns were well spaced so lodgings and the like should not be a problem.

He passed the time by working out where they would be each day. Derby to Nottingham was about fifteen miles. He wasn't usually good with numbers but he knew this one. The people of Derby spoke of it in awe and treated anyone who had made the journey as some great traveller. Those miles could be easily completed in a day. They were all keeping a very good pace when they didn't loiter for discussion, so they could press on beyond Nottingham if they wished.

After that would be Newark. Another twenty miles, or so he had heard from the really adventurous. There would go the best part of another day.

And then on to Lincoln. Hermitage knew Lincoln very well. And the less time he had to spend there, the better. Up to his arrival in Lincoln, a direct result of all the unpleasantness at De'Ath's Dingle, he had been a plain uncomfortable monk. Thereafter things rapidly deteriorated until he ended up King's Investigator. He somehow felt that it all started in Lincoln. If he hadn't been sent there in the first place, he wouldn't be here now.[The Heretics of De'Ath is becoming essential reading, isn't it? Why not buy the paperback?]

Perhaps they could skirt the town. If they arrived with time to spare.

And after that, on to Grimsby. He had no idea how far that place was. It must be at least as far as the old monastery, after all, they couldn't be that far apart. He stopped walking and his gaze fell to the north.

'Hermitage?' Wat asked. 'Something in your sandal?'

Hermitage slowly moved his face towards Wat, although this took a huge effort. 'De'Ath's Dingle,' he croaked.

'Beg pardon?'

Hermitage swallowed. 'De'Ath's Dingle,' he repeated.

'What about it?'

Hermitage could barely get the words out. 'We're going near De'Ath's Dingle.'

Wat frowned and gave it some thought. 'Not very. It's further west.'

'Not far enough,' Hermitage mumbled.

'We don't have to actually go there,' Cwen reassured him. 'Unless you'd like to?' she added, mischievously. 'I've heard all about it from you two and it would be fascinating to see what it's really like.'

'No it wouldn't,' Wat was very serious. 'Really, it wouldn't.'

'We'll be under their influence,' Hermitage shivered.

'I think you're getting carried away, Hermitage,' Wat said. 'They're hardly likely to be out scouring the countryside for missing monks, are they? Anyway, we don't know what the place is like these days. It might be charming.'

'It wasn't built to be charming,' Hermitage groaned.

'Surely the monks who were there will have gone by now?' Cwen asked.

Hermitage sighed heavily, 'They tended not to leave, even when they died. I was an exception.'

'Don't worry about it,' Wat insisted. 'We aren't going close and we've got the abbot with us this time. The monks of

De'Ath's Dingle aren't going to be going out at night to capture passers-by and drag them into the place screaming, are they?'

'Perhaps not any more,' Hermitage admitted. It could well be that the presence of the abbot would contain the most extreme practices of the monks who'd been in De'Ath's Dingle too long for their health.

And they had curtailed a lot of their work outside the monastery walls, even in his time. The rather special ministrations to the poor had certainly come to an end. Although that was only achieved when the poor besieged the place and secured the concession from the abbot of the time.

If he did have any close encounters with the place he would simply call upon the authority of Abbot Abbo.

'What are you all muttering about?' Abbo called back, clearly impatient that they weren't keeping up.

Hermitage skipped along and explained. 'We were just saying that the road might take us close to De'Ath's Dingle.' He waited for the abbot's dismissal of that as a problem.

Abbo looked thoughtful and even rubbed his chin for a few moments. Wat and Cwen joined them and watched as he took a breath. He crossed himself and explained his plan. 'We simply make sure we're not in the area after dark. And if we are, and someone grabs you, don't scream. It only upsets them.'

Caput VI: Journey of Avoidance

After days of travel, Hermitage looked out at their surroundings and a single thought dominated his mind. Thank the Lord. He was inclined to drop to his knees to make his gratitude explicit. A very long prayer would be the least he could offer and surely Wat and Cwen would join him in this.

The weaver had insisted, in the most direct manner imaginable, that they were not going to divert through York just to avoid one monastery. He had dealt with De'Ath's Dingle once and could do it again. The abbot and Hermitage had looked at him askance but he had assured them he would take full responsibility for anything that went wrong.

Hermitage had pointed out that a simple apology for things going wrong in a place like De'Ath's Dingle was unlikely to be much help at all. Nevertheless, they pressed on towards Grimsby.

And now, this. For once in his horrible existence as King's Investigator, perhaps for the first time ever, he had managed to get from one place to another without anything of note happening at all. Remarkable.

If he were going to make a record of all his travails at some point in the future, a sort of Chronicle if you will, this was going to be one tale that did not have to go on interminably about all the troubles of simply getting to the investigation in the first place. Pages of parchment could be saved and the reader would not be bothered by the host of diversions, distractions and the plain irrelevant that usually accompanied a relatively simple task.

Mind you, there was still a voyage in a boat to come. He'd

had a few of those and was not confident the smooth nature of the journey thus far would be maintained. Still, mustn't dwell on what might, or might not happen, as Wat told him. A pretty hopeless request in his case.

They had passed Nottingham without a peep. Newark had slid by with nary a murmur. Even Lincoln, the place that had troubled him so much in the past, was a mere place of note. Being able to note it from a distance as they climbed the hill well away from places of habitation had probably helped.

Wat had clearly shared some of Hermitage's trepidation at the prospect of travel. His approach to its practicalities had doubtless helped them get here. As soon as they saw anyone coming, they hid in the bushes.

Nights had even been spent in the open, rather than in the fine inns and hostelries Wat tended to favour. Cwen had been sent into the towns and villages to purchase food and drink, which she brought back to them at whatever hiding place they favoured that night.

Hermitage stood on the crest of the last of the gentle, green hills they had just passed through and gazed over a stretch of flat, marshy land. On the other side of this, only some five miles distant, the low dwellings of Grimsby could be made out. And beyond that, the sea. Hermitage preferred gentle, green hills.

'It's not actually the sea,' Wat explained. 'It's the estuary of the river. But across that, we should find the monastery.'

Hermitage wasn't sure whether crossing an estuary was worse or better than the sea. The sea sounded more final, somehow.

'I must say that our travel has been remarkably peaceful,' he said to Wat as they walked down the hill, the abbot ahead on his own, once more. 'I am grateful that you have put yourself out to ensure a smooth passage'

'Eh?'

'Not taking to the towns. I know how much you like your comforts. Staying out each night must have been an inconvenience.'

'Not really,' Wat dismissed the problem. 'However,' he said, with a heaviness that landed straight on the place Hermitage kept his worry.

'However?'

'Now that we are within sight of Grimsby and the people who may know the abbot, we need to be even more cautious.'

'Cautious?'

'Hermitage, you're repeating what I say.'

'Ah, yes. Sorry. I'm a bit lost, that's all.'

Cwen made a noise that said she was not surprised to hear this.

'There's a reason we've been staying out at night and not going into the towns,' Wat said.

'Save time and avoid interruption.' Hermitage thought this was perfectly clear.

'Not exactly.'

'Why else?' Hermitage looked at Cwen to see if she had any idea what was going on.

Wat took a deep breath. 'Someone wants the abbot to be dead.'

'Unless it's a mistake,' Hermitage replied, with a nod of assurance.

'And if it isn't?'

'Erm.'

'Let's just assume, for a moment, that it isn't a mistake.'

'Alright.' Hermitage was always willing to engage in a speculative argument.

'If it isn't a mistake, someone really wants him to be dead and has set out to make sure it comes to pass. So far we have his family, Brother Gad and probably the baker's wife as well, and then there's a whole monastery full of monks.'

'And possibly a bishop,' Cwen added.

Hermitage shook his head at this flight of fantasy.

'And what do you think these people would make of the fact that the abbot has gone and got the King's Investigator? Up until now, it was just the abbot on his own, wandering around telling people that he was alive. Easy to ignore one abbot.'

'Particularly a dead one,' Cwen said.

'But here comes the authority of King William.' Wat held out his arms to make it quite clear that Hermitage was the authority.

He'd never thought of himself as authority before. Authority always resided somewhere else. Whoever he was with, whatever situation he was in, there would always be someone in authority to issue instruction, and take responsibility. Authority was distant and impersonal. He couldn't possibly be authority. He hadn't a clue what to do himself most of the time, let alone be able to instruct anyone else.

'Obviously, they don't know you,' Wat added.

Hermitage wasn't sure if that was a compliment or an insult.

'But king's men generally tend to be trouble.'

Well, that definitely wasn't Hermitage.

'So?' Wat asked Hermitage to think this through for himself. 'Assuming that the abbot's death is a deliberate story?'

'Erm,' Hermitage stumbled.

'Whoever started the rumour now knows that the king's man is coming?' Cwen encouraged.

'Ah.' Hermitage had it for a moment and then lost it again.

'Will he be happy?' Wat asked. In a rather childlike tone. 'Will the man who wants the abbot dead be happy that the king's man is on his way?'

'No.' Hermitage thought that no one would be happy to hear one of William's men was on the way, whether he'd started a rumour that an abbot was dead or not.

'Exactly,' Wat gave a very heavy and rather dramatic sigh. 'So what will he do?'

Hermitage put on his thoughtful face.

'I would ask you what you would do in this situation,' Wat said. 'But I don't think that will get us anywhere.'

Wat clapped his hands to his sides after a few moments had passed. 'And you're the investigator,' he said, strangely. He held up a hand and counted fingers. 'One. You do nothing and hope that it all goes away, or the king's man doesn't find anything out.'

'Bit risky,' Cwen said. 'King's own Investigator coming? Bound to be an incisive and troublesome fellow. Like as not he'll have everyone executed, just to be on the safe side.'

'Two,' Wat went on before Hermitage could get a word in. 'You try and undo the rumour and put everything back the way it was.'

'Not likely,' Cwen explained. 'It's all gone a bit too far for that. Records updated, the rumour now a solid fact with a life of its own. Can't just say, oops, sorry, he's not dead, I meant someone else.'

'Three,' Wat gave a very meaningful glare. Quite what the meaning was, Hermitage would have to wait to find out. 'You make the abbot really dead.'

'What?' Hermitage was horrified to hear his friend think such a thing.

'What's the problem?' the weaver asked, sounding as if it were as hard a decision as whether to put your sandals on the right feet. 'The abbot's dead. Everyone knows it. The bishop knows it, his family knows it, the monastery knows it, the parchments say so.'

'But, they're wrong,' Hermitage complained.

'Not if the abbot is actually dead. Suddenly they become right.'

'And it can't be a sin or even a crime,' Cwen said. 'After all, the man's dead, you can't kill a dead man.'

'You could rob him, I suppose,' Wat said. 'But definitely not kill him.'

'Ah,' Cwen questioned Wat in a rather overt manner. 'But the abbot is already with the king's man. He knows the abbot is alive.'

'Have to kill the king's man as well then,' Wat said.

'Ooh, dangerous, that. Killing king's men? Surely no one would risk such a thing.'

'On the road?' Wat queried. 'Say from, I don't know, Derby to Grimsby for instance. Lots of spots for someone to get killed on a journey like that. And you'd never find out who did it. Could be an accident. Or robbers. Vikings, even.'

'Gosh.' Cwen and Wat both turned to face Hermitage with their arms folded.

'Surely you're not suggesting...,' Hermitage began, although he could see from their faces that they were. 'I think you are getting completely carried away.' He knew Wat and Cwen were both very creative, but really they should save that for tapestry. 'We haven't discovered anything about all this yet and you think people are prowling the roads ready to kill? All over the death of an abbot from one of the most obscure monasteries in the kingdom.'

'But we already know there are reasons,' Wat said. 'His family, Brother Gad.'

'If you're suggesting that Brother Gad, having run away from the monastery to live with a baker's wife, is now combing the land ready to kill, I think your reason has left you.'

'Please yourself,' Wat shrugged. 'Personally, I don't want to be murdered in my bed by an abbot-killer.'

Ah, now Hermitage got it. 'Hence keeping away from towns and sleeping in the open.'

Wat and Cwen gave him a quiet, but polite round of applause.

He shook his head, humouring their worries. 'You'll look very silly when this all turns out to be nothing at all.'

'Better silly than dead, I always say.' Wat strode off down the hill towards the path through the marsh and to Grimsby beyond.

. . .

The sight of the approaching town gave Hermitage a whole new topic to consider. Townsfolk. The place looked quite large, even from this distance, and would doubtless have a lively and inquisitive population. Being a fishing port, many of those townsfolk would also be seafaring.

Strangers wandering in from the marshes, even if two of them did wear the monk's garb, would be certain to attract attention. Any town would gather around newcomers to examine them and find out what they wanted, when they were leaving and whether they carried anything of value. The best they could hope for from a monk would be news.

Seafarers were different, somehow. In his few encounters, Hermitage had always found them to be quite direct in their examinations and enquiries. Positively rude, some of them. Perhaps it was that time spent on a small boat with just fish for company.

And seafaring folk in this part of the world would most likely share pretty common ancestry. Viking.

Hermitage had never coped very well with Vikings, but then neither had anyone. Until Harold defeated them at Stamford Bridge, they had had free rein over much of the country, even under Edward's rule, and ran large areas. In an earlier period, the now insignificant town of Gainsborough, not far from their current position, had been declared the capital of England and Denmark.

King Sweyn Forkbeard had done that. And then died five weeks later after falling off his horse. Perhaps thinking that the place was cursed, his son, King Canute, promptly left it to its own devices.

All of this was fascinating history to Hermitage, but it was packed with Vikings. And they can't all have left with Canute.

Even the name of the place was a worry. Grimsby, Grimm's By, the village of Grimm. What a name for a Viking, Grimm? Hermitage was already picturing a town crammed to the ditches with Grimms and Bloodaxes who were only waiting for some monk to wander in.

He told himself that the monastery had regularly traded with Grimsby so there wouldn't really be any problems. He reassured himself that he was with the abbot so there wouldn't be any trouble. He comforted himself that Wat was there as well, who could handle most things life threw at him.

Told, reassured and comforted, Hermitage trembled and shook as they passed the first dwellings.

It was mid-morning as they entered the town and hopefully, the seafaring folk would be out faring on the sea. A few faces looked from tasks of field or homestead, but most of them seemed too busy at their work to be interested in strangers. Which was a relief.

Hermitage reasoned that as the place was a port, it was very likely that strangers coming and going was a common occurrence. A new face would not be a surprise to these people. They probably saw far more exotic and exciting things than a couple of monks and two weavers. The trade of the world probably landed on these shores. Even Saracens might be a common sight. After all, over the water from here lay the rest of the world. And more Vikings.

He glanced back at the people who had paid no interest in him to see if he could spot any signs to worry about. As the few faces belonged exclusively to old women and not giant, axe-wielding warriors, he tried to relax a bit. Although what a giant, axe-wielding warrior would be doing digging weeds, he couldn't immediately imagine.

'The harbour is this way,' the abbot beckoned them to follow through the scattering of houses towards the coast, which was clearly visible.

There were no walls or defences to keep people out of the place. Instead, there was a large flat marsh. Anyone heading this way would have to come via the clear path that they had followed themselves and could be easily spotted. An attack from the sea was unlikely, as it was the attackers from the sea who still lived here.

Hermitage had to think that his current choices were to stay here and engage with the residents, whatever their opinions of monks, or get on a boat and head out into the choppy waters towards the monastery. Perhaps the locals weren't so bad, after all.

From what he could see, out away from the shore, the water actually looked surprisingly flat and calm. The sun was shining and only a gentle breeze blew from the sea. If ever there were a day for a voyage, perhaps this was it.

The abbot led them down to the edge of the town where a few boats were drawn up on the strand, doubtless for repair. Not one of them was a Viking longship.

As he started to breathe more easily, seeing that things were not as bad as the picture he had created in his mind, Hermitage saw that there was a reason the stretch of sea looked so calm and still. It was made entirely of mud.

He peered hard into the distance and could just about make out a ribbon of water, glistening in the distance, but between here and there was a very large expanse of nothing much. A huge, flat region of something not very inviting at all stretched out in front of them. It even looked slightly more dangerous than water, if that were possible. Hermitage imagined that it could swallow a monk in a single gloop.

'The sea is out.' The abbot was disappointed. 'We'll have to wait.'

Off across the distance, Hermitage could just make out the shape of the monastery as it disturbed the horizon. From here, and looking like nothing more than a blob, it appeared that some passing fisherman had dumped something quite unpleasant off the side of his boat and the gods of the deep had refused to take it.

The sight of the place gave him mixed feelings. The comfort he had felt there in the abbot's presence was disturbed by the new knowledge that he may have been in a position of some privilege. The fact that the building was close enough to see but far enough away not to worry about, did not help him resolve his dilemma. But then he preferred his dilemmas unresolved.

'Looks like it's at the lowest ebb though,' the abbot went on. 'Best to cross at the top of the waters, otherwise, you can be swept up-river or out to sea before you know it.'

If those had been intended as words of comfort, they had failed. "Top of the waters" and "swept out to sea" were not words Hermitage could take comfort from in any conceivable circumstance.

He distracted himself by examining the boats drawn up on the beach, checking them for seaworthiness and safety. As he wouldn't recognise a seaworthy boat if it sailed into him, he had to be satisfied that they didn't appear to have any holes where there shouldn't be.

There was no one attending any of them, so if they did need repair, it wasn't being done now. Perhaps their owners were out in other vessels, or in the town somewhere, waiting for the water to start rising.

'Do you know a trustworthy man for the crossing?' Wat asked; he too appraised the boats and didn't look very happy.

The abbot's pursed his lips in thought. 'We always sent our own across, rather than have to pay a boatman. I had heard of a fellow called More, who seemed to ply the water quite regularly.'

'More!' Hermitage blurted out before he could stop himself.

'Do you know him, Hermitage?' the abbot asked.

'It can't be the same one.'

The abbot looked to Wat and Cwen for enlightenment.

'We came across a boatman called More a while ago,' Wat

explained. 'Peculiar fellow and about as trustworthy as a rotten plank over a viper's nest.'[The tale of Hermitage, Wat and Some Druids covers this encounter. A descendant of More even appears in The Magna Carta (Or Is It?). You'd think he was the only man in history with a boat.]

'I see,' the abbot raised his eyebrows. 'I don't think that's our More. Been here for years, I gather.'

'We'll soon know,' Hermitage trembled slightly.

'We'd better go into the town.' The abbot beckoned them away from the sea. 'At least the significant people of the place will know of the abbot of Kilnsea. They'll be sure to help us out in selecting the right man for the journey. I shall speak with the Ealdorman.' The abbot nodded confidently at this as if only someone as important as an abbot would be allowed to have free conversation with the Ealdorman. And as if he would get special treatment in return.

As the abbot wandered away, Cwen held Wat and Hermitage back and they followed behind.

'What if he's dead here?' she said.

Hermitage just looked at her. The individual words alone made sense, but joined together it was nonsense.

'The abbot,' she explained. 'If everyone thinks that he's dead and won't give him alms and the like, won't the people of Grimsby be the same?'

That hadn't occurred to Hermitage, but now it did and he could see the problem. 'Perhaps they haven't heard over this side of the water?'

'I should think they were the first,' Wat said. 'As the monastery comes here for its supplies. First thing they're going to talk about, the dead abbot.'

'Ah, yes,' Hermitage had a bright flash of an idea. 'In fact, this could be the place that first heard. In which case we can ask who told them. Did it come from the monastery and, in which case, who from exactly?'

'Brother Gad?' Cwen suggested.

'Depends when he set off for the bakers,' Wat smirked.

They could get no further with their speculations as a great cry suddenly went up from somewhere in the middle of the town. Many voices were raised at once and it wasn't in surprise or alarm, it was more like awe.

They ran to follow the abbot's trail, Hermitage immediately thinking that Abbo's arrival had been unannounced and the town's people were shocked to see that the man was still alive.

When they arrived in what passed for a village square, they saw that the abbot was indeed the centre of attention. He was standing in the middle of the space, looking with some annoyance at the crowd that was gathered around. It wasn't large, maybe twenty or thirty people, but they were all gazing at the abbot, the awe that had found voice still clear on their faces.

While Hermitage, Wat and Cwen looked on, one of the crowd stepped tentatively forward and, after some vocal encouragement and no little cautious trepidation in his approach, eventually reached out and touched the edge of the abbot's habit.

He immediately leapt back and announced his findings to the assembly. 'It's true, it's true,' he cried out. 'It's really him.'

Hermitage was relieved that they had got over this. At least one town could now see that the abbot was alive.

The leader of the audience explained to those looking on, with a terrified shriek. 'It's really him. It's the dead abbot of Kilnsea. Run for your lives!'

Caput VII: Meet The Locals

Hermitage, Wat and Cwen continued to look on as the population of Grimsby ran in all directions, screaming at the tops of their voices and waving their arms in the air to ward off the evil 'fluence that must surely descend upon their heads at any moment.

'Oh, for goodness sake,' Hermitage complained.

The abbot just stood where he had been left and looked with resigned disappointment at the scattering crowd. 'See what I mean?' he called over.

In a few, very short moments they were on their own again. Hermitage suspected that the whole town would be empty soon, the more excitable residents probably running into the mud to escape their fate.

Superstition was a ridiculous encumbrance. Granted, these were simple folk but surely they could see that the abbot who had stood before them wasn't dead. By their own reasoning, they could conclude that everyone they met was dead.

The abbot joined them now and held out his hands to demonstrate that the problem was beyond his control.

'They certainly seem to have taken the news to heart,' Hermitage noted.

'Idiots,' Cwen snorted.

'At least it wasn't the whole town,' Wat said. 'The people in the fields didn't seem concerned. Perhaps we can find someone with a bit more sense in their heads.'

'In Grimsby?' the abbot asked, with some surprise.

'What about this Ealdorman?' Hermitage asked. 'Surely the head of the town will be open to a more sensible discussion.'

The abbot shrugged. 'I think the Ealdorman was the one telling them all to run.'

'You would think,' Hermitage went on, annoyed at these gullible folk, 'that practical people such as sailors, would not be swayed by such nonsense.'

'Sailors?' Wat sounded amazed. 'To get anyone more superstitious than a sailor, you'd need two sailors.'

Hermitage looked quizzical.

'Mermaids?' Wat suggested. 'Sirens? Never sailing on Candlemas? If this lot were told that the abbot had walked here from the monastery, they'd look to see if his feet were wet.'

Hermitage sighed. 'Perhaps we had better explore the town alone then.' He gave Abbo an apologetic look. 'If we three can find someone to talk to, we may get information about why they think the abbot is dead.'

'I think we'd better,' Wat said. 'If this is the way they behave when they see him standing in the middle of town, I can't imagine they're going to let him near a boat, let alone row him across the river.'

'I shall go and sit by the boats,' the abbot said, acknowledging the sense of the suggestion. 'My presence should scare anyone off the idea of escaping by sailing away.'

Leaving the abbot to make his way back to the shore, Hermitage, Wat and Cwen wandered off into the town.

It was a simple place but a busy one. Or it would be busy if the population hadn't run off to hide under their beds. From the number of buildings, Wat estimated that there must be nigh on two hundred people living here. A remarkable number.

What was also remarkable, at least to Hermitage, was that there was no sign of any Normans. He realised that this place was at the end of the road and no one would come here unless they had reason, but it was a port. Boats would come and go quite regularly and it wouldn't take long for a Norman vessel to spot a healthy-looking port, make straight for it and tell all the locals that they'd just been invaded.

Maybe it had already happened and the Normans had gone away again, but he thought that unlikely. It wasn't an approach they'd used anywhere else. Perhaps they just hadn't met the right people yet. If the place was under Norman control there was bound to be a few of them loitering about, threatening people.

They wound their way between the buildings, through narrow passages, which presumably offered some protection from the worst of the weather. The land was so flat here that if the wind blew the sea up, it would likely be in your lap before you knew it.

The river Haven ran through the town and made it the port it was, but this watercourse was more dripping ditch of mud than free-flowing thoroughfare at this state of the water.

At least they did see some signs of life. They got some very nervous looks and no one stopped to talk, but word of the arrival of the abbot had clearly not spread everywhere. Or if it had, it hadn't scared absolutely everyone out of their wits.

There were the humble dwellings of the peasant folk, wattle and daub for the better organised, or just plain sticks and straw for the others. There were one or two timber and lath constructions of the merchants and masters, whose great wealth and extravagance allowed them to live in much better conditions and to flaunt the fact.

Hermitage looked at the variation of living standards and thought that there was something fundamentally wrong with it. He couldn't put his finger on it exactly, the natural order of things was firmly in place, but something worried him.

It resolved neatly in his head as they rounded a corner and saw the solid stone tower of the church, looking down on everyone, peasant and merchant alike.

'Ah,' he called out. 'Here we will find sense and reason.'

'In the church?' Cwen did not sound convinced.

'Of course.' Hermitage strode up to the building and looked around for indications of the priest.

The place was as simple as a Saxon church should be. It was a tower. It was a large one though and the nave inside might accommodate the whole population of Grimsby, although it would be a squeeze. The tower was much more use as a tower. Climbing to the top of that would help the town spot Vikings coming from miles away. There would be plenty of time to warn everyone and then run away into the marshes.

That the Vikings had ruled this part of the country for many years proved either that the tower was ineffective, or that the running away had gone a bit too far.

Hermitage tried the simple door and found that it would not open. 'That's strange. Why would the church be shut? Surely they can't have great treasures in this place.'

'Great treasure?' Cwen asked with some obvious derision. 'In this place? Could be a particularly shiny rock.'

Hermitage just tutted and pushed hard at the door. He felt it give slightly, perhaps there was something jamming it. Putting his shoulder to the task he gave a great heave. Well, great for him. The door stayed shut.

'What do you want?' A timid sounding voice called from the inside.

'Ah, hello,' Hermitage called through the woodwork. 'We were just looking for the priest, only the door seems to be stuck.'

'Of course it's stuck,' the voice said. 'It's stuck shut.'

'I see,' Hermitage replied, not really seeing at all. 'Could it be unstuck?'

'I doubt it.'

'Well, could you direct us to the priest then?' Hermitage wasn't actually sure that he wanted to meet the owner of a voice that spoke from behind the stuck door of a church with one door.

'I could,' the voice sounded confident of this.

'Excellent,' Hermitage said after no further information was forthcoming. 'Where, erm, where is he then?'

'He's in here.'

'In there?'

'That's right.'

'With you?'

The voice had to think about this. 'Possibly.'

'Possibly?' Hermitage asked in surprise. Granted the church was large, but surely the man on the end of the voice would know if there was a priest in there with him? Particularly as he had just said the priest was in there.

'Depends who's asking,' the voice explained, which was no explanation at all.

Wat stepped up and moved Hermitage gently to one side.

'You've got a monk and two weavers out here,' he called at the door. 'Are we speaking to the priest?'

The voice thought some more. 'Possibly.' It seemed to be a favourite word. 'Have you got anyone from the town with you?' it asked.

'No, no,' Wat said. 'Just us.'

'You're sure?'

'Quite positive. We showed the townsfolk an abbot and

they all ran away.'

'Ha!' the voice called with some feeling. This was followed by a clattering from the inside of the church as whatever it was holding the door shut was moved out of the way. After this, the door opened just enough to show a pair of eyes peering out from the dark interior.

If the voice had been timid, these eyes looked like the church mouse was bullying them mercilessly.

'There's none of them with you?'

'Them?'

A timid arm emerged in front of the timid eyes and pointed, timidly, towards the town.

'No, no. It really is only us.'

The door was moved cautiously aside and the shape of the priest was revealed. The shape did not look in very good condition at all. The man was tall and thin, his clerical robe hanging from his shoulders as if it were about to give up and throw itself to the floor. He wore a stole over the top of this, but to say that it had seen better days would require a very long memory. Hermitage thought that he was probably young for a priest, thirty or so, but just at the moment, he looked about sixty.

The man beckoned them to enter the church quickly and immediately set about barring the door behind them.

When he turned to them again, Hermitage saw a face of worry. He knew what a face of worry looked like from the inside, but here was a demonstration of what others had to deal with. He knew that he could fret about most things with very little prompting, but he sincerely hoped he never got this bad.

The poor priest was wringing his hands and had even developed a slight twitch under the left eye. This became most active whenever he glanced at the door, at which point his feet joined in with a sort of hopping shuffle.

'Are you all right?' Cwen asked, looking a bit worried about him herself.

'Eeek,' the priest hopped backwards when he realised Cwen was there. 'You're a woman?' the man's voice quivered again.

'Er, yes,' Cwen said. She must be feeling sympathetic as she didn't berate the priest for such an obvious statement.

'They're the worst,' the priest explained. 'Apart from the men,' he added. 'And the children.'

'Worst at what?' Hermitage asked.

'Have you come to take me away?' The priest demanded, ignoring the question.

'Er, no,' Hermitage reassured him.

'Please take me away,' the priest now begged. 'I've been here long enough now. I'm allowed to go, surely?' He gave them a look as pleading as a sad-eyed puppy. 'In fact,' he went on, 'you can't make me stay. Aha! Now you're here I can go and you'll just have to work it all out for yourselves. There we are.' Although he had come to this conclusion all on his own, the priest didn't actually do anything about it. He just looked even more pleading, if that were possible.

'I think you'd better sit down.' Wat stepped up to take the priest by the elbow and lead him to the far end of the nave.

The priest did so, but still quivered and shook as he sat looking up at them all.

Wat gave Hermitage a rather hopeless look as if slightly crazed priests were something he was not equipped to deal with.

Hermitage took the prompt and sat next to the shaking man.

'We've come to find out about the supposed death of Abbot Abbo,' he said, as gently as he could.

'You've come to the right place then.' The priest had a good measure of desperation.

'Ah, is that right?' He looked up at Wat and Cwen, pleased that they had made a breakthrough this early. 'You know of it then?'

'Of course,' the priest seemed to find some life. 'Of course I know of it.'

'That's excellent. We're trying to find out how…'

'And I know who,' the priest interrupted, with a bit a wild glare to go with his twitch now. He raised his arm and pointed once more out of the church towards the town. 'They did it.'

Caput VIII: It Must Be Them

'They did it?' Hermitage asked, lost for a moment. 'They did what?'

'They killed the abbot.'

'But.'

'Bound to have done.' The priest hunched himself down as if trying to stop something getting him. 'It's the sort of thing they do.'

'I'm trying to tell you that the abbot is not dead.' Hermitage moved to get directly in the priest's line of sight, but the man's eyes were flying about all over the place.

As that news eventually made it into the priest's head, he frowned and his frantic fidgeting calmed slightly. 'Not dead?' he asked.

'No, Father. He's with us. I know him from old. I'm Brother Hermitage and we've come to find out where all the nonsense about his death came from.'

'Hermitage?' The priest looked like he was trying to draw on a deep memory, so deep that it had probably drowned some time ago.

'That's right. And what's your name, Father?' Hermitage asked quietly.

The priest looked around his church, perhaps checking that he dare say it out loud. In the event, it was as much as he could do to whisper it. 'Birinus,' he said.

'Ah,' Hermitage smiled while Wat and Cwen looked blank. 'After the blessed Birinus.' They still looked blank. 'Saint Birinus came from Rome and converted the Saxons in the west from their pagan ways,' he explained.

'Ha,' Birinus gave a desperate laugh.

'Why do you think the abbot's dead?' Cwen asked. 'And more than that, why do you think the folk of Grimsby did it?'

'Birinus,' Birinus said, which didn't seem much of a reply at all. 'At least he managed to convert his pagans.'

Hermitage, Wat and Cwen shared a look of alarmed insight. Even Hermitage got this one straight away.

'Are you saying the people of Grimsby are pagan?' he asked.

'This lot?' Birinus seemed to be relaxing a bit. 'They'd give pagans a bad name.'

'And they practise,' Hermitage found it hard to say the words, 'the "old religion"?'

'The abbot said they weren't very devout,' Cwen reminded them. 'Another example of his unique interpretations of events?'

'To be honest,' Birinus sagged, 'I'm not sure they practise anything properly. They certainly don't come to church, despite my warnings and imprecations. I've given up now. There's no point. Leave them to it, that's what I say.' The man's hysterics started to rise once more.

Hermitage shook his head in sympathy for Birinus's predicament and state of health. He wondered how long the poor man had been here, a priest on his own among pagans, trying to convert them without success. Doubtless, this church had a minster to report to but that was probably days' journey away.

'What makes you think they're still pagan then?' Hermitage asked, finding it hard to really believe that there were still pagans in England. Scotland and Wales, certainly, but not England. 'It could be that they are just lost souls.'

'I don't need to think they're still pagan,' Birinus gave a contemptuous nod towards the town. 'It's perfectly obvious.

When I tell them of God, I talk of the Father, Son and Holy Spirit.' Hermitage and Birinus made the sign of the Cross. 'When they talk of God it's Woden, Thunor and Tiw.'

'Oh dear.' Hermitage now appreciated why Birinus was in the condition he was.

'And another name for Woden is Grimm. Guess the name of the place where we live?' He gave a hollow laugh at this. 'And they have festivals on all the wrong days. They pray for the sun to come back after winter. They have bonefires and put things on them, including bones.' Birinus gave a little shiver. 'And they make sacrifices.'

Hermitage was horrified at this. 'Sacrifices?' he asked. Even Wat and Cwen looked a bit nervous at this. 'What sort of sacrifices?'

'I don't know, do I?' Birinus protested. 'I'm hardly going to go to them.'

'But you know of them?' Wat asked. 'Actual sacrifices? People or animals going missing?'

'Well,' Birinus didn't seem quite so sure now. 'It's the sort of thing pagans do.'

'But you've never actually seen one.' Wat looked to Cwen and Hermitage and raised his eyebrows.

'They do the prayers,' Birinus protested. 'And I've seen the bonefires. Great big things.'

'I think I'd have a big fire now and again if I lived out here,' Cwen said.

'So why do you think they killed the abbot?' Hermitage asked. 'Did they tell you they'd done it?

'Didn't need to,' Birinus replied with a shrug. 'I saw it for myself.'

'You saw it?' Hermitage knew poor Birinus was wrong now. 'But I told you he's alive. He came to us in Derby, he's down by the boats at this very moment.'

'Look,' Birinus said, in the manner of a lecturing prior. 'It's quite simple. That brother who used to come over in the boat for supplies.'

'Gad?'

'That's the one.'

'Didn't he notice they were pagans?' Cwen asked, quite rudely, in Hermitage's mind. He waved her to be quiet.

'The last time he came over was when the weather was good, doesn't happen much in these parts so I remember it well. It was also on a rising water, which I thought was a bit odd. He had to struggle against the current and gave himself a lot of work not to go straight up river. Anyway, he gathered up his goods as normal, paid everyone, right and proper and then gets ready to leave.'

'I see,' Hermitage said, not really knowing where this was going.

'But he's setting off on the rising water as well. Very peculiar, I thought, giving himself the trouble both ways. Then, just as he's pushing off from shore someone comes running down the beach from the town, hops in the boat with him and off they go. Well, I thought it was some fool who wanted the life of the monk. Probably young Lop, he's always moaning about his lot.'

'But it wasn't?' Hermitage asked, thinking that, for a priest, Birinus was getting a bit carried away with his gossip now.

'No, it wasn't. And do they head back to the monastery? No, they do not. Straight up the river, they go.'

'Aha.'

'Full speed on the rising water. And next thing is the baker comes shouting out of town, asking where his wife has gone.'

'Oh.' Hermitage, suddenly felt quite guilty, even though

94

none of this was anything to do with him.

'So that's where he got his baker's wife,' Cwen snorted.

Hermitage tried to ignore this. 'I'm not sure I see what this has to do with the death of the abbot.'

'I haven't finished yet,' Birinus snapped. 'You can imagine that the baker wants the next boat to go after her.'

Hermitage just nodded.

'But then we find that Gad has thrown all the oars into the water and they're heading off up the river with him and the wind is offshore so we'd never catch up.'

'Very difficult,' Hermitage felt he had to say something.

'So what can they do but curse him. A real pagan curse, then and there, right on the beach.'

'Terrible.'

'Of course, I try to tell them that curses aren't Christian and won't do anything anyway, except risk their eternal souls.'

'Naturally.'

'But they don't take any notice of me. Never have done. And then someone suggests that they should curse the monastery as well. They say as how it must all be the abbot's fault for not controlling his monks. So they curse the abbot too. They even had a special bonfire for that one.'

'And you think their curse killed the abbot?' Hermitage asked with disbelief.

'Of course it did,' Birinus confirmed. 'Next thing we hear is that the abbot is dead. So there you are.'

'That explains why they ran away when they saw him' Cwen said.

'Father, Father,' Hermitage tried to sound as sympathetic as he could. 'You said yourself that curses have no effect.'

'These were good ones,' Birinus complained.

'I'm sure. But they didn't work. The abbot is not dead. As far as we know, Gad is not dead either. The abbot reports that he is living in Brough with the baker's wife.'

Birinus frowned at this. 'Brough?' he asked. It was as if the name of a sensible, simple town tugged at him from the panic in which he lived.

'And the abbot has appeared in the town square,' Cwen reported. 'Scared the life out of your pagans.'

Birinus gave a half-hearted smile at this.

'We could probably get him to march through the place waving his arms about and moaning at people if you like,' Wat added.

'Now, now,' Hermitage calmed them. 'Let's not get as carried away as the superstitious folk who live here.'

Wat and Cwen looked disappointed at this as it seemed they had a number of other good ideas about what they could do with a dead abbot.

Hermitage turned back to the priest. 'How did you hear that the abbot was dead? It is plain to us that he isn't, but someone has spread reports that he is. We're trying to find out where these stories have come from.'

Birinus gave this some thought. 'Not sure, really. Everyone was talking about it. And about how successful their curse had been.'

'But who talked about it first? Can you recall who the first person to tell you was? Was it one of the monks?'

'From the monastery?' Birinus sounded surprised.

'Yes.'

'They're hardly likely to come back here, are they? Not when one of them ran off with our baker's wife. They'd have a very bad time of it. A curse would be the least they got away with.'

'I suppose so.'

'And Gad sailed off with their boat,' Birinus pointed out. 'They're a bit stuck themselves now.'

'Then who?'

Birinus looked to the ceiling, to see if that held any inspiration for him. 'I think I got it from the Ealdorman,' he said. 'None of the others come anywhere near me, so most likely him.'

'The Ealdorman,' Hermitage mused. 'Although he seems the worst of the community, he is the leader. He should be able to tell us something.'

'Going to be a bit tricky,' Wat said. 'Him running away and everything?'

'And is he likely to talk to us anyway?' Cwen asked. 'Us being the ones who brought the abbot back from the dead.'

'Now there's a thought.,' Wat had a rather troubling smile on his face.

'What?' Hermitage asked cautiously and slowly, knowing in his heart that this was going to be a very bad idea. Bad in every sense of the word.

'We go and find the Ealdorman, just us three, and say we need to talk to him urgently about the dead abbot.'

'And then?' Hermitage asked.

Wat's smile was broader now and had moved from troubling to a different realm altogether; a realm Hermitage had caught a glimpse of before, usually when there was an extremely rude tapestry involved.

'I'll tell you as we walk,' Wat tapped the side of his nose. 'Should be good though. And there's a special part for you.'

Caput IX: A Good Burning

Locating the Ealdorman was surprisingly easy. He was directing the creation of a large fire in the middle of the town. People emerged from the streets and the shadows of the houses to pile the supplies they were bringing onto the growing mound in the main space, while the Ealdorman fussed about, moving things; moving things from where they were perfectly satisfactory to another spot half an inch away, just to show who was Ealdorman.

There were a lot more people this time, it looked like most of the town had turned out for this event. Although a lot of them didn't actually look very happy in their work.

Much of the bonefire was made of scraps and larger pieces of wood, many of them washed up on the beach by the look. Some families seemed to be using the opportunity to get rid of a lot of their rubbish, dumping broken pots and bones, none of which would burn anyway. There was also much emptying of pots and buckets containing material that turned the nose up, even before it was on fire.

Hermitage, Wat and Cwen stood quietly in the corner of the square watching the building programme. One or two people noticed them, probably because they weren't putting anything on the fire, but they paid little heed.

The hardest looks Wat and Cwen were getting were from Hermitage, who remained very critical of the plan Wat had outlined.

One local shuffled past, perhaps on his way to the beach to find more wood. 'Another bloody fire eh?' he muttered at them, with a backward nod to the Ealdorman, accompanied by a very pained expression on his face.

'Looks like the Ealdorman likes a fire,' Wat said after the local had wandered on. 'Even if the rest aren't so keen.'

Hermitage had noticed something in the opposite corner of the square and tugged at Wat's sleeve to draw it to his attention.

'What's that?' he asked, a slight tremble in his voice.

'Don't know,' Wat replied. 'Pile of old rags, I think.'

'Pile of old rags in the shape of a habit, being stuffed with straw, I think you'll find.' Hermitage swallowed.

'Ah,' Cwen smiled. 'They're probably going to burn an effigy of the abbot. What with him coming back from the dead and all.'

Hermitage, pale of face and slack of jaw could only mumble. 'That's disgraceful. And sinful. How could they do such a thing?'

'Pagans?' Cwen reminded him. 'Building bonefires to ward off the evil of the dead coming back to life. Sounds pretty standard pagan to me.'

Hermitage shrank to the rear of the weavers, in case anyone spotted that there was a ready-filled habit just standing there.

As the fire grew, the Ealdorman stood back to admire all the work that he had not done. One other man was appraising the construction as well. This fellow approached the Ealdorman and, by the waving of arms and direction of pointing, seemed to be suggesting that the fire was a bit close to a nearby building. Most likely the building owned by the protester.

The Ealdorman waved these objections away in a rather peremptory manner, which was doing nothing for the temper of the building owner.

Clearly not satisfied that he was getting a fair hearing, the man started picking up pieces from the side of the fire nearest his house and throwing them across to the opposite side.

The Ealdorman interrupted this and tried to drag the man away, making imprecations to the sky at the same time, by the look of it.

The argument became so heated that the words rose to be heard across the whole area.

'You've built it too bloody high,' the man said. 'Again.' Perhaps this was a common failing of the Ealdorman. 'You're going to have my house down this time. Why don't you build the bloody things outside your own house for a change.'

'You fool,' the Ealdorman responded, with passion. 'The dead abbot has come back. Do you want him in your house? Well? Do you? Because that's what you'll get. First place he'll come back is the square. That's where he was before. And what'll he do then? He'll come into your house, it's nearest.'

'Not if it's burnt down he won't,' the man protested. 'And we've only got your word he's come back anyway.'

'I saw him, I touched him,' the Ealdorman almost screamed. And the others, they were here.' He gestured to the others in the square, now watching the altercation with interest.

There were a few nods from people who must have been there at the time.

'Well,' one quiet voice said, 'I think I saw an abbot. Or could have been a monk.'

'Shut up,' the Ealdorman instructed. 'I know a dead abbot when I see one walking about. The curse obviously didn't work completely. His shade has come back to taunt us. The fire will get rid of him once and for all.'

'What is it about you and fires?' the impudent building owner enquired. 'Every bloody day it's a fire for this and fire for that. It's no wonder we're all freezing in the winter. Got nothing left to burn.'

'And I should be mending my nets,' another voice called. 'Just get settled down and it's "got to build another fire for the Ealdorman." What's he warding off this time?'

'He's warding off the spirit of a dead abbot,' the Ealdorman snapped. 'The one you all cursed who has now come back to take you.'

'Well,' the thoughtful net-mender said, 'it wasn't actually us that cursed him was it? It was you and the baker.'

The home-owner took up the argument. 'Be a lot easier to let the dead abbot have them both and then we could get back to work.'

Wat nudged Hermitage, 'This could be our moment.' He stepped into the square, followed by Cwen. Hermitage felt it probably wise to keep his own inflammatory habit away from this excitable crowd. Particularly as he was in it at the moment.

The outlying layers of the crowd noticed the arrival of Wat and Cwen, and just gave them the looks any strangers would get if they wandered into the middle of pagan fire magic.

The weavers' appearance seemed to give the Ealdorman good reason to move away from the debate with his townsfolk. 'There they are,' he cried.

'That's not an abbot,' someone remarked.

'It's the ones who were with him though.' The Ealdorman scanned the crowd, giving them encouraging looks. Here was solid evidence that dead abbots really were infesting the town.

Wat made it to the Ealdorman without incident and laid an arm around the man's shoulder. The leader of Grimsby winced at this but held his ground.

Talking quietly into his ear, Wat gently led the Ealdorman away from the fire.

The crowd was quiet, waiting to see what was going to come of this. It was turning out to be quite an interesting day, even without the fire.

The Ealdorman and Wat stopped in their walk and the Ealdorman looked directly at Wat with a very questioning look on his face. Wat nodded back, very deliberately as if confirming something terribly significant. The man then looked to Cwen, who also nodded, most seriously.

The Ealdorman turned back to the square full of his people and raised his arms to get their attention. 'I will go and speak with these strangers. They may have word concerning the curse the abbot has put upon us. Wait here until I return. Nobody move and I will tell you what to do next.' He, Wat and Cwen now went to join Hermitage and they left the square.

Behind him, the people of the square almost immediately wandered off to get on with what they had been doing before all this started. Some of them even took back the wood they'd put on the fire in the first place.

Building-owner and net-mender strolled off together.

'I told him he was building it too close to the house, but would he listen?'

'And now it's the abbot who cursed us? Did you hear that? I ask you.'

'Between you and me I'm thinking it's time for another boating accident if you know what I mean.'

The net-mender sniggered at this.

. . .

102

The Ealdorman gave Hermitage a very close examination as they left the square. He seemed satisfied that this was not the dead abbot or some other dead monk.

'Is there somewhere we can go to talk?' Wat asked.

'I don't know,' the Ealdorman was heavy with suspicion. 'How do I know you're not in league with him?'

'I assure you we're not,' Wat explained. 'As I said, the abbot simply appeared in a vision at our door.'

'Why you?'

'Hermitage here,' Wat gestured at the monk at his side. Hermitage nodded acknowledgement.

The Ealdorman studied Hermitage once more. 'And you reckon you can get rid of him?' he checked.

'That's right.'

The Ealdorman seemed to make up his mind, albeit reluctantly, and he led them away through the streets until they arrived at a very well-appointed house. This was up a slight rise at the side of the town square, away from the site of the fire and any waters that might rise up and flood those lower down. It was small but solid, being a good timber frame with a fine oak door and glass in some of the windows.

Entering the place, the Ealdorman ushered them into the room on the right of the door. There was another room at the back, which it was clear they were not to enter. That the man had two rooms in his house indicated just how well off he was.

There were two simple wooden seats and a bench at a table by the empty fireplace. The Ealdorman took one of the chairs and Wat the other. Cwen and Hermitage perched themselves on the bench.

'My fire would do the job, just as well,' the Ealdorman sulked as if the conversation had never stopped.

'Possibly,' Wat admitted. 'But as we know, the abbot is a Christian. Pagan fire's no good on a Christian. You need a specialist.' He nodded towards Hermitage.

'And he's what, did you say?'

'Exorcist,' Wat said. 'And not just that. He's the king's Exorcist.'

Hermitage managed a smile but felt very bad about this deception. All of Wat's arguments that the man was a pagan and so it didn't matter were no help. Deception was deception.

Unfortunately, the Ealdorman was looking to Hermitage for some explanation. He didn't know if he'd be able to keep this up. Stick to the facts, he told himself.

'You see,' he said, 'there are two different orders in the church, major and minor. The major orders are subdeacon, deacon, priest and bishop. The minor orders are porter, lector, exorcist and acolyte.'

The Ealdorman did look quite impressed with this bandying about of titles.

'We have to work our way up through them all. So, before I can become an, erm, acolyte, I have to be an exorcist. It's the exorcist's job to cast out demons.'

'Done lots, have you?' the Ealdorman asked.

'Hermitage has been on the king's business many times. And on each occasion, he has rooted out the evil. Even to the satisfaction of the king.' said Wat.

Hermitage just smiled, weakly.

'Both kings as well,' Cwen added. 'Harold and William. He's famous, is Hermitage.'

'I've never heard of him.'

'Yes, but you're not Christian,' Cwen pointed out.

The Ealdorman seemed happy that he had not heard of

any famous Christians. 'And what do you two do? If he's the one who does the exercise?'

'Exorcism,' Wat corrected. 'We're his assistants. You can imagine getting rid of demons is a bit of a job. Not the sort of thing you want to do alone.'

'Especially in the dark,' Cwen kept a very straight face. 'Which is when most of them have to be done.'

Wat pursed his lips very hard indeed at this.

'And you know how to get rid of the dead abbot?'

'We're on our way to do just that,' Wat contained a bit of a coughing fit.

'We're going to expunge all record of his death, aren't we, Hermitage?' Cwen said.

'Er, yes, that's right,' Hermitage said. Of course it was right, just not exactly right.

'But we've got to get him across the water, back to the monastery, you see?' Wat explained.

It didn't look like the Ealdorman did see.

'That was where he was cursed by you in the first place. We have to take him there so we can finish the job. He's following us now, Hermitage being the Exorcist and all.'

The Ealdorman frowned. 'So if you leave, he'll go with you?'

'Exactly.'

'It's no good you setting a fire,' Cwen explained. 'It'll only make him cross. Hermitage has to take him home. Then we can deal with him.'

'Can't our priest do it?' the Ealdorman asked.

'Not an exorcist,' said Wat. 'Is he, Hermitage?'

'Er, no,' Hermitage was happy that this at least was true, if completely out of context and irrelevant. 'He's a priest. Major order, you see. He would have been an exorcist once, but not any more.'

'Hm.' The Ealdorman sat in contemplation.

Hermitage, Wat and Cwen tried to look encouraging and helpful. Hermitage managed blank, which he thought was best, in the circumstances.

'And you want a boatman to take you across to the monastery?' The Ealdorman asked.

'That's it. Quick row across and he can come straight back.'

'But you'll have the dead abbot in the boat with you.'

'Well, yes,' Wat accepted. 'So it will need a boatman of strong heart and courage.'

The Ealdorman seemed to have come to the conclusion that he was going to accept their plan. 'Only one man for the job then.'

'Full of strong heart and courage, is he?'

'More? No, he's completely mad. But he'll do anything for money. I assume there's money in it.'

'Er, yes, some, I suppose.' Wat didn't sound happy at this.

'More?' Hermitage asked, with real trepidation. 'Didn't used to run a ferry on the Thames, did he?'

'The Thames?' The Ealdorman asked. 'Where's that?'

'Not him then,' Hermitage was relieved.

'Good,' Wat clapped his hand loudly. 'We're agreed then.'

The Ealdorman silently nodded, looking a little disappointed that there was no excuse for a fire.

The silence was broken by a light tapping at the window of the room. Hermitage, Wat and Cwen seemed not to have heard it as they just sat with their own thoughts.

The Ealdorman did hear it though and looked up. And screamed as he jumped to his feet.

'Good God, what it is man?' Wat asked in alarm.

'It's, it's,' the Ealdorman spluttered out. He pointed a

shaking finger at the window and the figure that was blocking the light 'It's the abbot,' he wailed.

The others looked to the window as well.

'Where?' Cwen asked.

'At the window. At the bloody window,' the Ealdorman screamed as he tried to climb onto the table.

Wat went over to the window and pressed his nose against the glass. He peered left and right as if looking through fog. 'I can't see anything,' he reported, giving the abbot a wink as he did so.

'He's right there,' the Ealdorman was shouting and blubbing at the same time. 'The dead abbot. Can't you see him?'

'There's nothing there,' Cwen wandered over to the window and held out a hand to demonstrate the view of the buildings opposite.

'But, but,' the Ealdorman was now on his knees on the table, his head buried in his arms.

'Can you see him then?' Wat asked.

'Of course I can see him,' the Ealdorman howled. He risked a peek between his fingers to see if the abbot was still there. He was. And now he was holding out an arm and pointing. 'And he's pointing at me.' The leader of Grimsby was now shaking as the sobs of fear ran through him.

'Oh, dear.' Wat shook his head and sucked air through his teeth. 'Pointing eh? It's bad when they start pointing. This is bad, isn't it, Hermitage?'

'Yes,' Hermitage was quite pointed. 'It's very bad indeed.'

'See,' Cwen said. 'I think we'd better get on. If the abbot's appearing to you and pointing, I dread to think what will happen next.'

'Make him go away, make him go away,' the Ealdorman

begged.

'Not a problem,' Wat said. 'We'll just need that boat.'

'Anything, anything, just take him with you.'

'Of course,' Cwen added, just thinking of something. 'There will still be the problem of the time to get to the monastery and deal with the abbot.'

'Ah, yes.' Wat sounded upset that he had not spotted this.

'What? What?' the Ealdorman looked to them all, holding a hand up to shade his eyes from the still glaring abbot.

'While we're taking the abbot over, he'll still have all his powers.' Wat nodded at some pretty impressive powers.

'Powers?' What powers?' The Ealdorman really was in a terrible state now.

'We could apply some of the Exorcist's special measures, I suppose,' Cwen suggested.

'Special measures,' the Ealdorman was eager. 'Apply the special measures. Please.'

'Hm,' Wat was thoughtful. 'It's possible.' He looked hard at the Ealdorman. 'But you'd have to help.'

'Anything.' The man now climbed off the table and got onto his knees, the better to fawn at Wat's feet.

'There are two things then,' Wat sounded very cautious and careful. 'First of all, we'll need to know who brought you news of the abbot's death. Who was the first person to tell the town that the abbot was dead? Some of the ghastly powers can be re-directed towards him.'

'The prior,' the Ealdorman blurted, without a moment's hesitation. 'It was the prior. When Gad went off with the boat we went over to the monastery to complain, and make sure they were still going to get their supplies from here. The prior sent personal word that the abbot was dead. It was him. It was him. Make the powers go on him.'

'Very good.' Wat clapped his hands once more and rubbed them with satisfaction

'What else?'

'Second, and this is most important, you have to go to the church and pray until this is all over.'

'The church.' The Ealdorman nodded enthusiastically. 'Pray. Yes, pray. Of course.'

'Being a Christian abbot, only Christian prayer will save you.' Cwen said.

Hermitage had his head in his hands at this point and was shaking it slowly from side to side.

'And no more fires,' Wat added. 'They really annoy demons.'

'No more fires,' the Ealdorman agreed.

'There you are, not so difficult. And I bet the abbot has gone now.'

The Ealdorman risked a very sideways look at his window. 'He has,' he shouted with joy. 'He's gone, He's gone.' He even skipped around the room a bit. 'I'll go and get More,' he said as he very cautiously opened the front door. Happy that there were no dead abbots out there, he glanced back. 'Help yourselves to anything, and thank you. Thank you so much.' He skipped off to find More the mad boatman.

'That was disgraceful,' the abbot said as he walked in through the door once the Ealdorman had gone. 'I don't know why I let myself get talked into that.'

'Absolutely,' Hermitage agreed. 'What falsehoods. Taking just about everything in vain.'

'Worked though,' Wat smiled. 'We now know that word of the death came from the prior. And we've got a boat to take us to him.'

Hermitage and the abbot looked like they thought the

price was not worth paying.

'And you never know,' Cwen said. 'That could be how the original Birinus converted his pagans in the first place.'

'I very much doubt that,' Hermitage huffed.

'You'd better disappear again,' Wat said to the abbot. 'Don't know how long it's going to take to find this More the boatman. Can't have the Ealdorman turning up to find you chatting with us by the fireside.'

'Hm,' the abbot scornfully left them to it.

'We'll bring some supplies,' Cwen said. 'After all, he said we could help ourselves.'

It wasn't long at all before the Ealdorman returned with the boatman. Overly happy that his problem with the dead abbot was being dealt with, the man seemed on the edge of hysterics. 'Here you are then,' he grinned broadly. 'This is More, he'll get you across.'

'Hello,' a bright and squeaky voice emanated from the body of a tiny, wizened old man with a grey beard that stretched out from his chin as if someone had nailed it there.

'Oh, no,' Hermitage, Wat and Cwen said in unison.

'It can't be,' Cwen breathed.

'It's not possible,' Wat said.

'How did you get here?' Hermitage asked the boatman.

'Eh?' More asked, his eyes bright with something or other. It wasn't intelligence or enthusiasm but was more like eagerness for things decent people shouldn't be eager for.

Hermitage felt his hopes sag. 'You were on the Thames. You took us in a boat and nearly killed us. How did you get here?'

'The Thames? Never heard of it. You're mad, you are,' More was a fine one to talk. 'I've lived here all me life.'

'Then you've got a twin,' said Cwen.

'Oh, yes,' More nodded and grinned a grin more gap than tooth. 'I've got a twin.'

'And what does he do?' Hermitage asked, already knowing the answer.

'He's a ferryman on the Thames,' More smiled and nodded at them all.

'There must be someone else,' Hermitage pleaded with the Ealdorman.

'Not to take you over there with a dead abbot there isn't. No one will go near. More's the only one.'

'Oh, well,' Hermitage said. 'That's that then. We're doomed.'

Caput X: Water Water

As the reluctant voyagers helped More push what was at least a waterproof boat into the small waters of the River Haven, the townsfolk of Grimsby kept their distance, having been warned that if the dead abbot caught a glimpse of them, he might decide to stay.

Hermitage had been quietly pleased with their vessel. It had three rows of wooden seats with Cwen accompanying him at the rear. Wat and the abbot sat in the front to balance the weight in the water, and More pulled steadily on the oars to move them out of the town.

Wat was not so pleased, as he was the one who had had to part with a shilling for this trip. 'A whole shilling,' he had complained. I could buy a boat for that.' Cwen had told him to shut up, having pointed out that he had spent twice that much on buttons for his jerkin.

The old man seemed not in the least concerned about having an apparently dead abbot in his boat. He even helped him to his seat.

'You do know who this is?' Hermitage checked. 'It's the abbot.'

'Oh,' More gave a little curtsy. 'How do you do.'

'The abbot who's supposed to be dead,' Hermitage pointed out.

More leaned over to Hermitage and nodded back towards the abbot. 'Has anyone told him?'

Although the water was now rising there was still very little of it, surely barely enough to float their boat. Hermitage knew nothing of such matters but even he thought that he shouldn't be able to reach over the side of the boat and touch the mud in places.

After one stroke from More's oars, they moved beyond the edge of the town wall and out of the river, at which point they came to a complete standstill.

'What's the matter?' Hermitage asked, in some alarm.

'Don't worry,' More beamed. 'It's only the mud. The water's not high enough yet.'

'What do we do then?'

'Wait until it is,' More and his beard nodded happily.

'Couldn't we have done that on the shore?' Wat asked. 'Instead of sitting out here on the mud, in a boat.'

'Oh, yes,' More marvelled at such an innovative idea.

'In fact,' Hermitage noted, remembering something from Birinus's explanation. 'If we leave on a rising water, won't we get driven up river?'

'Oh,' More grinned. 'I can tell you're a boating man. But I've got a special method I use in these circumstances.'

'Really?'

'I'll tell you if you promise not to pass it on.'

'Oh, I promise.' Hermitage was confident that this special method was going to be something very stupid indeed.

'Yis,' More said. 'I row straight out to sea.'

'You, what?' Hermitage did not like the sound of that at all.

'That's right. I row straight out to sea and the rising water brings me back in again. Clever, innit?'

'And it it doesn't bring you in again?' Hermitage asked, always able to see the worst in any situation.

'Have you ever been to Germania?' More asked.

Hermitage looked to the others for help. Perhaps there was still time to get out and walk back to town through the mud.

'He is right,' the abbot said. 'Surprisingly. If the waters are on the move, it pays to aim up or down stream, let the current do the work.'

No one else seemed ready to get out, so Hermitage resigned himself to a pointless wait. During which he could worry about the sea and currents and rivers and everything that went with them.

They made themselves comfortable and Cwen distributed some of the supplies she had taken from the Ealdorman's house.

More sat at his oars as if ready to pull away at any moment. Even though it was probably going to be at least an hour before they floated free.

. . .

Up at the church, Father Birinus had barricaded the door once more and was cowering as far away from it as possible. 'Go away,' he cried, in tones of terror.

'Open the door,' the crowd outside called back.

So this was it, they had finally had enough and were coming to put Birinus on one of their fires. Perhaps he would go to heaven and sit with the martyrs. But only if he were caught first. There was no other way out but he thought that he might be able to climb the tower and then get out by a rope down the outside. Naturally, he didn't have a rope.

'You have to let us in,' a strong voice called through the door. The voice of the Ealdorman, the worst of the lot.

'Why?'

'Because we want to pray.'

'Not in my church you don't. Wait. You want to what?'

. . .

The water of the Humber estuary, as reluctant as a self-respecting river should be to go anywhere with More the boatman, took its time lifting the vessel from the body of the mud. When it did though, it clearly wanted to get the whole thing over as quickly as possible. The level of the sea and the river rose very speedily indeed. For once, Hermitage was quite pleased that he was in a boat. Anyone trapped in the mud would have to run to get away from the advancing flood.

True to his word, More heaved away and directed the party straight out to sea. Despite the apparent frailty of the old man, Grimsby was soon disappearing to the rear while the shape of the monastery stayed pretty much where it was.

Rather than head straight for it, More kept it on their left and appeared to be heading down the coast. It still took a lot of strength to move boat and people against the incoming waters, but More smiled and nodded and cackled, which Hermitage imagined was a good sign.

'Easier rowing down the shore,' More explained. 'Don't get caught between Condatis and Nodens.'

'I beg your pardon?' Hermitage asked, thinking these might be the names of rocks or some other sea feature people had to have names for.

'That's why it's so rough here,' More went on with a happy laugh. 'Condatis, God of the river, is fighting Nodens, God of the sea. Nodens is trying to get up the river you see. Well, Condatis isn't going to have any of that sort of thing now, is he?'

'What a load of nonsense,' Hermitage shook his head.

'Ooh, you mustn't say that. One of them could have us out of the boat.'

'They could have one of us out of the boat if they like,' Wat observed.

The abbot was just rolling his eyes at the ideas of the boatman.

'Once we get down the coast a bit we'll be out of Condatis's realm. Then we head out to Nodens who'll drop us off at the monastery, see?'

'All very straightforward,' Hermitage said. 'I'm glad you explained it.'

After rowing on quietly for a few more minutes, More seemed satisfied that they'd passed out of one god's realm and so he headed for the next.

This did alarm Hermitage as they now moved steadily and directly out to sea. He kept looking back over his shoulder to watch the coastline recede. The coast line that he could walk on, even if it was mostly mud. If something went wrong now, they'd never make it back alive. He gave a silent prayer to the one true God. The one he trusted to look after him when he was in a boat.

When the shore was a distant hope he looked forward once more. 'Well, I never,' he said.

The others looked around and sure enough, More's rowing and the force of the incoming water was driving them directly towards the monastery.

'Told you so,' More grinned his pride.

'There's still plenty of room to drown between here and there,' Hermitage noted.

'Only if you get out,' More said.

As they drew closer, Hermitage looked upon the monastery and felt mixed emotions. Here was the place where he had felt as comfortable as anywhere in the world. Discussions with the others now made him realise that this was largely down to the presence of Abbot Abbo. No one else there was enjoying themselves at all. As he approached

116

from the sea, it now looked like one of the most uncomfortable places he could imagine. But then he'd never seen it from this side before.

The sea was still not full, but even so, it was lapping at the lower stones of the place. Perched on this insubstantial outcrop of sand and shingle, and not much more, the building looked as if it were just waiting for a particularly heavy wave to carry it away.

Why anyone had even built a monastery in this precarious spot was a constant subject of debate among the brothers. The usual conclusion was that it must be some sort of punishment. A punishment for the builders who were sent out here to put it up and then a punishment for those who had to live in it. And then a second punishment for some new builders who had to come along quite regularly to stop it being washed away - the first lot of builders having sensibly vanished.

That these first builders had managed to get a foundation of stone out to this spot was widely regarded as a miracle. That they'd stopped as soon as they got above the high water line, was no surprise. On top of the higgledy-piggledy foundations, which looked like nothing more than an accident in a quarry, wooden structures had been built. These had been added to over the years until the monastery constituted one of the most bizarre constructions in Christendom.

As the waters washed away some particularly vulnerable spot, or it simply gave up through months of pounding and rot, a replacement was installed. Frequently by the brothers, none of whom had any skill in building.

There was an outer wall, which was refurbished on a daily rota, but inside, a variety of buildings stood, hung, balanced or wobbled, according to their construction. The centre of the place, the abbot's rooms and the library, were protected from the worst of the wind and weather and were at least firmly bedded on solid ground. After that, it was everyone for themselves.

On one truly awful night of the most ferocious winds and waves, when no one was able to get any sleep, the brothers had been alarmed by a terrible cracking and splintering noise. They all headed straight for the source of the commotion and found that a whole section of the monastery had been torn free. It was now simply floating away from the main body of the building, like some huge lobster pot, lost overboard by a careless fisherman.

Even worse, this particular pot contained not lobsters, but three of the brothers of the monastery who were all calling and shouting back to their fellows.

In horror and despair at their awful fate, one of the brothers, it might have been Gad, acted quickly and found a good length of rope. He tied one end to a firm section of the masonry and hurled the other out towards the stranded brothers. With the aid of the Hand of God the rope landed squarely on the lost section of the building where the floating brothers could reach it.

The words of one them were caught by the gale and delivered to the ears of the rescuers. 'No thank you, we'll take our chances,' he called as he threw the rope back into the sea.

Despite these horrors, which were now springing back into Hermitage's mind, his time with the abbot had been a happy one, working through manuscripts, putting order into the small but interesting library, jotting down his early thoughts for that work on the post-Exodus prophets. But as the wooden ramparts looked down on him, he recalled that physical comfort had not been a notable feature.

The wind whistled through gaps in the walls whenever it blew hard enough, which was constantly. The whole place had the constant tang of the sea in the atmosphere and the taste of it in all the food. And when the waters receded and took the sea away, the whole place reeked of rotting seaweed.

It was virtually impossible to get in and out without serious risk to life and limb and, needless to say, no one ever visited. Well, not out of choice anyway.

Despite his protestations, the abbot and the other brothers had insisted that it was actually safer to take a boat across to Grimsby than try and walk along the headland back to Kilnsea. It was all very well looking out of a high window and seeing a clear path back to the village, but by the time you got down there it would be gone; which was particularly troublesome if you happened to be standing on the clear pathway just as it disappeared beneath the waves.

Even taking the boat was no mean feat. There were only certain states of the water during which a vessel could land and anyone get on it before it was swept away. There was a small outcrop of stone at the foot of one of the walls, which everyone said was the landing stage. Some others said that it had been a mistake with some left-over stone, but whatever the cause, it was a means of embarkation.

More was making for this now and Hermitage thought that he could see a cowled figure, standing on the jetty, waiting to receive them. This wouldn't be a surprise as most of the brothers spent a lot of their time looking out of the windows wishing that someone would come.

Any successful mooring required speed of hand and good coordination. A rope would have to be made fast very quickly if the boat was to be able to halt its progress and not be carried away up river, or out to sea. If that happened they'd have to go round and try again, usually the next day.

Hermitage thought that the brothers must be missing Gad, who seemed to have an innate ability to see the motion of the waters and time his movements accordingly. Hermitage had watched his skill on quite a few occasions - from a distance and through a window.

More might be mad, but he could certainly handle a boat. Despite the rise and fall and the rush of the waters, he delivered the prow of his craft to the wall of stone, from where Wat could throw a rope to the monk waiting to receive them.

With the boat safely secured to a metal ring, hammered into the rock for the purpose, the occupants clambered and staggered their way to shore. More stood on his seat, helping Cwen and Hermitage through, as if he were pinned to the seabed.

'I expect there's some things for me to take back,' More called to the monk, hopefully.

The monk threw his cowl back and revealed the face of the prior. He looked puzzled and worried as he noted Hermitage and the abbot. He was of middling age and clearly intelligent as contemplation of this development ran across his face. He also had a look of confident entitlement about him. As if he were graciously letting the arrivals step ashore.

'There are some letters,' the prior agreed.

'Tuppence,' More said.

'Yes, we know,' the prior replied with some resignation. 'But if you get halfway across and find Brother Stigand in the bottom of the boat again, you bring him straight back, not a week later, like last time.'

More grumbled something that sounded a bit like

agreement.

'Come,' the prior beckoned that they should all follow.

It was actually quite a nice day still. The sun shone, the air was clear and the wind was moderate. Still, no one in their right mind would loiter outside.

The prior led the way up a winding series of steps in the rock that led away from the water's edge. They weren't purpose-made steps, just gaps in the stonework that served the same purpose.

Once at the top of the stones, the prior pulled on a large and heavy gate set into a strong wooden wall of half tree trunks with a scattering of driftwood. Closing this behind them a sense of relative peace and calm descended. The noise of the sea could be heard clearly, but at least it couldn't be seen as well.

The prior didn't pause but led them on through the maze of huts, shacks and lean-tos towards the centre of the place and the abbot's lodging.

Hermitage thought it strange that he had made no comment at the sight of the abbot, or of Hermitage, returning after all these years - particularly in these circumstances. Doubtless, he had already had many discussions with the abbot about the death and had already decided there was nothing he could do.

'Where are all the monks?' Cwen hissed in his ear, looking around and seeing no one else about.

'The brothers tend to spend much of their time indoors,' Hermitage explained. 'There's no garden or fields to attend to and once you've gazed out to sea a few times, there seems little point in doing it again. And of course, the weather is not usually welcoming.'

'What a marvellous spot for a monastery,' Cwen observed.

Once they entered the calm of the abbot's chamber, the prior bade them sit while he searched out the letters for More.

The room brought back many happy memories for Hermitage. The comfort of the thick straw on the floor and the warmth of the fire in the hearth. The smell of parchment and quill and the quiet scrape as the prior wrote some last few words on one missive.

Satisfied that he had everything together, he bundled a collection of documents together and wrapped them in a thick leather sheet which he tied securely. He held it out for More, who grabbed it happily, but the prior did not let go.

'This one gets to the other side,' he instructed, firmly.

'Of course,' More and his grin acknowledged.

'There's no "of course" about it. One of the brothers will be watching you from the high window and if he reports that anything dropped over the side of your boat before you got to Grimsby, I shall walk over there and pull your beard out myself. Clear?'

'Oh yis,' More nodded happily.

'Right.' The prior handed over the leather roll and the tuppence and More skipped merrily back to his boat.

The prior did now sit, in the abbot's chair, behind the desk. He looked at them all. The abbot was giving him a particularly unfriendly scowl. 'Prior Godric,' he nodded as if the term was one of abuse.

'Brother Hermitage,' the prior ignored his abbot. 'What brings you to this sorry business?' He cast a glance at Wat and Cwen, clearly intending to get to them next.

'Sorry business,' the abbot scoffed. 'Not spent the time since I left working out how a perfectly living abbot can be called dead then?'

The prior gave a heavy sigh. He had clearly been through this many times before. 'Nothing has changed.' He held out his hands as if their emptiness proved that there was nothing to do.

'You can see that I'm alive, man,' the abbot protested.

'But officially, you're dead,' the prior retorted in what was obviously a repeating argument.

'Officially, eh?' the abbot said, with a very knowing tone. 'Perhaps you'd better reacquaint yourself with Brother Hermitage then.'

The prior looked very puzzled at this. 'I'm not sure what Brother Hermitage is going to be able to do about this. A lecture on the post-Exodus prophets is hardly going to shed light on anything - not even the post-Exodus prophets.'

Hermitage had forgotten how rude the prior could be.

'And who are these two?' The prior waved a hand at Wat and Cwen.

'They come as a set,' the abbot smiled a smile which obviously gave the prior some cause for concern.

'A set of what?' he asked.

'You tell him, Hermitage.'

'Aha, yes, well.'

'Straight to the point, as usual, eh Hermitage?' the prior gave a hollow laugh.

Something in the prior's tone got to Hermitage in a way it never had before. Perhaps this was because he had been away too long, or perhaps because the experiences he had had since leaving this place had changed him. Either way, he suddenly felt quite proud of the title he'd been trying to get rid of only a few days ago.

He looked the prior in the eye. 'I am the King's Investigator,' he announced. 'Appointed by King Harold and again by King William. And I have come to get to the bottom of this.'

The prior suddenly looked a bit pale. Then he frowned. Then he looked sideways at Hermitage. 'The king's what?' he asked.

'Investigator,' Hermitage repeated. 'From vestigare, to track. The king has me investigate for him.' He could see that the prior was on the verge of dismissing all this as nonsense. 'Most of the time it's murder of course,' he said, nonchalantly. 'Dealing with the king's Court, Le Pedvin, that sort of thing. We've not been back long from Normandy where the king sent us upon his authority to deal with a Norman noble. I think the small matter of a mistaken death will be fairly straightforward.'

As he said this he could feel himself shaking inside. It was actually months and months since he had been in Normandy, and that had gone as horribly as all his other investigations.[Hermitage, Wat and Some Murder or Other, in case you were wondering....] And he already knew in his heart that this mistaken death wouldn't be straightforward at all. He had heard the words coming out of his mouth, even though he couldn't believe that anyone would be taken in.

'And this is Wat the Weaver and Cwen. They assist me in the investigations.'

'And deal with any trouble,' Cwen added, with one of her most effective glares.

'Wat the Weaver?' The prior sounded disgusted at this. He neatly ignored Hermitage's announcements and turned his nose up.

'That's right,' Wat beamed. 'And it's Prior Godric, isn't it?'

'Erm, yes,' the prior was very cautious.

'I thought so,' Wat said. 'A little work entitled The Lady

124

Undone ring any bells?'

The prior made a noise like a mouse. A soon-to-be-dead one.

'Naughty Prior,' Cwen grinned.

The abbot growled.

'It was for a friend,' the prior said, a lot less sure of himself now. 'And I never got it from him,' he gestured at Wat.

'It's a small world, Prior Godric,' Wat said. 'You should never touch strange tapestry. You don't know where it's been.'

'Well,' the abbot clapped his hands. 'Now we've got all of the pleasantries out of the way, perhaps we can get on.' He stepped up to his old chair and brushed Prior Godric from it as he would a piece of lint.

'Erm, erm,' muttered the prior as he moved out of the way.

'We know from Grimsby that it was you who told the town that the abbot was dead,' Cwen said.

'Why did you do that then?' Wat asked.

Prior Godric didn't have anywhere to turn. He looked in all directions but was surrounded. He collapsed into a spare seat. 'Because it was true,' he said. 'Why else would I say someone was dead when they weren't? Particularly my own abbot.'

'Take over yourself?' Cwen suggested.

'I had word,' Godric protested. 'The abbot had been away for weeks. We had no idea what had happened to him. It was quite possible he was dead. He might even have drowned just walking back to Kilnsea.'

'Who did you have word from?' the abbot asked.

'The office of the bishop, of course.'

'In a letter?' Hermitage enquired.

'Of course in a letter. I wouldn't go making this up.'

'Not that it's done you any harm,' Cwen looked around the room.

'Do you still have the letter?' Hermitage asked.

'Yes, I do,' Godric replied. 'Just because you aren't here any more doesn't mean we can't look after letters and the like.' He turned to the shelves at the back of the room and started to go through loose parchments that were piled there, doubtless trying to find the letter.

Hermitage noted that if he'd been in charge still, he'd have known exactly where it was.

'Ha!' the prior called out after a few moments. 'Here it is. Here's the very letter.' He returned to the centre of the room, brandishing a parchment.

'Why didn't you show me this before?' the abbot demanded.

'You were dead. Remember?' Godric handed the letter to Hermitage who examined it carefully.

'But not dead, really,' the abbot pointed out.

'Dead officially. Which is more important.'

'Hm,' Hermitage said, in disappointment at the contents of the letter.

'What does it say then?' Cwen asked.

'It's just a standard missive informing of the fact that the abbot is dead. No detail, no information, just "we are sad to inform you of the passing of Father Abbo." Then some instruction as to the care of the monastery and the steps to be taken as the body can't be found.'

'Interesting,' Wat said. 'Doesn't say where or when or how he died?'

'No, nothing helpful like that at all.' He stood and handed the letter to the abbot. He thought that Abbo would be interested to read the report of his own death.

Everyone sat in quiet consideration of the letter and its implications.

'So,' Hermitage said, eventually. 'We have to trace it back to the bishop's office.'

'If that's where it came from,' Cwen was in accusatory mood.

'What do you mean?' the prior demanded.

'Well, we've only got your word that the bishop sent it. You could have written it yourself.'

'I did no such thing, how dare you?' Godric did sound genuinely offended at this.

'Get to be abbot though, don't you? Convenient, eh?'

'Why don't you read the rest of the letter,' Godric suggested, his own voice finding its aggression.

They looked to the abbot who raised a hand for quiet as he read. 'Your personal instructions are to maintain order and discipline until the new abbot can take over.'

'Well,' Hermitage said, 'that could be months or even years. When an abbot passes on or moves, monasteries are frequently left alone for prolonged periods until a new appointment can be made.'

The abbot's hand was still up.

'Until the new abbot can take over,' he read on. 'The candidate will be there within the month.'

'Oh,' Hermitage said. 'That's very quick.'

'Yes,' Wat drawled. 'It is, isn't it.'

'You could almost think they had someone ready and waiting,' Cwen said. 'Ready and waiting for the old abbot to die.'

'And if he couldn't be trusted to get on and do it himself, just send a letter, same effect.'

'What are you suggesting?' Hermitage asked.

'Just that it will be very interesting to see who this new abbot is,' Wat said. 'And to see what he does when he finds that the old one isn't as dead as he should be.'

Caput XI: Explanations of No Value

'What's to do then?' Hermitage asked.

The three of them had been given adjoining accommodations next to the abbot's lodging. Not close enough to the sea to worry about being swept away, but not entirely safe from truly fierce weather.

They had left the abbot doing his best to take his monastery over again, dead or not. The prior definitely seemed to be on the back foot and could only keep waving his letter from the bishop.

'The abbot seems quite happy,' Cwen said. 'Just leave him to it?'

'All very well until another abbot turns up,' Wat replied. 'Especially one sent by the bishop on the understanding that the previous incumbent is the more dead of the two.'

'Just send him away again?' Hermitage suggested. 'Tell him it's all been a horrible mistake and that the abbot is a lot better now.'

'Not sure it's going to be that simple,' Wat put his feet up on his pack.

Although they were in the guests' quarters, the part of the monastery set aside for travellers, the rooms were not comfortable. Of course, no room in a monastery should be comfortable anyway, but this was a place where any traveller turning up at the door would have to be seriously lost. If the rooms had been found without the monastery around them, someone would assume they were just some big old boxes, washed up by the sea.

The simple cots in the rooms were occasionally called into use when one of the more outlying rooms disappeared into the sea, but other than that they were left to fester. At least they had managed to locate some fresh straw, or rather Cwen had, much to Hermitage's puzzlement as he had never seen any fresh straw in the monastery before.

Other than the cot and the straw there was nothing. Only Cwen's room had a window, and that looked straight out onto a wall two feet away. They had all gathered here, as it was slightly less oppressive than sitting in the dark.

'A new abbot might solve the whole thing,' Hermitage sounded hopeful. 'The new one finds the old one still alive, reports back to the bishop and everything gets back to normal.'

'Except, of course, that the bishop has sent this new man in the first place, and the strong suspicion is that it's all been arranged in advance,' Cwen said. 'Chances are that if the new abbot finds the old abbot isn't actually dead, he'll make him so.'

'What?' Hermitage was horrified.

'Give you a chance to investigate a murder first hand,' Wat smiled.

'But it can't be murder,' Cwen reminded them, 'because the abbot is already dead.'

Hermitage sighed, heavily. He should have known that this whole matter wouldn't turn out to be a simple mistake. He never got simple things. Even the actual murders he'd had to look into were not simple. Just once in a while couldn't two people just have a fight with swords? That would be easy. Now, if this new abbot turned up with a sword... He castigated himself for such thoughts.

'Should we go to the bishop's office then?' he suggested. 'If that's the source of the letter, let's go and find out what motivated it.'

'And where do we find that?' Cwen asked. 'Don't say Grimsby,' she sighed.

'Grimsby?' Hermitage gave a light laugh. 'No, not Grimsby. Bishop of Grimsby? That would be a thing.'

'Well, where then?' Cwen pressed, with some irritation. 'York, I assume.'

'Not necessarily.'

'Not necessarily? What does that mean?'

Hermitage saw that this was a simple question; unfortunately, the answer was not. 'It's all a bit changeable at the moment,' he said.

'Changeable?' Wat asked, sounding surprised. 'How can bishops be changeable?'

'Oh, it's quite common,' Hermitage explained, looking forward to an interesting discussion on the reforms to church organisation over the last couple of hundred years. 'Even in Saxon times, the Episcopal sees were moved according to need. Usually, they needed to run away from the Vikings.'

'So where is the bishop's office now?' Cwen pressed.

'Well,' Hermitage said, 'we'd better check with the prior, but the letter did come from York.'

'No getting away from the place,' Wat observed.

'Unless it's moved since then. And of course, the current bishop is away in Rome, so perhaps it's Dorchester now.'

'Dorchester?' Wat asked in alarm. 'We'd be quicker going to Denmark.'

'And then the Normans have their own ideas. I have heard suggestion that Lincoln itself may be granted a bishop.'

'The Lincoln we just walked past?' Cwen complained.

'Yes, but there isn't a bishop there yet,' Hermitage smiled.

'And there's still no telling that the bishop himself knows anything about this,' Wat said. 'If the letter came from York, that's where we have to start.'

'Or we wait for the mysterious new abbot to turn up and explain everything,' Cwen said.

'Who would actually want to be abbot of this place,' Wat turned up his nose. 'Having seen it now, I understand this whole business even less.'

'Any abbot is a significant figure,' Hermitage said.

'I'm sure. But here? Who wants to be significant on the end of a rock?'

'It could still be a mistake?' Hermitage suggested although he didn't really believe it himself.

'I don't think the office of the bishop would go to the trouble of a letter and have a new abbot waiting to step in for a mistake. I imagine that if a monk or even an abbot disappears on a journey, you don't normally get people acting this quickly?'

'Well, no,' Hermitage had to admit. 'There is the tale of old abbot Hean of Abingdon who vanished from Bradfield Abbey in a storm one night. It took some time to get his death confirmed and a replacement appointed.'

'How long?' Cwen asked, with only mild interest.

'A hundred and fifty years.'

'What?' Wat's feet fell off his pack.

'Well, they never found the body, apparently.'

'And so assumed he was still out there somewhere, a hundred and fifty years later?'

'He was a holy man,' Hermitage explained.

Wat stood now and went over to the window, perhaps to gather his thoughts. He sat down again, having examined the view for about the fifth time. 'What is it about this place or this abbot, or both, that makes it so interesting then?'

Hermitage and Cwen gave it careful thought.

'Good place to spot any invaders coming,' Cwen suggested.

'In which case simply build a castle,' Wat said. 'William's doing it all over the place. I'm sure he wouldn't hesitate if he wanted one here.'

'Maybe the abbot annoyed someone,' was Cwen's next idea.

'That, I can imagine.'

'You don't go to all the trouble of declaring someone dead just because they annoy you,' Hermitage said. 'Even Normans don't do that, they just make people who annoy them dead for real.'

Wat put his hand across his mouth and frowned hard. 'It must be something that the abbot has. Something that can only pass to a new abbot.' He looked to Hermitage for any ideas.

'The abbot doesn't have any possessions,' he explained. 'None of us do.'

'Which might bring us back to his family again?' Wat sounded hopeful. 'If they had him declared dead and then replaced, there could be no threat to the household. A new abbot quickly in place would mean there could be no going back. No undoing anything later. The abbot is dead and not even an abbot any more.'

Hermitage had a horrible thought that might be relevant. As he shaped this in his mind he saw that there might also be a horrible truth inside the horrible thought.

'Things are changing now,' he started, 'bishops and the Pope are more and more often becoming the ones who appoint abbots. In older times and older places, the monks appointed their own abbot. Once such a man is installed it is for life. The abbot holds his appointment from God. He would have to die for a new abbot to be put in place by someone of authority.'

'And this is one of those places?' Cwen asked.

'I don't know. It's not very ancient, but it is pretty much forgotten, I think. Perhaps the rule of this place was never changed. The abbot was already here when I joined, but I'm sure we could find out if he was appointed by the brothers.'

'It would explain a lot,' said Wat. 'But still doesn't explain why anyone would actually want to be abbot of this forsaken place. It must be personal to this abbot. Someone wants rid of Abbo, specifically.'

'Where do we find out?' Cwen asked.

'In the Scriptorium,' Hermitage said, with a shiver of excitement at the thought of going back to that marvellous place.

'Lead on,' Wat stood up and held his arm out.

Hermitage beamed as if he'd just been given a habit with no fleas.

. . .

The scriptorium of the monastery was just as Hermitage had left it. Almost exactly as Hermitage had left it. And he'd been gone for years. Had no one done any work at all?

When re-entering the block of the monastery comprising the abbot's lodgings, Wat had suggested that they avoid being spotted by the abbot or prior. If Godric was mixed up in this somehow, they didn't want him knowing what they were looking for.

For once, Hermitage did not think the best of a man of the church. He recalled the Godric of old and was happy not to have another conversation with him.

'This is disgraceful,' he said as he pottered happily about the shelves and tables of his old demesne. 'It's almost as if the work of the place ground to a complete halt the moment I walked out of the door.'

'The abbot would have kept things going, surely?' Wat looked around the place, not really knowing what he was looking at.

'He left all that side of things to me,' Hermitage explained. 'He took more of an interest in the discipline of the orders of the day. Making sure the brothers did their duty, that sort of thing.'

'And they appointed him?' Cwen sounded rather surprised.

'Disciplined into it, most likely,' Wat suggested.

'At least I'll be able to find things,' Hermitage said. 'Probably all exactly where I left it.'

'There were some parchments in the abbot's chamber,' Wat said. 'The letter from the bishop included.'

'Indeed. But I suspect that was only the material that has arrived since I left. It certainly doesn't look as if anyone has bothered to put anything new away where it ought to be. Can you believe they may not have recorded communications in the day book, or catalogued any new acquisitions or even added them to the master record?'

'Surely not,' Cwen sounded appalled. 'How awful.'

'Unbelievable,' Wat added. 'Absolutely shocking.'

Hermitage was glad they agreed.

'So,' he rubbed his hands. 'The section on the organisation of the monastery is over here.' He went to a far corner of what was a fairly small room anyway. At least the walls and floor of the place were solid and well made. It had to be the best room in the monastery, Hermitage had explained. After all, the documents must be protected above all.

This part of the scriptorium was little used as there was seldom any change to the organisation of the monastery. The abbot had added a small work on discipline, but apart from that, Hermitage couldn't recall dealing with much material here at all. This could take some time. How wonderful.

He took an armful of parchment, some loose, some bound and some simply rolled and tied. The dust rose from works that had probably not been moved since they had were put down in the first place. Hermitage was enthralled by the thought that he would be opening parchments and revealing words that had not been seen since their scribe laid them down.

He wondered about the life of the unread word. Was there some secret place that they went once they were closed off from the world? Did they only materialise when there were eyes to see them? Did they undergo some change while away from the sight of men?

'When you're ready?' Cwen called, dragging Hermitage back from the daze in which he stood clutching an armful of precious words, all of them crying out for his personal attention.

'Sorry,' he woke himself and moved over to the main desk where he carefully deposited his fragile cargo.

'Do you know what's here then?' Wat asked, looking at the quite large selection that faced them.

'No,' Hermitage said, terribly excited by the prospect. 'Never had call to examine it before.'

'So we have to look at them all?' Cwen asked, sounding quite despairing.

'Yes,' Hermitage wasn't despairing at all. 'Isn't it wonderful?'

'Wonderful.' Cwen said. 'Yes, definitely wonderful. That's just the word.' She picked up one of the pieces of parchment and scanned the close and complex writing. 'What's this?' she asked, in some disbelief.

Hermitage glanced over and quickly took it in. 'Looks like an addendum to the grant of the monastic house. Covering rights of landing of vessels, if I'm not much mistaken.'

'No. I mean what language is it?'

'What language?' Hermitage didn't quite understand the question. 'It's Ecclesiastical Latin, of course.'

'I can't read Ecclesiastical Latin,' she said as if so much should be blindingly obvious. 'I'm a weaver. I can read enough to get the order for a tapestry and get it paid for. How am I supposed to read this lot?'

'Ah,' Hermitage said. He looked to Wat.

'The odd word here and there,' the weaver replied, casting his eye over another piece of writing. 'Something about feast days, I think.'

'There might be some Saxon documents,' Hermitage sighed. 'The older ones, perhaps.' Just for a moment, he thought that he could teach them Ecclesiastical Latin, but he soon accepted that there wouldn't be the time. 'Very well,' he said. 'Just bring me the documents one at a time put them on a shelf when I've checked them.

'I hope this is worth it,' Cwen said as she handed Hermitage the sheet she was holding. 'Not sure what help it's going to be though, knowing whether the abbot was appointed or not.'

'It will be further proof that there is clear deliberation behind the abbot's death. If the only way to remove him from his position is for him to die, we'll have a good idea why it's been done,' Hermitage explained.

'It might explain why he had to be dead,' Wat grumbled as he chose a particularly colourful parchment from the bottom of the pile. 'Still won't know why anyone would want this place at all. I still think it's personal.'

Hermitage made himself comfortable at the desk and studied the parchment Cwen had selected. 'Yes, definitely about the movement of vessels and mooring rights. If you put this on one side, we'll start a pile called transport. There will probably be more to come.'

'Transport, right,' Wat absent-mindedly took the parchment from Hermitage and threw it on a shelf at random.

Hermitage considered the colourful piece from Wat. 'Ah, now, this is interesting.'

'Is it?' Wat sounded happy to have found something so soon.

'Absolutely. This is the charter giving right of access over the beach from Kilnsea to the monastery.'

'Handy,' Cwen said.

'As long as the beach is still there of course,' Wat said, throwing it on the shelf in disappointment.

'No, no,' Hermitage said. 'That's not transport, is it? Start another pile. We'll call this one Rights.'

Wat made great play of carefully moving the parchment from one spot on the shelf to another.

'Rights will go to the left of transport, won't it?' Hermitage pointed out.

'Beg pardon, I'm sure,' Wat moved the parchment again. This time with a great sigh.

They continued in this manner for some time, the individual piles increasing in number as Hermitage decided that a fresh one was needed every time he read something new.

'We're going to need a bigger shelf soon,' Cwen reported as she started another heap called Clothing and Supplies.'

'We're not getting anywhere,' Wat complained. 'We haven't even come close to anything about the appointment of the abbot.'

'Yes,' Hermitage acknowledged, 'but look how many more documents we've got to get through.' He considered the heap of those still waiting review with real enthusiasm.

'I think we'll have to talk to the abbot and prior,' Wat said. 'Be blowed with keeping the prior out of it. We could be at this all day.'

Hermitage thought that sounded wonderful, but he forced himself to acknowledge that they were here to get to the bottom of the abbot's death, not the bottom of a fascinating collection of parchment.

He looked wistfully at the pile yet to be approached, at all those words peeping out, calling to him. 'Just one more,' he pleaded.

'All right, just one,' Wat agreed. 'But the last one, and choose it carefully.'

Like a child facing three pots of honey, Hermitage dithered over where to go. He shuffled the parchments around a bit until something caught his eye.

It was a large, illuminated capital. An "A", it looked like. "A" was always hopeful as it could be the start of Ad gratiam Dei, by the grace of God. Only serious works began with Ad gratiam Dei.

It was an "A", and it was Ad gratiam Dei, how exciting.

He scanned the whole page and then started reading word by word, his lips moving with the joy of translation.

'Oh,' he said in disappointment.

'Nothing about the abbot then?' Cwen asked.

'No,' Hermitage cast the parchment aside, having found the honey had gone off. 'You'd better start another pile,' he sighed.

'What do I call this one?'

'Oh, I don't know. Monastery land and estates perhaps. It can go between Jurisdiction and Orders.' He gazed at the unread works, convinced that there would be something of interest in there. Perhaps nothing about the abbot, but still of interest.

Wat was looking at him very intently, which gave him the distinct feeling that he had just done something wrong. As he hadn't done anything at all, he couldn't immediately think what the problem was.

'Monastery what, did you say?' the weaver said, very slowly.

'Erm, land and estates?' Hermitage repeated.

'Monastery land and estates?'

'Yes, land and estates. It was a charter granting the land and estates.'

'What land and estates, Hermitage?' Wat sounded very serious all of a sudden.

'Well, the monastery land and estates.' Even Hermitage thought that should be obvious.

'The monastery has land and estates?'

'Of course it does. Before it had the land it would have to rely on donations just to keep going. That would be very precarious.'

Wat dropped his head into his hands and ran his fingers through his hair, looking like he was trying to pull it out by the roots. 'You never mentioned any land and estates.'

'Didn't I?'

'No, you didn't.'

This conversation was sounding very important to Hermitage. The tone and manner of Wat's enquiries gave it a deep significance. What that importance and significance was, he had not a clue.

'How much land does the monastery have? How many estates?'

Hermitage shrugged. 'I don't know how to compare. Monastic landholding has never been my area. I know that the land is owned by the monastery but worked by farmers and the like who pay their dues. The land was probably gifted by some noble or other.'

'The charter you just looked at then,' Wat prompted. 'How much land did that involve.'

'Oh, that was just along the north coast of the river from here.'

'How far along the north coast from here? Exactly?'

Hermitage turned and reached for the parchment again, which Cwen placed in his hand. He quickly read again and translated with little interest. 'Erm, for so far as five miles inland from the high watermark of the river.'

'Yes? And how far along the river?'

'Ah, I saw that somewhere.' He ran his finger down the lines. 'Here we are. Between the southern boundary of the monastery and erm, York.'

Wat and Cwen suddenly looked quite alarmed.

'What?' Hermitage asked.

'Brother Hermitage,' Wat addressed him very formally. 'I know you are not a man concerned by the worldliness around you. Your mind is on higher things, at least I think they're higher.'

Hermitage smiled.

'But consider. This monastery owns all the land along the river between the sea and York. You may not appreciate this, but that is a lot of land. A lot. A huge amount. A swathe. A tract. An expanse. It's the sort of land the kings of old would go to war over. In fact, it probably had its own king, once upon a time.'

'Really?'

'Yes, really. And if this abbot is in charge of the place until his death, he has ownership of the land?'

'Well, not really ownership, as such. Command, perhaps? Although that might be specified in one of the other documents if we could just examine them.'

'The point is,' Wat interrupted, 'that if kings were prepared to kill one another over the land, just think what the Normans would do to a lone abbot.'

Hermitage looked from Wat to Cwen as the thought permeated his mind.

'I think he was lucky to get away with just being declared dead, instead of being actually made dead,' Cwen said.

'If he did go on one of his wandering pilgrimages, maybe they just couldn't find him to do the job properly,' Wat speculated.

'Either way, we now know why the abbot has been told he's dead.'

Hermitage was still looking.

'The land, Hermitage. The land,' Wat spoke quite loudly now.

'Ah, right.' Hermitage nodded. He understood it now. He still didn't quite see why you would go to all this trouble, but he did accept that he wasn't strong on the machinations of landed folk.

'And I'd bet my best pair of boots that the next abbot is a Norman,' Wat added.

'That'd be for the bishop to decide, or even the Pope,' Hermitage explained. 'Always assuming that the brothers have their right of appointment taken away.'

'I think we'll find that if the bishop doesn't make the right decision, there'll be a new bishop as well.'

'What's to be done then?' Hermitage asked. 'For the abbot, I mean.'

Wat gave this a moment's thought, but only a short moment. 'I think we tell him to be grateful he's only dead on parchment and to find somewhere to go and hide for the rest of his life. Preferably somewhere he never has to say hello to a Norman.'

Hermitage shook his head gently. Surely simple avarice could not be at the root of all this. He had to admit that a large amount of land might be a temptation to many but still could not shake off the idea that there was a simple mistake somewhere to be found. As for the Normans getting involved in the appointment of a remote abbot, that was just ridiculous.

Caput XII: You Might Have Said

'So, Father abbot,' Wat said when they managed to get the man on his own, Godric having gone to deal with More, who had turned up again, unexpectedly. 'Do you, in fact, own a large part of the country between here and York?'

The abbot frowned at him. 'Own land? No of course I don't own land. I have renounced all worldly possessions.'

'You are not the abbot of the monastery that has these lands granted by charter then?'

'Well, yes, of course I'm that. I don't see what this has to do with anything though. Why are you asking about the monastery estates?'

'Because up to now we didn't know the monastery had any estates at all.' Wat sounded quite annoyed. 'And no one thought to mention the fact. We thought all it had was some rocks and the sea that kept hitting them.'

'The estates belong to the monastery, not to me.' the abbot flipped the problem away with a wave of the hand.

'Bear with me,' Wat went on. 'We also need to know if you were appointed by the brothers or put in place by the king, or the Pope.' He looked to Hermitage to check that he had asked the right question and got a nod in response.

'I was appointed by the brothers of the monastery, of course.'

'I won't pause to ask why,' Wat gave a disbelieving shake of the head. 'As I understand it, or rather as Hermitage has explained it, that means that you cannot be removed from office. You have to die.' He just raised his eyebrows at this, leaving the abbot to draw the right conclusion.

The abbot did manage that, although he looked like he

found the idea ridiculous. 'Are you suggesting that someone has declared me dead just to get at the monastery land?'

'Just to get at a swathe of country the size of a decent kingdom? Yes, that's the idea.'

'Nonsense,' the abbot concluded.

'And if I were to have to pick a group who might do something like that. I think I'd go for Normans. What do you think, Cwen?'

Cwen appeared to give this careful thought. 'Yes, I think Normans as well, funnily enough.'

'I'm sure that the Normans are quite capable of simply coming and taking what they want,' the abbot protested. 'Why bother with all the subterfuge?'

'Who knows?' Wat replied. 'That's what investigations are for. Perhaps the bishops and popes don't take kindly to having their land simply taken. Even by the likes of William.'

'It was you suggested there was some devilment in all of this,' Cwen pointed out. 'What more devilish than taking land from the church?'

'I meant that there was someone covering up an error, or making mischief, not that there was a scheme to steal the property of the monastery.' The abbot shut his eyes and held his hands up to indicate that he had finished listening. 'Once the new abbot arrives we can sort all of this out.'

'Unless the new abbot turns out to be a Norman, of course,' Cwen said.

'Probably a Norman who wouldn't know a monastery if he floated past one,' Wat added.

. . .

'Roger FitzGilbert,' the abbot announced, reading from the

freshly delivered letter; delivered at great profit by More who had only just arrived in Grimsby when Father Birinus told him to turn round and go back again. Godric stood by, listening in quiet obedience, or what looked like obedience, anyway. 'The new abbot is to be Roger FitzGilbert.'

'Who?' Hermitage asked. He racked his brains to recall which existing prior or abbot bore that name.

'The Norman, Roger FitzGilbert,' Wat said. 'Fought at Hastings I believe. Quite effectively, from what I hear.'

'Erm,' said Hermitage.

'Before you confuse yourself, Hermitage, no, he is not a monk. Nor is he a prior or an abbot or held any religious office at all, I imagine. He has been made abbot Roger by King William, who can do that sort of thing. And he has been appointed to get the land.'

'I would not have believed it.' The abbot sounded crestfallen. 'It all becomes clear. I was in the way of simple Norman greed and have been brushed aside.'

'You were lucky to just get brushed,' Cwen said.

'There remains the question of who administered my death. Someone declared me dead while doubtless knowing that I wasn't. And then they refused to correct the error. The Normans may be the power in the land but they do not control the clerical records of the church, as far as I am aware. This could still have required the connivance of others.' He gave Prior Godric a glance at this, but the man made no sign of it having made any impact.

'I suspect that if a Norman stands over you and tells you to write a letter saying that someone is dead, you probably do it,' Wat observed

'Maybe they're a friend?' Cwen suggested. 'Did you a favour.'

'How so?'

'Well, if this Norman comes along and says I'd like this or that abbot dead, they probably expect it to be the real thing. You know, "show me the body" sort of arrangement. In this case, all someone did was make you dead on parchment. Much more healthy way to die.'

'Even if that were so,' the abbot said, 'there is still corruption at heart.'

'Corruption?' Wat said. 'In the Church and amongst the Normans? Whatever next?'

'But,' Hermitage was sure that there was something to be done. He just needed someone else to come up with it.

Abbot Abbo sighed. 'You're telling me I should be grateful that someone declared me dead and robbed me of my role and my purpose just to let some Norman lord have what he wanted.'

'Yes,' Cwen said. 'That's it. Well done.'

'The Normans may yet turn up at the monastery gate with their swords in hand,' the abbot cautioned. 'We may all come out the worse from that encounter, previously dead, or not.'

'I can't imagine this FitzGilbert is really going to turn up,' Cwen said. 'Probably just take possession of the land and get you to send the tithes and dues. You could stay here and no one would know.'

'He is going to come,' the abbot reported, reading further down the letter. 'In fact, he is on his way.'

They all expressed some surprise at this, apart from Hermitage, who expressed some worry.

'Apparently, he feels it his Christian duty to inspect the monastery and all its holdings, to make sure that they are in a good condition to   serve God.'

'I'll bet he does,' Wat snorted. 'Still, it might be as Cwen says. 'Just keep out of the way while he has a prowl around. Then, when he goes back to court, or whatever other bit of the country it is he's been given, you can come out again. You could disguise yourself as a monk,' he mischievously suggested.

The abbot did not look happy at this idea.

'You can be sure of one thing. He's not going to want to live here.' She gave the room a disparaging appraisal, which looked like it went beyond the walls to encompass the whole monastery.

'Or you just tell him you're dead,' Wat offered.

Hermitage had a bit of coughing fit at that idea.

'I'm sure he won't mind. As long as you aren't going to make any claim against his lands. Simply tell him that you've been declared dead and that your rights as abbot have passed over to him and that's that. Go and do some more pilgrimages.' Wat smiled at the suggestion of being able to spend the rest of your life on pilgrimage. It was a pretty thin and insincere smile.

The abbot released a great sigh and shook his head, which gave the others some encouragement that this could all end quietly. 'Hide from the sight of the Norman, or capitulate in the face of his deceitful scheme.'

'Got it again,' Cwen said.

'Of course,' Abbot Abbo nodded to himself. 'This path is laid out clearly before me. Naturally, I shall not follow it.'

'Eh?' Wat looked like he had not heard properly.

'Give way before deception, greed and theft? What sort of abbot would I be if I calmly stepped aside and let some Norman ride roughshod over this house of God?'

'A living one?' Cwen proposed.

'One of shame and cowardice,' the abbot corrected.

'One of arms and legs,' Wat suggested.

'Let the Norman deal with me as he will, I will not relinquish my God-given task. I have protested the matter and I will continue to do so. Until the day I die I am truly abbot of this place.'

'That'll be the day FitzGilbert arrives then,' Cwen folded her arms as if there was no more to be said.

'You talk to him Hermitage,' Wat said. 'He seems to listen to you.'

Hermitage gazed at the floor in sadness at these developments. Of course, he wanted his abbot alive, it was unthinkable that he should even consider the alternative. But then there was principle involved here. What would he do in these circumstances, if he were an abbot, facing the arrival of a Norman warrior?

He knew what he did as a monk facing the arrival of Norman warriors and suspected that the outcome would be the same. All good for the Norman warrior, not so good for the monk.

'Having dealt with the Normans for some time, Father,' he began, 'I can be pretty confident in assuring you that your sacrifice, noble, pure and well-intentioned though it be, would make absolutely no difference whatsoever. In fact, most of the Normans I know would be quite happy to have someone to kill.'

The abbot made a grumbling noise.

'I'm sure they even consider the existence of the monastery itself as nothing more than a bit of a nuisance. Once they have the land they will doubtless leave the place alone.'

'Leave it alone to collapse into ruin,' the abbot pointed out. 'Without the land to support us, what future do we have? The Saxon benefactors are no more. We can't even catch fish now that Gad has gone.'

The abbot threw the letter down on the table and sat back in his chair gazing into space.

'Well, if your mind's made up, that's that,' Wat was bright with acceptance of the decision. 'We can wait with you if you like. For Hermitage's old time's sake and all that. FitzGilbert turns up, you greet him, he kills you, we all go home. Shouldn't take long.'

'And when is he going to arrive?' Hermitage asked, glancing over the contents of the letter the abbot had put aside.

'More has gone back to get him,' Godric said.

'He's here already?' Hermitage gulped.

'He and the letter arrived at the same time, apparently.'

'So why didn't More bring them over together?'

'Tuppence, probably,' Godric said. 'Although if I know More he's probably charging the Norman a pound.'

'Is it a force?' Hermitage fretted. 'Surely not just one lone Norman. How are they all going to get in the boat?'

'Just three of them, it seems.'

'Three's not many,' Cwen noted, her eyes saying that she might be able to come up with a plan for just three Normans.

'They're probably expecting a monastery full of monks and a dead abbot,' Wat said. 'Why send more?'

The abbot got to his feet. 'We had best make the guest quarters ready. Note of my death may be an error but this new abbot appears to have been properly appointed. We must prepare to receive him.'

Wat coughed and shook his head. 'I can see where Hermitage gets it from. I'm not sure even he would go so far as seeing the best in the person who's just had him killed.'

'I am a servant of God.' The abbot made his position clear.

'We shall wait upon His will and see what befalls.'

'I know one thing that's very likely to befall,' Cwen said. 'Or one person, rather.'

'And what's that about the guest quarters?' Wat asked. 'I thought that was where we were staying.'

'You're absolutely right,' said Godric, with a smile. 'You were.'

. . .

The arrival of Roger FitzGilbert was a noisy affair with much shouting and loud expressions of anger, together with threats of the most unwholesome kind. Gloved fingers were pointed and promises made which, if carried out, would require the most extreme penance, probably under the direction of a Cardinal at least.

All of this was directed by three large, solid, well-armed and fierce-looking Normans towards their boatman.

The boatman himself just sat there grinning at them all, holding out his hand for the payment he looked confident would come.

More curses were thrown to the sea breeze, some of which made even the seagulls wheel away in raucous offence.

For reasons that were not entirely clear, one of the Normans handed over a pile of coins to the boatman, spitting into the sea while doing so and driving a small but sharp dagger hard into the rail of the boat, very close to More's hand.

'Thank you very much,' More said as if this were normal behaviour from his passengers. 'See you on the way back.' With the Normans safely ashore, he pulled the craft away from the monastery and headed back to Grimsby once more, whistling at what a profitable day it had been.

The Normans stood on the monastery dock variously shaking their fists at the departing boat, or throwing their gloves to the floor.

Godric was alone to welcome his new abbot, the others thought it prudent that Abbo should keep away for now. Wat said that saving him would be tricky if the Norman simply stabbed him and threw him into the sea.

They also thought that Hermitage should stay away. If he had to introduce himself, this FitzGilbert might recognise the name as that of his King's Investigator. Explaining what he was doing here could be tricky. Hermitage pointed out that he was a monk in a monastery and so tended to blend in, but Wat said it was too much of a risk.

A well-dressed weaver and a young woman on the other hand, would be a strange sight for any monastery. They definitely needed to keep out of sight.

Which neatly led to the whole party sitting in one of the farthermost outcrops of the monastery, in a wooden room which Hermitage said was a dormitory that had been abandoned when it started creaking more than normal in a high wind. They sat very close to the door.

Prior Godric bowed acknowledgement to his visitors and led the way up to the main gate, a babble of Norman conversation at his back. You didn't have to speak Norman to know that these were not happy visitors.

Once escorted all the way to the abbot's chamber, the Normans threw down their packs, dropped travelling cloaks on chairs and unbuckled weapons. Whichever one of these was Roger FitzGilbert, he would certainly be the most heavily armed abbot in the monastery's history.

'Who are you?' one of them asked as he sat himself in the

abbot's chair, it being the largest in the room. This Norman was not the largest of the lot but looked the youngest, and his size hardly mattered anyway. As first to speak and sit, this was probably FitzGilbert. He spoke clearly, although a strong measure of Norman tainted his accent. The two with him looked very blank indeed as if they hadn't understood even that.

Godric bowed. 'I am Prior Godric.'

'Ah, the prior,' FitzGilbert said. 'I've been told about you.'

'Of course, Father,' Godric replied.

'Father?' FitzGilbert sounded confused. 'You call me sire, or my lord,' he instructed.

'You are my abbot,' Godric pointed out.

'What? Oh, yes, right. Father then. But try not to use it too often.'

'No, Father.'

'I imagine the abbot has wine?' FitzGilbert asked as if this should have been thought of before now.

'Yes, of course.' Godric busied himself getting cups of wine and handing them out to the Normans.

'So,' FitzGilbert looked around the room. 'Where's the land then? It can't be out near this God-forsaken hole.'

'No indeed, Fath…, erm, no. The land is away along the north bank of the river.'

'Excellent. Don't want to spend any more time here than I need to. You live here all the time?' It was clear that he found this hard to believe. And hard to stomach.

'All the time, yes,' Godric explained to this idiot that he didn't have a summer lodge somewhere nicer.

'How many?'

'There are twenty-five brothers in all.'

'Twenty-five?' The Norman sounded impressed. 'What on

earth do you do all day?'

'Pray,' Godric said, plainly.

'Oh, yes. I suppose you would.'

One of the Normans gabbled something at FitzGilbert, who shrugged in return. He turned to Godric and translated 'Do we have to get on that wretched boat again to see this land?'

'Ah, no. We can walk from here, but we will need to wait for the waters to recede before it is safe.'

'Walk?' FitzGilbert complained. 'Where are your horses?'

'Horses?' Godric sounded like he'd never heard of horses.

'What a place,' the Norman sagged in his chair. 'As soon as we reach a village we'll take some horses.'

Godric didn't like to point out that they'd have to walk a very long way to find a village that owned a horse.

'When the waters fall we'll be off. How long?'

'Oh, er,' Godric was a bit nonplussed by this. 'The sea is still rising, so at least six hours, Father.'

'Six hours!'

'And the dawn should be with us by then. It's certainly not safe to venture out after dark.'

'Robbers? Rebels?' FitzGilbert asked, with some excitement.

'No,' Godric explained. 'You just can't see where the land is.'

'What are we going to do for six hours?' FitzGilbert threw his arms up.

'There is the business of the monastery. Father,' said Godric. 'And the Orders of the day to be performed.'

FitzGilbert waved him away. 'You can deal with that. We might as well eat and rest.'

'Eat and rest, yes Father,'

'Enough of "Father".'

Godric just nodded.

'So, erm, Father,' Godric asked. 'It is not your intention to take on the duties of abbot. The daily, weekly and monthly duties.'

'Good God, no.' FitzGilbert sounded stunned by the very idea. 'I didn't become an abbot for all that. Didn't want to be an abbot at all, but William said I had to. I'll just look after the land and you can handle the monastery.'

'The previous abbot…,' Godric began.

'The dead one,' FitzGilbert confirmed.

'Just so.'

'He is dead? We are sure?'

'I have it on the very highest authority.'

'Hm,' FitzGilbert frowned. 'The people over there,' he waved a hand towards Grimsby. 'Who seem completely mad, by the way, some of them were shouting about seeing the abbot walking the streets.'

'They probably claim they've seen the dead abbot walking the streets,' Godric corrected. 'A superstitious people.'

'Yes,' the Norman acknowledged. 'They did seem to think he was dead at the time. Don't know about superstitious though. They were queueing up to get into church when I left.'

Godric looked very surprised at this.

'Don't want him popping up again, the abbot.' FitzGilbert made his expectations very clear.

'Indeed,' Godric said. 'As I was saying, the previous abbot conducted the Orders of the day and was most firm that all brothers attend.'

'Not very firm now, is he?' Robert FitzGilbert burst into a disgusting laugh. He then translated his comment for his companions who also found it very funny. One of them even made flopping motions with his arms, which was presumably supposed to resemble a dead abbot.

'And as Compline approaches…,' Godric suggested.

'Look, Godford,' FitzGilbert stopped laughing and glared at the prior. He even picked one of his smaller daggers from somewhere and made sure the prior got the point. 'You look after the monastery. I don't want to hear any more about it. Clear?'

'Quite clear,' said Godric. 'Father,' he added, pointedly.

'Good. Now you can take us to our rooms, send wine and food and we'll wait while your wretched sea goes down. Then we leave.'

Godric bowed.

'And never come back.'

. . .

'Abbot Roger seems only lightly engaged with the duties and responsibilities of the role,' Godric explained to the others after he had deposited the Normans and most of the monastery wine supply in the guest quarters.

'No surprise there, then,' Wat gave a resigned shrug.

'And he most definitely believes the abbot to be dead. I think that he would not take it well to discover otherwise.'

'Hm,' the abbot grumbled.

'I even made the suggestion that, as evening approaches and Compline is due, he might like to attend.'

'And?'

'He threatened me with a knife.'

'Didn't stick it in?' Cwen asked. 'He must like you.'

'As soon as the light and the waters allow, we are to leave

on an inspection of the estates.'

'That'll give us a chance to head back to Grimsby, then,' said Wat. 'If we can summon More again. And afford his fare.'

The abbot's face was stern.

'You can't go after him,' Wat read the look. 'He very much wants you to be dead.'

'And what will you do if you catch him?' Cwen pressed. 'Have a word and ask him if he'd very much mind giving the land back and going home?'

Hermitage gave the abbot a pleading look. 'If we leave, at least you will be alive, Father,' he said. 'And there may still be a way to get the record of your death corrected.'

'Really?' Cwen didn't sound at all convinced of this, or even that it mattered very much.

'Of course. Once FitzGilbert is established and the business of your death is forgotten, we may be able to persuade the bishop's office to discover that you are alive after all. It will be too late to reinstate you here...,'

'As if you'd want to be,' Wat interrupted.

'But you could be placed in another monastery perhaps?' Hermitage suggested. 'One far away from any Normans.'

'Good luck finding one of them,' Cwen said.

The abbot sighed, heavily. 'It is surrender in the face of evil-doers. It is giving in to force when we should stand against it.'

'It is staying alive and living to face another day,' Cwen said. 'After all, you never know with Normans. One good falling out with the king and it could be FitzGilbert who finds himself getting a letter telling him he's dead. A letter wrapped around a great big sword.'

Caput XIII: The Norman Dead?

'Roger FitzGilbert is dead,' Godric wailed at the top of his voice, bursting through the door of the dangerous dormitory.

'What?' Wat leapt to his feet, quickly joined by the others.

'What do you mean, dead?' Hermitage asked.

'Dead,' Godric repeated, clearly in quite a frantic state, wringing his hands and pacing up and down. 'And I don't mean dead by correspondence, I mean really dead. Dead, dead. Bodily dead.'

'He can't be dead.' Hermitage knew that, of course, he could be dead, it just didn't seem possible as the Normans had only arrived last night.

'You go and tell him then,' Godric retorted.

'Calm yourself, Brother,' the abbot said, soothingly. 'Tell us exactly what has happened.'

Godric looked at them all and took a deep breath. 'The Normans went to their chambers last night, along with most of the monastery wine. I was to wake them as soon as it was safe to take the walk to Kilnsea. As you know Father, you can never be too sure of that path, so once the water had dropped sufficiently, I gave it another two hours, just to make sure.'

'Very wise,' Cwen said. 'Losing Norman nobles is never advisable.'

Godric looked even more horrified at that comment. 'If I'd roused them earlier they would have insisted on setting off straight away. When I did go to call FitzGilbert, I couldn't. Because he was dead.'

'And the others?' Abbo asked.

'I've not called them yet. I was going to let FitzGilbert do that, as they don't speak our language.'

'And you're sure he's dead?' Wat asked.

'As sure as Brother Anselm.'

'Brother Anselm?'

'Brother Anselm had an accident,' the abbot explained. 'A very nasty one,' he went no further. 'Suffice to say it is now common parlance to refer to something as being as dead as Brother Anselm. Even if it is an inappropriate expression.' He gave the prior a frown of disappointment. 'Presumably, the Norman is still in one piece?'

'Oh yes,' said Godric. 'He's not as dead as Brother Anselm like that.'

Brother Anselm must have been after Hermitage's time, for which he was quite grateful. 'Any sign of how he died?' he asked.

'Oh, yes,' Godric replied. 'He was chopping wood with the large axe, which he said he'd repaired…,'

'I meant FitzGilbert,' Hermitage cut in.

'Oh, right. Yes. Knife wound, I think.'

'Knife wound eh?' Hermitage pondered. 'Plenty of blood then?' He didn't relish dealing with a freshly stabbed body.

'Yes,' Godric confirmed. 'And a knife sticking out of him.'

'Actually sticking out of him?' Wat gaped. 'Whose knife?'

'No idea,' Godric replied, with some irritation. 'I didn't wait to have an inspection.'

'I think we'd better go and look,' Wat said. 'Before the other Normans wake up and decide to take action.'

'Unless it was one of them,' Cwen shrugged. 'You know what they're like.'

'I don't think even Normans would get up in the night, stab their leader and then go back to bed.'

'If they're still here at all?' the abbot suggested.

'They've not gone,' Godric said. 'No one has left by the

coast path and there's been no boat overnight.'

'To the body then,' Wat said.

Godric hesitated to move as if going back would only confirm what was bound to be an awful lot of trouble.

'You know where it is,' Wat urged.

They filed out of the room, Godric reluctantly leading the way with the abbot close behind. Cwen followed with Wat and Hermitage at the rear.

'There you are then, Hermitage,' Wat nudged him in the ribs. 'Now you've got a real death to go with the wrong one.'

Hermitage sighed. 'Is it me?' he despaired.

'Getting up in the night to stab a Norman? I very much doubt it.'

'No. Is it me attracting murders? I can understand that being King's Investigator means I have to go and deal with them, deeply unpleasant though that be. I don't expect them to start following me around.'

'As only we know who you are, it's unlikely. And I don't think a killer in his right mind would wait until the King's Investigator was stuck in the same monastery with them before doing the deed.'

Hermitage nodded that this sounded sensible.

'Although most killers probably aren't in their right minds anyway.' Wat gave Hermitage a friendly thump on the back.

. . .

Roger FitzGilbert was dead.

The group had had differing views on a number of points over the last few days; the motivation behind the administrative death of the abbot, if there was one; the morality of getting that same abbot to pretend he was dead to frighten some pagans; even on whether they should set off to investigate the whole problem in the first place. They were all now in accord. The Norman laying on his cot with a knife sticking out of his chest was dead.

And it appeared that he had not been dead for long. While he was rather pale and well, dead-looking, he actually appeared to be quite comfortable. Naturally, he was still fully clothed. No one would take any clothes off at night in this part of the world, not when the wind and waves might be coming to join you at any moment. He looked restful and at peace, almost like the figure of a noble atop his tomb. Which he would be, fairly soon.

'Someone sneaked up and did for him while he was asleep then,' Cwen said. 'No sign of struggle, no sign that he's moved at all since he went to bed.' She shivered slightly as the bed with the dead Norman in it had been hers just a few hours ago.

'And it looks like his knife.' Wat took a look at the empty sheath at FitzGilbert's waist.

'Who would do such a thing?' Godric fretted, his pacing starting to speed up now.

'Most likely another Norman.' Cwen didn't fret at all. 'I mean,' she explained to the puzzled looks she was getting, 'how many murders have there been here up to now?'

'None,' Godric protested, angrily. 'None at all.'

'Exactly. So the first one happens when there are three Normans staying here. And it's one of them who gets to be the victim. I can't imagine any of your monks would do it?'

'Absolutely not,' Godric was not coping with this very well at all.

'There's always the abbot,' Hermitage pointed out.

'I don't think it was him,' Cwen said. 'We were all in the

same room together.'

The abbot scowled at her.

'No, no,' Hermitage shook his head in some irritation. 'Of course, it wasn't him. I mean there is also the death of the abbot to consider.'

'The death that didn't involve anyone actually dying?'

'That's the one. Perhaps there's a connection. First of all the abbot is declared dead, then the Norman is made dead. That's two abbots of the same monastery dead within weeks of one another. Very suspicious.'

'I think you've been investigating too long,' Cwen looked at him askance. 'This is a Norman. They die all the time. Get killed on most of those occasions, I imagine. It just so happened he was here at the time. In a monastery with two other Normans in it.'

'Perhaps,' the abbot was forceful. 'Perhaps we could deal with the issue of the dead Norman in our guest quarters before having a lengthy debate about the mortality of Normans in general.'

'Ah, right, yes,' Hermitage acknowledged.

'And I think there is no alternative to rousing the other Normans. I don't think we want them waking up and finding their leader has been dead for a while but we hadn't mentioned it.'

'They're going to be trouble,' Cwen warned.

'Wouldn't you be, if you woke up and found Master Wat was dead?' the abbot asked, quite pointedly.

'Well, yes, of course.' Cwen admitted. 'Not that he's our leader,' she added, just to make things perfectly clear.

'Thank you very much,' Wat said.

'And who's going to talk to them?' Godric asked. 'That language of theirs doesn't sound like anything I've ever heard.'

'Could be Breton,' Wat speculated. 'Strange tongue. Bit like they speak down in Cornwall.'

Godric didn't seem to think this was helping much. 'And you speak it, do you?'

Wat looked slightly confused by the question. 'Of course not,' he said. 'No one does.'

'Once again,' the abbot spoke, loud and clear. 'The linguistic preferences of sleeping Normans is not entirely relevant to the dead Norman in front of us. Godric, go and wake them.'

'Yes, Father,' Godric nodded and left.

'I still think...,' Cwen began.

The abbot held up a hand. 'Brother Hermitage. What are your thoughts.'

Cwen glared.

'We have the King's Investigator here,' the abbot reminded them. 'Perhaps his view of this event will be more useful than that of a weaver?'

'I wouldn't count on it,' Cwen muttered but invited Hermitage to go ahead.

That was fine, except Hermitage didn't really have anything to go ahead with. It had all been said. Perhaps just repeating it would help. 'I think it is as Cwen has explained,' he smiled at Cwen. She bounced this straight on to the abbot with "I told you so" written all over her face.

'It really is most likely that the other Normans have something to do with this. After all, as Godric told us, no one has left the monastery this morning so the killer must be here. Hardly likely that one of the brothers would do it. Even though gossip has probably spread so that everyone knows the Normans are in residence.' He looked at FitzGilbert. 'Even if there's one fewer in residence this morning.'

'Why would they wait until now?' the abbot asked. 'Surely they have had plenty of opportunity. They could have thrown him off More's boat and watched the body disappear.' He frowned at this thought. 'Wouldn't be the first time people have not been seen again after travelling with that man.'

'Sounds like we're about to find out,' Cwen nodded towards the clattering and complaining from the corridor outside, which was loud and incoherent.

Godric entered the room first, almost pushed aside by the two Normans, or Bretons, who bundled in behind him.

The others all made way so that the men could see their compatriot and take in the fact of his death.

Hermitage made as much way as he could. His experience of Normans was that they tended to grab him by the scruff of the neck and shake him about a bit. Granted, that was mainly the king, and these two fellows did not know who he was. Still, they were generally a violent people and being faced with something like this was bound to bring out the worst in them. What was on the surface was mostly horrible so the worst didn't really bear thinking about.

The now crowded room stood in silence, the heads of the Saxons respectfully bowed in the presence of the deceased. Or perhaps in the hope that they wouldn't catch the eye of a Norman.

The two men still looked bleary-eyed from the night and were clearly confused about the sight before them. They looked at one another and then back at the body again.

'Hon Tad, c'hwi hag a zo en Neñv,' said one of them, in a very sombre tone.

'What on earth does that mean?' Cwen hissed.

Wat shrugged, 'No idea, but it's definitely Breton.'

Hermitage was rubbing the back of his head. 'If I had to guess, I would say it was Our Father, who art in heaven.'

'Why?' Cwen asked, sounding as if this was a ridiculous guess.

'It just sounded like it. The tone, the pattern of the words. And the last one sounded like heaven. A bit.'

The others were humouring him but the now confirmed Breton who had spoken turned and pointed at Hermitage with a vigorous nod. ''Eaven,' he said.

'There you are.' Hermitage was quite pleased that he could now speak Breton. 'Heaven,' he said to the Breton in a very loud voice and with his own exaggerated nod.

The Breton turned back to face his leader's deathbed.

The other reached out and gently touched FitzGilbert's shoulder, to which, of course, there was no reaction.

The first one pulled his fellow back and pointed to the knife that was still sticking out of the chest. They both bent to examine this closely and then one pointed out the empty sheath at the waist.

Reaching a clear conclusion of some sort, they stepped back from the edge of the bed, looked one another long and hard in the eye, and then burst out laughing.

To say that this was not the reaction Hermitage had been expecting would be to use the word expect in entirely the wrong circumstances. Unexpected didn't even come close to encapsulating his confusion. He thought he was in the wrong room for a moment, that there wasn't a body on the bed and that if asked his own name, he would probably have to go and look it up. At least he could see that the others were in no better state.

And it got worse. One of the Bretons now started doing a little mime of someone lying in bed and being stabbed with his own knife. He pulled all sorts of horrible faces, each one of which got more laughter and even applause from his fellow.

This made them both double up as they slapped their knees and dragged their breath in through the gales of laughter. Tears were streaming down eyes now and one of them even had to sit on the deathbed to avoid collapsing completely. As mark of the hilarity he was affording them, he slapped FitzGilbert heartily on the leg several times, almost as if he expected the corpse to join in.

The other Breton had to sit on a rickety chair that was in the corner of the room and they both panted and shook as they gradually controlled themselves.

The Saxons looked on in a rich mix of amazement, offence and just plain confusion. Reduced to the occasional chuckle, it only took another glance towards the body to set the Bretons off again.

When things had been calm for a few moments, Wat put his hand up to ask a question. 'Did you, erm?' he nodded towards FitzGilbert.

'Huh?' One of the Bretons asked, clearly not understanding.

Wat did his own mime of taking the knife from FitzGilbert's belt and putting it in his chest. He made a nice gurgling noise to get the point properly across.

This just set the men off laughing again. They each repeated Wat's actions, including the gurgle, and clearly found it hilarious. Eventually, one of them took a few very deep breaths and managed to shake his head. 'Nann,' he said. 'Marv?'

'Marv?' Wat repeated.

The Norman leaned back in his chair with his tongue

hanging out, doing a passable impression of a dead man.

'I imagine it means dead,' Hermitage noted.

'Oh, marv,' Wat said. 'Yes, did you marv?' he asked the Breton, repeating his stabbing mime.

'Nann,' the man repeated, smiling broadly. 'FitzGilbert marv,' he clapped his hands.

'FitzGilbert marv,' the other echoed, shaking his head as if unable to believe his luck.

They both stood, now that they were able, and still shaking from the remains of the laughter seemed about to take their leave.

'But, FitzGilbert?' Hermitage asked. 'What about FitzGilbert? Don't you want to take him with you?'

The Bretons just looked at him so he did his own mime of picking up the body and handing it to them to take away.

'Nann trugarez,' said the Breton, sounding pretty disgusted at the suggestion.

'No thank you?' Cwen tried a translation.

'FitzGilbert marv,' the man explained slowly, accompanying it with his own mime of taking the body from the bed, and throwing it into the sea. He even added a show of looking off into the distance and waving goodbye as the corpse sailed over the horizon. 'FitzGilbert Norman,' the man pronounced in a very loud voice, as if volume would aid translation. He then slapped his own chest and the shoulder of his compatriot. 'Breton,' he said.

'Told you so,' said Wat, with a smile.

With one last look at Roger FitzGilbert, as if trying to fix the image in their minds, the Bretons slapped one another on the back. 'Kenavo,' they called, still chortling as they left the room.

'Well I never,' Hermitage was the first to speak.

'Quite extraordinary,' the abbot shook his head at their behaviour.

'Why would they be glad to see one of their own dead like this?' Godric just looked stunned. Having gone from finding a dead body in his monastery to discovering that it was the funniest thing to have happened in years, was not something he could handle.

'Obvious,' said Wat. 'Not Normans at all.'

'What's not Normans?'

'Those two. FitzGilbert here is a Norman. Was a Norman. Those two are Bretons.'

'So?' Godric's understanding of geography beyond the Humber was obviously pretty weak.

'Different people altogether. They could have been bound in service to FitzGilbert. They could have been hostages from some family in thrall to the Normans. They could have been his slaves for all we knew. No wonder they're glad he's dead. If they were tied to him that could end with his death. And even better, they didn't do it. That probably would cause trouble.'

'Surely they're going to have to explain something when they get home?' Cwen reasoned. 'If you're in the household of a Norman I expect you have to give a good reason for leaving. Death's probably fine, but people might think they did it.'

'Could be,' Wat accepted. 'Although I imagine they will just go home and say FitzGilbert is dead. Killed in some monastery.'

'Oh, heavens.' Godric started fretting once more.

'And I don't think the Bretons will care much where FitzGilbert is, or what happened to him, but the Normans will probably be quite interested. The real Normans that is. King William and Le Pedvin and the like.'

Godric's hands were going round and round again. 'And they've just left it to be our problem,' he whined.

'Well,' the abbot was thoughtful. 'It is a problem, you're quite right. A big one, I should say. Dead Norman in a monastery, just as he's turned up to take over as abbot and with it get control of all the land? Can't imagine they come much bigger.' He gave Godric an encouraging smile. 'Still, not to worry.'

Godric seemed to take some heart from this.

'It's your problem after all. I'm dead, remember?'

Caput XIV: Show Some Respect

As they gathered back in the abbot's chamber, Hermitage was worried that Godric might be about to jump out of a window and let the sea do its worst. This situation was so far beyond the prior's experience that he clearly had not a clue what to do. He did seem to have reached the conclusion that it was all going to reflect badly on him though. Probably reflect in the gleaming blade of a Norman sword as it took his head off.

If pacing, hand wringing and whimpering resolved problems then FitzGilbert would probably get up and walk home at any moment.

The abbot had taken to his old seat and was looking on with calm superiority. Hermitage, Wat and Cwen sat on various chairs and tables, although it was as much as Hermitage could do to stop himself going round reading any parchment that stayed still long enough.

'So,' the abbot said.

Godric looked up in hope as if this simple word was the answer to all his problems.

'A difficult situation.'

'What do we do?' Any pretence of authority was now forming a pool at Godric's feet.

'I would imagine that as prior, with the second dead abbot in as many months, you probably need to send word to the bishop asking for yet another one. A difficult request to fulfil, I would think. Mind you, with the Normans showing such an interest in the place they could probably find a replacement quite quickly.'

'They sent three people last time,' Wat pointed out. 'As

that didn't turn out very well it will probably be quite a force next time.'

Godric dropped into the nearest chair at this, the shaking of his legs making standing up a bit of a problem.

'I'm sure it will all work out,' the abbot was nonchalant. 'One way or another.' It sounded very much as if both of those ways would not be comfortable for Godric. 'And we'll hear all about it. In a month or so, I expect. We should be back in Derby by then.'

Godric looked around the room at the faces staring in at him. 'Help,' he whimpered.

'Pardon?'

'Help,' Godric whimpered a little louder.

'Ah, help, yes, I see.' The abbot steepled his finger and looked deep in thought. 'Help eh? Well, well. What's to be done? What can be done?' He looked to the others, although Hermitage had the distinct impression that the abbot knew exactly what he was going to do. Why he was taking so long about was a bit of a mystery.

'I suppose,' the abbot began.

'Yes?' Godric jumped in, eagerly.

'You see the problem we have is my being dead,' he sounded truly perplexed by this. 'It's so difficult to do anything when one is dead.'

Godric got it straight away. Hermitage took a bit longer.

'Silly mistake,' the prior announced. 'Clearly an error in the bishop's office.'

'Really?'

'Absolutely. I'm sure if I sent word that you had turned up alive and well things would be straightened out in no time.'

'Straightened out with the bishop, perhaps,' Cwen said. 'Not sure the Normans will be so keen.'

'And it was simply the letter from the bishop that convinced you I was dead?' The abbot sounded quite business-like now.

'Of course,' Godric nodded, eagerly. 'You'd been gone on pilgrimage for several weeks. We'd heard nothing until the letter came from the bishop. We were all quite sorry to hear it, held special services and everything. It seemed quite reasonable. Deaths happen all the time, and you are quite old.'

The abbot scowled.

'Erm, older than many who do pilgrimage,' Godric recovered, slowly and carefully.

'But then I turned up. How could you still believe I was dead when I came back?'

'Ah,' Godric was a touch less eager now.

'Yes? We need to get this sorted out before we do anything about the dead Norman in your monastery.'

'It was a messenger,' Godric blurted out. It seemed that he was more scared of dead Normans than he was of messengers who weren't here anymore.

'A messenger?'

'Yes. He came soon after the bishop's letter.'

'Who was this messenger?'

'Never seen him before. Not one of the regulars.'

'And what did he have to say?'

There was a slight hesitation before Godric went on, but it was only slight. 'He told us that you really were dead. It was official, the bishop had put everything in place and that a replacement would be on the way very soon.'

'That's all?'

'Ah. He also said that there was someone going around pretending to be you and that we should not be taken in.'

They all gaped at this.

'He said it was the bishop's personal word,' Godric explained and excused the inexplicable and the inexcusable. 'He said that if someone came along claiming to be you, we should ignore them.'

'But you could see it was me, you fool. I wasn't pretending. If someone was pretending to be me they wouldn't be me, would they?'

'Well, no. I suppose not.'

'So?'

Godric spoke into his chin. 'He said that even if we were sure that it really was you we should send you on your way. You were officially dead and that was that. No going back.'

'Only a messenger and a letter though?' Cwen asked, staring at Godric with some hostility. Cwen's stares with hostility were a force of nature. 'Hardly enough to persuade you that the abbot standing in front of you was dead, I'd have thought.'

'Mumble, mumble,' said Godric.

'We didn't hear that.'

'He said I could be abbot,' Godric flopped back in his chair, utterly defeated.

'Aha.' The abbot was utterly victorious.

'The new abbot wouldn't want to stay and so I would take over when he left.'

'The new abbot didn't even make it through his first night,' Wat observed.

Prior Godric was a beaten man and sat in his chair as if his habit had been taken out and thoroughly trampled.

'Not only did the bishop send word that you were dead,' Wat went on, 'he sent a messenger to make sure you stayed dead.'

'All at the behest of the Normans, no doubt,' Cwen said. 'They must have put pressure on the bishop to declare you dead so they could get the land.'

'And it wouldn't do the bishop any good in the eyes of the Normans if you popped up again,' Wat continued. 'Either he sent the messenger on his own initiative, or the Normans told him to. Doesn't matter really.'

'But now the abbot's dead,' Godric muttered. 'The new one I mean.'

'Yes, he is, isn't he.'

'So what do we do?' Godric beseeched. He even put his hands together in prayer.

The abbot nodded to himself. 'I have been giving this some thought.'

Hermitage was keen to hear what the abbot's ideas about this were. He was used to dealing with dead people when Normans were involved. It would be fascinating to see how someone else approached the problem, particularly someone he respected and looked up to.

'Brother Hermitage will deal with it.'

'Well,' Hermitage said. 'What?!' he added as the words sank in. 'Me?'

'Who better? You are the King's Investigator, young Hermitage.'

'Well, yes, but.' Hermitage knew he should have stayed in Derby.

'And your companions are with you.' The abbot said "companions" as if they were something that had come in on the bottom of his sandals.

The companions were looking very resigned and disappointed.

'Your experience of this sort of thing far outweighs anyone

174

here. This will be grist to your mill, I'm sure.'

'Grist,' Hermitage said. 'Mill.'

'And,' the abbot had a happy new thought. 'What would King William do anyway, when he had word of FitzGilbert's death?'

'Burn something to the ground?' Hermitage suggested. 'It's what he usually does when he gets bad news.'

'Unless he also hated FitzGilbert, of course,' Cwen put in with an inappropriate smile.

'No, no' the abbot beamed. 'He'd send his Investigator wouldn't he?' He held his arms out just to make sure everyone knew which investigator in the room he was talking about.

'Ah.'

'You are the only one, I assume?'

'Oh, yes,' Hermitage said, with profound sadness.

'And I will be fascinated to see how this all works at first hand with a real dead body.'

Wat suddenly developed a nasty cough, which took some time to clear.

'Still,' the abbot nodded as he thought, 'at least we know that it must have been someone in the monastery. Of course, it could have been those two Normans,'

'Bretons,' Wat corrected.

'Quite.' The abbot was clearly not happy at being interrupted. 'But as no one else has come and gone, we must have the killer in our midst.' He sounded quite excited at the prospect.

Hermitage was unfortunately familiar with having killers in his midst, and it was not something to be recommended. He gave a great sigh. Here he was again. No Normans battering him into it, no warriors coming to take him away in the middle of the day and drag him to some awful event. No king or Le Pedvin threatening him with death if he didn't sort their problems out for them. No. Here he was, with his old friend the abbot, in his old monastery where he had spent many a happy hour. And now the whole place was ruined.

He suspected that if he had gone on pilgrimage instead of coming here he'd have suddenly found half the other pilgrims murdered. Then a group of armed Normans would turn up demanding that he investigate.

If he went and hid in a cave and became the hermit he secretly longed to be, he would find a dead body at the back, under some leaves.

In a monastery literally at the ends of the earth, what did he find? A murder to investigate. How much further did he have to go to get away from the things? The bottom of the sea? Even then he'd probably be brought dead fish to be looked into.

He was getting carried away. Back to the matter in hand. He looked about and saw that the rest of the room was waiting for him to speak. Well, the abbot and prior looked expectant. Wat and Cwen looked rather bored and fed up.

'I don't think it was the Bretons,' he said.

'Fascinating.' The abbot sounded genuinely interested. 'How so?'

'Although they were happy at the event, they were clearly very surprised. I don't think anyone could laugh so genuinely at a dead body if they already knew it was there.'

'I see.' The abbot was impressed.

'And while they had motive to get rid of FitzGilbert, they would probably not risk the wrath of King William by doing so themselves. It was as you said, Father, if they had wanted to they could have done it any time. Why wait until they were here?'

'If not the Bretons,' the abbot pronounced "Breton" carefully, his irritation with Wat still lingering. 'It must be someone still here. Who on earth in this place would dream of stabbing a Norman with his own knife? I know the brothers well and there isn't one who is capable of such an action.'

Hermitage had to agree with this. In his time the brothers had been a talkative and rather impudent group on occasion, but they had never strayed into violence. Those who came to this place were usually happy to live in solitude and took little interest in outside events. They weren't happy with the place itself of course, but unhappiness was a relative concept for most monks. Perhaps many of these didn't know any better. He suspected that Brother Limney, who seldom appeared at all, wouldn't even know who the Normans were.

But if not someone here, who? Could FitzGilbert have done it himself? Or rolled over in the night and accidentally stabbed himself to death. He thought that unlikely as the man was lying on his back with the knife firmly in his chest.

'Aha,' he said.

'There we are,' Wat said.

'There we are what?' the abbot demanded.

'Hermitage,' Wat explained. 'It's what he does. First, you take your death, or murder or whatever and we all have a jolly good think about it. We work through all sorts of possibilities and generally come up with nothing.'

'And then, out of nowhere,' Cwen went on, 'Hermitage says "Aha" and that's that.'

'That's that?'

'Problem solved. And then he explains it all, and we go "aha" as well. He always gets there first.'

'Didn't take long this time,' Wat smiled.

'He knows who did it?' Godric asked, sounding very impressed.

'No,' Hermitage had to put them straight, which seemed to be a bit of a letdown. 'But it could be someone who is not here.'

'How so?' the abbot asked.

'Because Prior Godric told us that the path to Kilnsea had been open for at least two hours before he went to rouse FitzGilbert.'

'So?'

'Plenty of time for someone to enter the monastery, find FitzGilbert and, erm, you know.'

'Kill him?'

'Quite. And then leave again.'

'Really?' The abbot sounded sceptical.

'Of course. It's only about two miles to Kilnsea. Easy, if someone was in a hurry.'

'Or arrived by boat?' Cwen suggested.

'Unlikely,' Hermitage said. 'It's almost impossible to land from a boat single-handed. Someone from the monastery would have to go down and help.'

'Perhaps there's more than one person involved?'

'Ah, yes, could be I suppose. But I still agree with the abbot that the brothers here are very unlikely to assist in such a matter.'

'So, someone sneaks in from the village, kills the Norman and then sneaks away again,' Wat summarised. 'Who?'

Hermitage paused. 'No idea,' he said. 'And we don't know that they sneaked away again. They could still be here.'

Prior Godric let out one of his whimpers at this.

'A fairly minor "aha" then,' Cwen rolled her eyes.

178

'But it must be someone who knew he was here or was coming,' Hermitage's thoughts went on. 'And who wanted him dead.'

'Well, obviously,' Wat said. 'Bit of a mistake to put a knife in someone's chest if you don't want them dead.'

'I mean him specifically. Either FitzGilbert the Norman, or FitzGilbert the appointed abbot.'

'Or any Norman at all,' Cwen seemed keen on the idea. 'He was probably the only one for miles around. Could be some Saxons resisting the Normans just did for him because he was handy.'

'If that were the case they'd have killed the Bretons as well,' Wat shrugged. 'I can't imagine these Saxons resisting the Normans are well enough informed to tell a Breton apart.'

'We don't seem to be getting very far,' the abbot observed. 'It could be this or it could be that or it might be neither. Isn't investigation supposed to come to some sort of conclusion?'

'Generally, yes,' Hermitage said. 'Although I've never found the conclusions particularly satisfying. Or pleasant.'

'Hardly surprising, I'd have thought. When there are dead people involved.'

'What's to do then?' Hermitage asked no one and everyone. Having come up with a thought, quite a good one, he considered it unfair that he was expected to know what to do about it.

'I think that's the nub of it.' The abbot adopted a thoughtful look.

Everyone sat gazing at one another for far longer than was conducive to the progress of any investigation. On several occasions fingers were raised as an idea occurred, only to be lowered again when the owner of the finger realised their suggestion was useless.

Godric stood to go and look out of the window as if the answer would be somewhere in the monastery.

Eventually, Hermitage did speak up. 'I think we need to at least gather the brothers together and see if there is anything that they know. Even if none of them had anything to do with this, they may have seen someone coming or going. It is an unusual sight in this place, after all.'

With no one having anything better to propose, it at least gave them something positive to do.

'They should all be gathering for Terce now,' the abbot said. 'Unless that's no longer the way of things.' He cast this accusation at the prior.

'Everyone gathers for every service, as is right and proper,' Godric bit back.

'Excellent.' The abbot stood and led the way from the room.

. . .

The chapel at the monastery was not where Hermitage remembered it. In the old place, the bright light from the sea had shone through a very small piece of stained glass that they'd had. The abbot had brought it back from one of his journeys, reporting that it was a left-over bit of the prophet Daniel, who was being built for a church in Germania. With such an exotic heritage the glass, which was as large as a man's thumb, attracted real devotion.

In answer to Hermitage's question about the move of the building, the abbot explained that they had all been in chapel one day when the light from the sea became increasingly bright. Some assumed this was a miracle, but those running for the door said that it was because the sea was about to come to mass.

They were proved correct as the chapel, the glass and old Brother Renard's sandals were swept away. Fretting that the glass had been lost, the abbot calmed the community by pointing out that the life of Brother Renard had been spared. The one who suggested that Brother Renard could be thrown into the sea to look for the glass was treated to a private conversation with the abbot.

As was usual practice, the new chapel was built further away from the sea. The problem was that space further away from the sea was becoming increasingly scarce. This new building could accommodate all the brothers, but only if they came and left in single file, and no one wanted to sit down.

Terce was indeed about to begin when the abbot's party arrived and so they had to push their way to the front of the simple wooden room.

There were some mutters and exclamations as the abbot made his way through. Hardly surprising, thought Hermitage, when they must all have thought him dead.

There was also muttering at the sight of Brother Hermitage, with a barely contained "Oh no, not him again", coming from the back somewhere.

Gasps, plain and simple accompanied the arrival of Cwen, several of the brothers crossing themselves vigorously.

The abbot had reached the front of the room and raised his arms for attention.

'Brothers, brothers,' he called. 'As you can see, reports of my death are about to be stamped on with my heaviest sandal. There has been contrivance and conspiracy in removing me from my office which I and Brother Hermitage here,' he gestured to Hermitage, 'are to resolve. Brother Hermitage is now no less than the king's own Investigator.'

Hermitage looked to the ground, modestly. He thought he heard someone say "dirty devil", but he could have been wrong.

'The proof of the wrong-doing surrounding my supposed death is that a new abbot turned up almost immediately.'

This brought the conversation in the room to life. The abbot waved it quiet. 'A Norman, by the name of FitzGilbert arrived with More the boatman last night.' He paused, significantly. 'That Norman is now dead. Murdered.'

The room now burst into unbridled hubbub. Some of the more audible comments included "That'll teach him to get in a boat with More" and "What's a Norman?" from Brother Limney.

'Brothers, brothers, calm yourselves.' They did as they were told, slowly and with the clear indication that this was going to be the main topic of conversation for months to come.

'What we need to know is whether anyone saw anything last night, or early this morning, once the road to Kilnsea was safe? Any strangers coming or going? Anyone in the monastery that you did not recognise?'

A fresh murmur of discussion was generated, but no one had anything positive to say. Brother Ignor claimed to have seen a mysterious shape on the roof of his cell, but the brothers had been ignoring the things Brother Ignor claimed to have seen for years now.

'No one?' The abbot checked. 'No one saw anything?'

Brother Welton, who was the most senior of the community, or at least the most senior who could still talk sense, stepped forward. 'We saw nothing Father,' he said, sounding as if he really was trying to help. 'We spend our evenings after Compline in the refectory.'

'The refectory?' The abbot sounded shocked at the implied

laxity. 'Doing what, may I ask?'

'Oh,' Welton was evasive. 'Nothing really. Just sort of waiting for Matins.'

'Hm.' The abbot did not sound convinced. 'And you attended Matins as normal?'

'Oh, yes,' Brother Welton confirmed, happily. 'And then to work. Didn't even know there was a Norman here. Might have been quite interesting to see one.'

The abbot scanned the faces before him and seemed satisfied that they all looked largely blank. 'If anyone does remember anything, come and see me in my chamber.' He stepped away from the front and started to press through towards the door once more.

'Erm,' Hermitage spoke up. 'Shouldn't we stay for Terce?'

'I think we have more pressing matters, Hermitage,' the abbot led the way out.

Hermitage should have said "couldn't" they stay for Terce. It had been so long since he had attended service in chapel he had forgotten how fulfilling they could be. He knew that Wat and Cwen would not want to stay but at least an abbot and a prior ought to be a bit less keen to get out. He supposed the abbot was right, the murder of a Norman in your monastery probably did take precedence.

. . .

Back in the abbot's room once more, Hermitage had returned to the parchment that had caused all this trouble in the first place. He read it again and again without getting anything new from the words before him. It was as Prior Godric had said, a straightforward message.

He looked to the bottom of parchment and examined the

florid mark of the bishop. 'I wonder who signed this,' he said, with mild interest in the calligraphy.

'Who signed it?' Cwen asked. 'Some bishop I hope. Otherwise, its caused an awful lot of trouble for nothing.'

'Well, of course it's the bishop,' Hermitage explained. 'But it won't actually have been the bishop.'

'The bishop but not the bishop. That's clear then.'

'The bishop would not sign routine letters such as this himself.'

'Routine?' Wat clearly didn't think this was routine.

'Abbots die all the time. There's a lot of them.' He studied the letter again. 'What I mean is that this would have been dealt with by someone for the bishop, and despatched on his behalf. An amanuensis.'

'I thought it was a letter?' Cwen queried.

Hermitage and the abbot exchanged looks of mild hopelessness. 'An amanuensis is an assistant, someone who copies manuscripts or assists a senior person in producing works they don't have the time for. Interestingly enough, it has a fascinating Latin origin. Servus a manu, means a servant at hand, for writing, you know, and ensis, means belonging to. Somewhere along the line, it all got shortened to a manu ensis, amanuensis, see?'

Cwen was shaking her head, a look of serious thought on her face. 'I think you're wrong there,' she said.

'Wrong?' Hermitage was taken aback, had Cwen some additional knowledge of the etymology.

'It is neither interesting nor fascinating,' she declared.

Wat snorted. 'You're saying that the bishop did not sign this,' he got in before Hermitage could react. 'Not in person.'

'That's right,' Hermitage threw a sidelong glance at Cwen, reproving her levity.

'So would the bishop have even seen it?'

'Probably not, although he would have been told about it. I expect. Although, then again, he might delegate all such matters.'

'Let me get this straight.' Wat was staring at Hermitage rather intently. This was probably more bad news. 'First of all, we find out that this monastery actually has an awful lot of very valuable land that can be taken if the current abbot is dead.'

Hermitage didn't feel the need to confirm this.

'Now you tell us that the bishop who is supposed to have declared said abbot dead, might not have done so at all.'

'It's quite normal,' Hermitage explained.

'So anyone could have written that,' Wat gestured at the parchment in Hermitage's hand.

'Someone from the bishop's office, yes.'

'Why the bishop's office? Why not anyone with a bit of parchment and a quill?'

'Erm,' Hermitage couldn't quite see what Wat was getting at.

'Someone could have made it up, Hermitage,' Cwen explained, slowly and clearly. 'Like Godric, although he says not.' She still didn't believe this, and Godric was no longer in any state to protest other than to give a weary shake of his head.

'It's an official letter,' Hermitage was in a complete quandary. 'It has the right form of words. It says here, Episcopus me fecit, the bishop made me.'

'And no one but a bishop's office could write that down?' Wat asked. 'If I gave you a quill and a parchment, I expect you could do it right now.'

'Well, I could. But I wouldn't,' Hermitage protested at

such dishonesty.

'The same as you wouldn't declare an abbot dead when he wasn't.'

Wat and Cwen simply stared at Hermitage until the ideas they had planted made him raise his hand to his open mouth. 'You mean this is a, a,' he tried to come up with the right word, but a piece of writing that was a lie ought to have its very own title. A very bad one. Something so appalling that it would never be repeated in polite company.

'Someone made it up,' Wat repeated, even more slowly this time.

'And you said the messenger who came later wasn't known to you?' Cwen asked Godric.

'That's right. But as Brother Hermitage says, it looks very much like a bishop's letter. And it did arrive by the normal process.'

'Which is?' Wat enquired.

'Occasionally a messenger will come via Kilnsea, but it's a long way. More the boatman delivers such things, now Gad's taken our boat.'

'Ah, yes,' Wat nodded, thoughtfully. 'The More who will do anything for money.'

Hermitage looked puzzled, mainly because he was.

'Oh, for goodness sake, Hermitage, try and keep up,' Wat huffed. 'The letter would look like a real one, wouldn't it? The person who has made this whole tale up isn't going to produce a bad letter. Doubtless, it was the Normans. Maybe the bishop wouldn't go along with them so they ignored him altogether and did their own letter and paid More to deliver it. Then they sent their own messenger to ram it home. There you are. One dead abbot, many leagues of land fall into Norman hands without a scratch on a battleaxe.'

'Then who killed the Norman?' Hermitage asked.

Wat settled back into his chair. 'That is a good question.'

'Still could be another Norman,' Cwen said. 'One who found the land was going to FitzGilbert but had a much better idea. FitzGilbert should be dead and it should go to them instead. Seems to be their normal way of exchanging property.'

'If we carry on at this rate, it'll be dead bodies all the way from here to York,' Wat despaired.

'What do we do then? Wait until the next Norman turns up and see who kills him?'

With no one having anything constructive to suggest, there was relief at the sound of a gentle tap on the door.

'Enter,' the abbot called.

The tap repeated, only more gently this time.

'Come in Brother Ronof,' the abbot gave a clear instruction, albeit with a sigh of recognition.

The door opened a very small amount and a very small head appeared around the corner. 'Shall I come in?' a tiny, timid voice enquired of the important people within.

'Yes, yes, come in. What is it?'

Brother Ronof entered the room and looked apologetic from his sandals up. He clearly hated to disturb his superiors, and people he didn't even know, and probably the dust in the room. He said something so quiet no one could make it out.

Hermitage smiled encouragement at Brother Ronof. During his time in the monastery, young Ronof was the only one who was reported as finding Hermitage quite scary.

'You really must learn to speak up, Brother,' the abbot instructed. Brother Ronof was obviously a feature of the establishment.

'Ahem, you asked us to come and tell you if we'd seen

anything unusual,' Brother Ronof breathed. 'And I didn't like to speak up in chapel.'

'Nothing's changed there then,' the abbot muttered quietly. 'And what have you seen?' he asked, loudly.

'Oh, probably nothing,' Ronof looked to the floor.

'Well, tell us what it was anyway.' The abbot was clearly having a hard time controlling his irritation.

Ronof looked very nervous and reluctant but managed to take his courage in hand. 'It was just that this morning, when I was on my way to chapel I saw some people leaving across the causeway to Kilnsea. It's probably nothing, I shouldn't have bothered you. I'm so sorry. I'll go now.'

The abbot held up his hand to stop Ronof running from the room, or simpering away under the door.

'The Bretons,' said Wat.

'Ah, there you are then, Bretons,' Ronof was relieved that his news was of absolutely no significance whatsoever, even though it sounded like he had no idea what a Breton was.

'Yes Brother,' the abbot boomed, perhaps trying to impart some volume into this mouse-like monk. 'There were two men here with the Norman, but they left. We know about them.'

'Excellent,' Ronof whispered as he bowed and scraped and backed towards the door which he was clearly hoping was exactly where he had left it.

'But thank you for telling us,' the abbot was almost shouting now, which was probably doing nothing for Ronof's state of mind.

Ronof had his hand on the door now and was sliding it gently open so that he could leave without causing it any inconvenience.

'And the one following them was probably a Breton as well

then,' he sighed as he left.

Caput XV: Answer The Question

Poor Brother Ronof was now sitting in a chair, in the abbot's room, with his superiors looking down on him, along with Brother Hermitage and two strangers, one of them a woman. His nervousness was like an extra person in the room.

Each of them had had a go at questioning him. He had shied away from the abbot, twitched at Godric and squirmed before Brother Hermitage. Wat had generated a look of plain fear while Cwen just caused confusion.

Without discussion, they all concluded that confusion was probably the best they were going to get so Cwen pulled up a chair.

'What did this third person look like?' she asked in a gentle and kind voice, a warm smile playing across her face and her eyes twinkling in the light that danced through the window.

Wat and Hermitage looked on in astonishment.

'A monk,' Ronof said, not looking at Cwen, but staring at his lap.

'Not a monk you recognised?' she encouraged.

'I could only see the back of him and he had his cowl up.'

'Did it look like he was with them? Did they know he was there?'

'I don't think so,' Brother Ronof's voice dropped into apologetic silence.

'Was he trying to avoid them? Was he sort of sneaking along, making sure he wasn't seen?' Cwen's voice quietened as well as if it was just the two of them alone in the room.

Ronof just nodded, all power of speech having vanished.

'And is there a monk missing from the monastery? Anyone

not here who should be?'

Ronof shook his head at this question.

'You're sure? Have you seen everyone today?'

'At Terce.'

'So it was a stranger?'

A nod.

'Our killer?' Wat suggested.

A whimper.

'Very likely, I'd say,' the abbot confirmed. 'Don't get strangers coming here at all, not if they've got any sense.'

'He probably wasn't even a monk,' Hermitage said. 'Just someone dressed as one.'

'Good Lord.' The abbot baulked as if such deception had never occurred to him. 'Then we must get after him. Straight away.'

This brought a blub from Brother Ronof.

'Not you, Ronof,' the abbot was amazed that the idea had even been contemplated.

'Ah, chase the killer, eh?' Hermitage made his voice sound keen and eager for such a chase. He was neither.

'How long ago was this?' Cwen was quietly kind and calm.

He mumbled something into his habit which Cwen had to lean forward to hear. She put a hand on the monk's knee to balance herself.

Brother Ronof simply turned bright red and ran from the room.

'What was that all about?' she asked.

'Gentle Cwen,' Wat grinned. 'Now we know she's in there, somewhere.'

The familiar scowl returned and it was clear Wat was going to be on the receiving end of some very specific instruction as soon as they were alone. 'He said it was at least two hours ago,' she told the assembly.

'He'll be well to Kilnsea and beyond,' Godric said. 'But the people there will have seen him pass by. Knowing that place they'll all have gathered in the street to point at the strangers.'

'Come then,' the abbot commanded.

'We can manage this,' Wat indicated Cwen and Hermitage. 'Are you sure you're up to a chase across the sand and shingle and an encounter with someone who stabs Normans in the night?'

'I can handle myself, master weaver.' the abbot made it clear he was not going to miss out on this.

'It is our daily business. King's Investigator chasing killers and all that.'

Hermitage tried to recall a time when they had actually had to chase a killer anywhere. They were usually there all along, you just had to spot them. Spotting killers was a lot less hard work than going after one who was running away.

'This wretch,' the abbot explained, 'whoever he may be, has something to do with my death, I'm sure of it. I will have the truth.'

'Please yourself,' Wat shrugged.

'Perhaps I'll stay here,' Godric offered. 'In case he comes back.'

'Someone will be coming back, Prior Godric.' The abbot's words were very pointed and well-aimed.

Godric did the right thing and just gulped, nervously. 'What do I do with FitzGilbert?' he asked. 'I've got a dead Norman lying in bed. I can't just leave him there. He'll ruin the cot.'

'It is another problem,' the abbot mused. 'One that any potential abbot would have to sort out for himself.' He made it quite clear that Godric was not going to get any help with this one.

'I suppose there is one thing to be said for chasing a killer across the headland into the village,' Hermitage said, as they left the room to gather possessions, Godric now pacing the floor, nervously. 'We won't have to get on another boat with More.'

. . .

The way across the headland was not easy. The waters had receded and left a path of sorts, but it was clear that they would be back to inundate that path at the first opportunity. And it was a bit generous to call it a path at all. It was simply a strip of land that wasn't actually underwater.

Stones and shingle and patches of sand comprised the way, with the occasional outcrop of sparse and sturdy grass indicating that one day this place might be reclaimed from the sea.

At this moment though, the sea looked like it considered anything foolish enough to step out here was fair game.

Hermitage could see across wide stretches of sand to his right where the main body of the sea lay in the morning light. To his left, very similar stretches of a more muddy consistency led to the river which now lay low in its banks. He had had the distinct impression that both bodies of water were watching him. Just waiting until he got to the perfect spot, that place where he would be unable to run forward or back. Then they would jump on him.

But, he told himself, he had made this journey before. When this monastery was his abode he had travelled to Kilnsea three or four times. And each of those journeys had been successful. And he'd been terrified all the way then as well.

Wat and Cwen had seemed eager to run from the monastery and make best speed to Kilnsea before the trail of the Bretons and their follower was lost. Not that a trail was visible, or even necessary. Unless their quarry had walked into the sea or the river, there was only one direction they could have gone.

The abbot had also assured them that two Bretons and a mystery monk would not pass through this land without the whole countryside coming out to watch. He also pointed out that the land over which they moved was potentially dangerous. Soft areas of sand and holes where the sea still lurked could catch out a reckless traveller. Finally, he acknowledged that at his age he couldn't actually run anywhere anyway.

Cwen gave this one of her smaller "tuts" indicating that they really should have left him behind.

As the halfway point of their journey to Kilnsea approached, Hermitage felt his familiar discomfort. The shape of the monastery was still clear behind them but it looked an awfully long way away. The village in front was still not visible, its low buildings hiding below the sands and grasses. It was just here that he could well imagine the sea to his right conspiring with the river to his left.

He forced himself to focus on Wat, who was striding ahead, and soon the moment of greatest peril was passed. He heaved a sigh as the normal, regular level of peril reasserted itself.

The first indications of arrival in Kilnsea were not encouraging. A simple wooden jetty stood on precarious stilts as it tiptoed into the river on the left-hand side of the headland where it joined the main body of the river bank.

Doubtless, when the river was full, this would provide a useful spot for the embarkation of boats, or for fishing.

Just at the moment it was deserted and looked like nothing more than a haphazard collection of logs that had been washed up by the river and left here; a collection of such decrepit decay that the river probably realised it had better things to wash out to sea.

'Kilnsea harbour,' Hermitage pointed out.

'Harbour?' Wat seemed to think that Hermitage had used the wrong word.

'Well, landing, maybe.' Hermitage acknowledged that the most generous, optimistic and perhaps drunk mariner would find the word harbour hard to justify.

Beyond this great port of Kilnsea, the first simple dwelling could be seen. This was actually a marked contrast to the village's riverfront area. It was a well-presented hut, mainly made of sticks and mud but a few solid timbers could be made out, probably delivered by the river from more wholesome parts of the country upstream.

The outside of the place was well ordered, with the tools and implements of a fishing community neatly stacked, clean and ready for action. A small vegetable patch circled the place and this too was tidy and looked well maintained,

A wisp of smoke rose from the central hole in the roof of rough thatch and the smell of smoking fish was prominent, the odour wholesome and appetizing.

'The dwelling of Master Scur,' the abbot explained. 'And Mistress Engel.'

'They look after the place well,' Wat observed.

'They do indeed. Very proud of their dwelling. NO!' the abbot cried out, urgently.

Wat stopped as he had been about to step forward.

'You can't just walk up to the door like that,' the abbot breathed again.

'That's what it's for, surely?'

The abbot just held his hand up, beckoning Wat to wait. 'Master Scur?' he called.

They stood and waited for Master Scur to make an appearance.

After they had waited for a few minutes without any sign of anyone, Wat gave the abbot a look of bewilderment.

'He'll be preparing himself,' the abbot whispered.

Wat shook his head in bemused confusion. 'While he's getting ready, our killer is getting further away.'

Eventually, there was a movement in the doorway and a thick animal skin was lifted to one side as Master Scur and Mistress Engel appeared.

Unsurprisingly they were as neat and well ordered as their house. Hermitage knew that they were both young, and devoted to one another, as well as to maintaining the best house in the village. He had been given fair warning never to approach the front without invitation in case he made a mess of the path. He should have mentioned it to Wat and Cwen, but it had completely slipped his mind. Or he had forced it out.

Their clothes were the simple garb of any peasant who worked the land, but it looked like theirs had been washed for some reason. Mistress Engel brushed the front of her long skirt and ordered it so that it sat neatly on each side. Master Scur tugged at the bottom of his jerkin so that it was straight and flat.

There was no smile for the arrival of visitors, but these were faces that did not tolerate smiles.

'Master abbot,' Scur, bowed and gave his dignitary all due

respect.

Mistress Engel gave a little curtsy.

Scur's face turned puzzled, 'I thought you were dead?' he accused the abbot.

'All a mistake,' the abbot responded.

'Amazing what abbots can do,' Mistress Engel observed, blankly.

'I beg your pardon?'

'Being dead and then it being a mistake and being alive again. Still, I suppose that what comes of being holy.' She seemed happy to accept the resurrection of abbots as the normal way of the world.

'No, no. I wasn't actually dead at all.'

Scur frowned at this. 'A bit careless, surely. Not to be dead at all but to let word get out.' He sounded as if the abbot should have done the decent thing and be dead, just to keep everything in order.

'We suspect someone else has declared the abbot dead, out of some malicious scheme,' Hermitage said.

'Is that Brother Hermitage?' Mistress Engel asked. She didn't sound all that happy about it.

'It is,' Hermitage confirmed.

'Tut,' Mistress Engel complained.

Hermitage now recalled why he might have wiped memory of this couple from his mind. He had seen Master Scur on one of his journeys to Kilnsea, on the jetty, when the water was high. He had stopped for conversation and Scur had called Engel to join them so that they could discuss the matters of the day with the learned Brother from the monastery.

The discussion soon descended into a comprehensive criticism of Hermitage for his lax and un-Godly ways.

Spending all his time reading and writing would surely lead to the most vigorous punishments in the hereafter.

Hermitage had tried to point out that he was a monk and so had devoted his life to the Lord, but this didn't seem to cut any ice with the couple.

He also recalled why Scur and Engel lived away from the rest of the village. No one else could stand them.

'And strangers.' Scur nodded to Wat and Cwen as if strangers were generally washed up on the river bank after heavy rain.

'We seek information about three men who passed by?' the abbot asked.

'How did strangers get here?' Scur ignored him.

The abbot sighed.

'We did not see you pass,' Scur went on. 'And we have been appointed by God to keep watch on all the comings and goings from the monastery.'

Hermitage could have sworn he heard the abbot mutter, 'Appointed by yourselves, you mean,' but he must have been wrong.

'We came from Grimsby,' Cwen said.

'Grimsby!' Scur declared in the utmost horror.

The abbot now had his face in his hands and was clearly mumbling, 'Why did you have to mention Grimsby?'

'We will have no dealings with people who come from that place of evil.' Scur declared in his most declamatory voice.

'We don't come from there,' Cwen was defiant. 'We just passed through.'

'You passed through the dwelling place of the devil,' Engel joined in the declarations.

'Quite probably,' Wat nodded, which surprised everyone. It gave Scur and Engel pause, anyway. 'We are on the king's business rooting out evil.' he explained, with some relish. 'And we have been chasing it across the land. We harried it though the terrible pagan town across the water, and struck fear into the hearts of those who dwell there.'

Scur looked to be quite happy with striking fear into people. There was no outward expression of happiness, of course, just the slightest softening of his rigid expression.

'In fact, we drove them to the church so that Father Birinus might deal with them.'

Scur even raised his eyebrows at this.

'And then we arrived at the monastery in pursuit of the evil that has declared the abbot dead when he is not.'

The couple seemed much happier with the idea that there was evil involved in this, instead of just an abbot who couldn't manage his own affairs properly.

'But the evil was ahead of us,' Wat went on, in dark and exciting tones. 'And,' he paused for effect, 'there was a murder.'

'No,' Scur gasped as Mistress Engel took a step back and clutched her husband's arm.

'Yes. And the one who committed the crime fled the place, in pursuit of two more strangers who had come from over the sea.' Wat raised his arm to indicate which direction over the sea he was referring to.

'We saw them, we saw them,' Mistress Engel cried, sounding very happy to have escaped with their lives. 'Two men talking in a strange tongue. They stopped here and tried to speak to us, but we would have nothing to do with them. They were probably possessed.'

'Quite likely,' Wat agreed. 'You did well.'

Scur and Engel looked quite pleased about this. 'And then a monk passed by soon after. He would not even speak at all,'

Engel was obviously offended at this rudeness.

'Which way did they go?' Wat asked.

'West. They took the river path and doubtless passed through the village.' She said the word "village" as if it was only a slight improvement on Grimsby.

'Excellent. We will be on our way and detain you no longer.

'Would you care to join us in prayer?' Scur offered. 'For the safe delivery of your mission.'

'Normally, of course, but today the pursuit of the evil which plagues us must take precedence.'

Scur nodded that he understood this sacrifice and gave Wat a solemn nod.

Engel curtsied again and they took their leave.

. . .

'I've never been invited in for prayer,' the abbot grumbled, as they took the river path, leaving Scur and Engel to pray for them.

'And what was that all about anyway?' Cwen asked. 'What a performance.'

'Oh, I've met their type before,' Wat said. 'I usually manage to sell them a nice big tapestry full of images of evil that they can fret and worry about.'

'If they only knew,' Hermitage sighed. 'If they only knew that it was Wat the Weaver they have just sent off with their blessing. I know that they can be a difficult couple, but if they ever find out, it could be the death of them.'

'And that would be no bad thing,' the abbot muttered.

'Father!' Hermitage chastised him.

'Well,' Abbo complained. 'You didn't have to deal with them. Every day there was something. Did I know that a visitor had passed towards the monastery? Yes, I did, because I met him. Did I know that they'd left again? Was I aware that the bell for Lauds had been rung slightly too late? Did I think it was significant that the pebbles on the beach were making noises? Honestly.'

'They think that they have been put here by God,' Hermitage was sympathetic.

'They could be right,' the abbot agreed. 'The Lord would be wise to put those two somewhere remote.'

'At least we know which way to go now,' Wat said, interrupting the stream of complaint about master Scur and mistress Engel. He strode along the path.

'I wonder why our killer is still following the Bretons?' Hermitage asked

'He wants to know where they're going?' Wat suggested.

'What if he wants to do them harm?' Hermitage's alarm woke up. Here they were, following someone who was suspected of killing a Norman. And that person was following others. 'Good Lord, he may want to kill them as well. We must hurry.' He really didn't want to arrive on the scene after two more murders.

'Could well be,' Wat had a lot less urgency. 'But why? While he was in the mood for stabbing people in their beds he could have done the Bretons as well. Perhaps they're of no interest? Not being abbots and all?'

'Perhaps he only fears being reported,' the abbot suggested. 'He may not know that they are actually delighted about the Norman's death. He could believe they are on their way to report a murder.'

'Good reason to kill some more people,' Cwen said, with alarming nonchalance. 'You know. Kill someone, then kill the people who know you killed the first one. Stands to reason.

'Course, you'd probably have to then kill the ones who knew you'd killed the ones who knew you'd killed the first one, and it could all get out of hand.' She frowned at the mountain of death she was building. 'Just a bit too difficult to do when they were in the monastery?' she shrugged. 'Get them on the path and throw them in the river.'

Hermitage shook his head in despair that such thoughts could occur to anyone. 'Or maybe he's just going the same way,' his hope was forlorn and he didn't really believe it. 'Just a coincidence.'

'Pretty big coincidence, a suspected killer following the only two people to leave the monastery.'

'But there isn't anywhere else to go,' Hermitage pointed out. 'If you want to leave the monastery you either take the boat or come this way. And I can't imagine that he would want to wait around in the monastery. We might have caught him.'

'Hm,' Wat said, 'Where will they be going though? Much easier to follow if we know that.'

'Bretonland?' Cwen suggested.

'Brittany,' Wat corrected.

'They could go there as well.'

Wat didn't bother to correct again. 'They could catch a boat I'd have thought. Quickest way to get anywhere.'

'From here?' Cwen nodded her head to point out the paucity of sea-going vessels just waiting for passengers.

'And they might be stopped by Normans if they tried to sail south,' Wat admitted. 'Perhaps they'd head for Wales and get safe passage to Cornwall and then on home. Avoid being in Norman country as much as possible.'

'Maybe the killer is a Breton as well?' Hermitage suggested, with no little excitement. It was also a theory that would avoid any more killing. 'They could all be in league. You know. The Bretons want FitzGilbert dead but daren't do it themselves. So they get someone else to do it for them. Someone unknown. Then they all escape together.'

'I still maintain that this is more to do with the abbot of the monastery,' the abbot of the monastery said, sounding rather sulky that his own death was being forgotten. 'Poor FitzGilbert was just the wrong Norman in the wrong monastery at the wrong time.'

'Catch the mysterious, disappearing monk, that's the only thing to do,' Wat said.

Having left the rigorous Scur and Engel behind they now walked through the small collection of dwellings that was Kilnsea itself. Hermitage doubted that five houses could be even called a village, but they were a proud people, the more imaginative inhabitants even referring to it as Great Kilnsea as if there was a lesser one somewhere.

'What's all this then?' a voice called as they passed the opening of the first simple home.

'Not again,' Wat muttered. 'Just passing through,' he called to the fellow who was now leaning against his doorpost. Well, resting very gently against the bound stand of sticks that constituted his doorpost.

'That's all well and good my lad,' the man replied. 'But it's getting ridiculous. We can't have hundreds of people tramping through the town like this.'

Hermitage recognised the imaginative village head, Ekvar. He was convinced that the man had a strong streak of Viking blood in him, so had always been careful to give him a wide passage. And to accept without question whatever ludicrous claims he had for his village

'Hundreds?' Cwen's disbelief rang clear.

'Hundreds,' Ekvar repeated.

'Two Bretons, and a monk and now four of us.'

'That's right.'

'Hundreds,' Cwen snorted.

'What's going on, that's what I want to know?' Ekvar asked, ignoring the maths. 'Oh,' he noticed the abbot. 'Hello, Father. I thought you were dead?'

'I am.'

'Eh?' Ekvar was obviously torn between not believing this and getting ready to run.

'Oh yes. It's all official. I have a letter from the bishop and everything.'

'Is that right?' Ekvar had stopped leaning on his house now.

'And, of course, being dead I get special rights and privileges.'

'Oh, ar?'

'Absolutely.' Abbot Abbo said this with such intensity, accompanied by a powerful stare of borderline insanity, that Ekvar started to retreat into his house.

'I expect you'll be on your way, then,' Ekvar said, hopefully.

'Oh,' the abbot sounded disappointed that he hadn't been able to exercise any of his powers and privileges on Ekvar. 'I suppose we will.'

'Well, goodbye,' Ekvar retreated fully.

'Are all the villages going to be like this?' Wat asked. 'We're never going to get anywhere if we get interrupted at every hovel.'

'Once you get away from the sea they do change' the abbot explained. 'They start getting rather peculiar.'

Caput XVI: A Journey Through Some Places

While their quarry had been reported as taking the river road, this was actually a well-trodden path quite a long way from the river. Both the abbot and Hermitage confirmed that to go any closer to the river itself was to invite certain death. The land and the water hadn't quite worked out which of them was in charge and the result was a collection of bogs and pools that would swallow an unwary traveller with one lonesome gulp.

That and the speed with which the water would rise meant that even unwary travellers might take one step towards the river before taking ten back again. If your footstep sank into mud you knew it was already too late to get out again.

After Kilnsea they skirted the community of Easington. Quite a big place, according to Hermitage. It had six houses. If the Bretons and the monk were following the river, they would head west from here, towards Weeton, instead of north towards Dimlington.

Hermitage and the abbot were quite clear that no one would go to Dimlington unless they were lost. And even then it wasn't advisable.

When pressed on just what it was about Dimlington, they refused to say any more. Only that it was not the sort of place innocent travellers should come across.

Wat looked like he was making a note to visit Dimlington.

At Weeton, it felt that they had arrived back in the real world. Houses, traders, animals and people moved about the place, showing little interest in the small party that wandered in out of the wetlands. They asked a variety of people if they had seen the Bretons and the monk, with no success. Perhaps they had skirted the town; the Bretons avoiding large habitations for fear of coming across Normans.

They did find the head of the town, who politely asked the abbot why he wasn't dead but did report that a shepherd in one of the outer fields had sent word of unusual movements. Apparently, that old man's report was of three extra sheep, each of them with only two legs, that had been spotted crossing the bottom of his pasture heading west.

They were hopeful that this might have happened recently and so asked for directions to the pasture. The town head satisfied them that as this news had been so remarkable, the shepherd had dispatched his boy to the town to spread the word immediately. Wasting no time at all, the young lad had only stopped at three or four places to gossip and had got the message back to the town in only a few hours.

Disappointed that the pursued seemed to be so far ahead, but satisfied that this must be them, they pressed on. More encouragement was in the confirmation that one of the sheep was dressed as a monk.

'At least he hasn't killed the Bretons yet,' Hermitage said. 'If he's going to.'

'How far are we going to get before dark?' Wat asked. 'Always assuming the Bretons will stop with the dark.'

The abbot gave this some thought. 'At the current rate we could make Torn, I think.'

'Ah,' Hermitage sighed.

'Problem?' Wat asked.

'No, no. Busy little place. Bound to get word of any strangers there.'

Wat gave the abbot a questioning look, clearly thinking that Hermitage was hiding something.

'In Torn,' the abbot explained, 'you might think you were

in Denmark.'

'Ah,' now Wat understood. 'Vikings, eh?'

'The Vikings clearly established the place many years ago, and a lot of them settled. But it is as Hermitage says, a busy little place and the people are friendly. They're just a bit more Viking than most other folk around here.'

'Doesn't sound too bad,' Cwen said.

'No, it isn't.' The abbot directed these words to Hermitage. 'Despite best efforts, some of them still worship the wrong Gods and the ships they build are still a bit, well, Viking.'

'Sounds like Grimsby.'

'Oh, no,' the abbot defended the place. 'Not at all. The people of Torn are quite normal. Although the town badge remains a Viking helmet.'

Wat gave this some thought. 'The Bretons might take refuge there. Safe from the Normans.'

'It's possible.'

'Will there be somewhere to stay?' Cwen asked. 'An inn or the like?'

'There will be somewhere, I am sure of it,' the abbot sounded as if he knew more about Torn than he was saying.

. . .

After Weeton, probably another three miles or so down the road, they came to Patrington. This was another quite large town, strategically placed where the road to the north-east crossed their path and the highway to the west became more substantial.

Quite what strategy would lead to anyone building in this spot wasn't clear. The road to the northeast was probably a favoured route for the Vikings as they got off their boats and started to look for plunder and treasure. They'd have to look pretty hard in this neck of the woods.

They did get news that they seemed to have closed the gap to the Bretons and the monk though. No one had actually noticed any Bretons but they definitely recalled the monk.

Doubtless, the two in front were trying to avoid notice and so would slip through a town without drawing attention. At least they were dressed normally, even if they couldn't speak the language.

The monk was also dressed normally, for a monk, and apparently did speak the language, but not in a nice way. Seeing a lone monk passing through the town, thinking that he must be on some holy pilgrimage, the town moot had offered him rest and sustenance. That a monk of the cloth should tell them where to put their rest and sustenance in quite such an earthy manner had been unexpected, to say the least.

The things he then said to the children, who had only asked where he was going, after all, were disgraceful. Then he approached Mistress Lora in a very personal manner and got in a fight with her betrothed. They all thought he might be ill.

Cwen suggested that he might not actually be a monk at all, but the town headsman thought that was highly unlikely. The man had a habit on, after all.

They had thought of detaining him, for his own good, in case he did himself harm on his journey, but he persuaded them otherwise. He persuaded them by punching one of the smallholders on the nose and bowling the priest over when he tried to get in his way.

The abbot had to spend quite a bit of time assuring the townsfolk that this monk was nothing to do with him, and in fact, he was chasing after the man for just such behaviour.

At least the disturbance in the town seemed to have delayed the monk a little and they might now only be an hour or two behind.

Wished Godspeed by the townsfolk and "give that monk a smack in the face for me" from Mistress Lora's betrothed, they returned to the road.

'Doesn't sound like any monk I know,' Hermitage was disgusted at the reported antics.

'Apart from Brother Wigan,' the abbot replied.

'Oh, Lord, yes, apart from Brother Wigan. But surely they haven't let him out again.'

'Not after last time.'

Wat and Cwen looked on, bemused, as they got no further information about what Brother Wigan got up to.

'So where's next?' Cwen asked.

'That'd be Winestead,' the abbot answered. 'Only a mile or so along   and we can rely on the folk there for news if there is any.'

'Reliable, trustworthy folk, or just nosy?' Wat enquired.

'The Hildegardis family are one of the most respected in the land.' The abbot chastised Wat for his impertinence and walked on ahead.

'Hildegardis,' Wat was thoughtful as he, Hermitage and Cwen walked on together. 'Sounds like the abbot knows this Hildegardis family well.' He considered this information and came to a conclusion. 'Don't want to delay our pursuit by having long discussions with old friends though. Perhaps you can find out anything with the abbot while I walk on and see if I can make progress on catching our murderous monk. No point in all three of us waiting about.'

'That could be a good idea.' Hermitage knew that Wat

could handle himself if the need arose. 'If we get delayed by long reminiscences, this fellow will only get further away.'

Cwen was looking at Wat with a very particular look on her face. 'What did you do to the Hildegardis family?' she sounded resigned to hearing about something rather distasteful.

'Nothing.'

'Nothing.' Cwen clearly did not believe this. 'So why the sudden urge to go chasing after the killer monk on your own?'

'Only trying to be helpful. Make best use of our assets and all that.'

'You know what,' Cwen pressed, 'I don't believe you. I think that if the Hildegardis family get wind that Wat the Weaver is in their town, there will be trouble.'

Hermitage looked on at the two of them, trying to work out what was going on. He knew Wat's reputation preceded him, and that sometimes this was a bad thing. He had made no secret of the fact that he could not visit Leamington anymore and that his own guild had invoked their sternest rituals to expel him, but one small village out here?[The Tapestry of Death explores the peculiarities of the weaver's guild. And they were very peculiar.] What could possibly have gone on that Wat needed to keep away?

Actually, he had quite a good idea what could have gone on. 'I still think it might be sensible,' he repeated. 'If this family do have some, erm, issues they want to take up with Wat, that could only delay us further.'

'See,' Wat pointed out. 'Hermitage knows best.'

That wasn't something Hermitage had heard from the weaver before.

'Hm,' Cwen frowned. 'I suppose there's no point in raking over dead charcoal.'

'And I wouldn't mention charcoal either if I were you,' Wat advised.

'Some early sketches?' Cwen suggested. 'Perhaps some charcoals of the Hildegardis family that they weren't too happy about?'

'Not the whole family,' Wat was insulted by the very suggestion. 'But if there's a woman called Alodia in residence, I shouldn't mention weaving at all, or tapestry.'

'Really.'

Wat nodded. 'Or charcoal, country walks, resting by the river and dancing around the maypole.' He shrugged.

'Wat, really,' Hermitage shook his head. 'I think you'd better get on,' he waved him away.

'Where are you going?' the abbot called as Wat passed him.

'Just going to get ahead, see if I can close the distance to our man.' He gave a friendly wave as he strode quickly off.

'Seems rash. But then nothing would surprise me.'

'I wouldn't count on that,' muttered Cwen.

The outlying dwellings of Winestead came into view and towards the back of these quite a fine house poked its head above its surroundings. Obviously made of solid timbers, with a good thatch roof, this must be the house of the master of the manor, or some such. The Hildegardis residence, Hermitage assumed.

'We'll go straight to the house,' the abbot directed. 'Master Cynweard should be able to give us help if there is any to be given.'

Cynweard Hildegardis, Hermitage mused. Rather surprising to find someone with a name like that still in possession of anything in this Norman country. But then, if these were the lands that ultimately belonged to the monastery, becoming abbot would have put them in FitzGilbert's hands anyway. With that plan failing, what with FitzGilbert going and dying like that, he suspected it wouldn't be long before a force of Normans turned up and did the usual. One of Wat's tapestries would be the least the Hildegardis family had to worry about.

As they approached the house the door was already open and an elderly man stood on the step, waiting to greet them. Presumably Cynweard. He was certainly dressed well enough to be Lord of the Manor and didn't look like he'd actually lifted a tool or driven a plough for a single day in his long life.

'Abbo, Abbo,' the old fellow called, happily, holding his arms out to welcome his visitors.

The abbot approached the door and the two men shared embraces and pats on the back for so long that Hermitage and Cwen started to exchange looks. This seemed more than the simple greeting of a landowner for his abbot.

Hermitage wondered why the man had not called out to Abbot Abbo. Using the name alone seemed a little disrespectful.

Once the men had extracted themselves from their greeting, the abbot turned and indicated his companions. 'This is Brother Hermitage,' Abbo said, with some pride. 'Once a brother with me, he now holds high office with the king.'

Cynweard looked very impressed with this. Hermitage found himself thinking it sounded quite good as well.

'And this is...'

'Leofcwen,' Cwen burst out, giving a short bow. Hermitage was surprised to hear her full name, she so seldom used it. 'I assist Brother Hermitage in his work.' She gave the abbot a forceful nod, telling him not to contradict her.

The abbot just shrugged and looked confused at what

young people got up to these days, but he said no more.

'Come, come,' Cynweard beckoned them indoors. 'It is so long since I have seen my old friend Abbo. There is much to catch up on.'

'Regretfully, there is little time,' the abbot explained. 'We are on the trail of a possible killer.'

'A killer?' Cynweard sounded truly shocked. 'In Winestead?'

'What's amiss, grandfather?' A young woman appeared at Cynweard's shoulder. She was certainly a great beauty, with a bright, intelligent gleam in her eyes and a look that invited conversation and most likely friendship. Doubtless, this was Alodia.

Hermitage immediately looked to the ground, feeling deeply ashamed of whatever it was that Wat had done. He tried desperately not to imagine what it had been, but several things popped into the front of his mind that he didn't even know had been at the back.

Even Cwen gave a nod of acknowledgement and then took to studying the timber frame of the building.

'See, it is our old friend Abbo,' Cynweard announced. 'But it sounds that he is here on a matter of some awful import. You had best go inside, child. I would not have your ears sullied by our conversation.'

Talk of sullying Alodia only made Hermitage feel worse.

'Oh grandfather,' Alodia chided, in her charming way. 'I'm sure there is nothing I have not heard before. You shelter me too much.' She touched the old man's arm lightly and he took her hand protectively, a look of fierce pride on his face.

If Wat turned up, he'd be dead.

'We seek a monk, travelling alone, mistress,' the abbot said. 'There has been some trouble at the monastery and it is most

213

urgent that we find him.'

'An escapee?' Alodia laughed, lightly. 'Whatever has become of the place.'

'Not a Brother of ours, I assure you.'

'How mysterious,' Alodia sounded thoroughly fascinated. 'A monk in the wrong monastery, there must be some rule against that.'

'Indeed there is. So if either of you has seen anyone, any strangers at all?'

'I've seen no one,' Cynweard said. 'But then I do not get out as once I did. I rely on others for news and no one has told me of strangers yet.'

'I had a charming conversation with two gentlemen from Brittany this morning,' Alodia said, without concern.

'You told me nothing of this,' Cynweard had tension in his voice.

'Grandfather,' Alodia comforted him. 'They were simple travellers who passed by while I was tending one of the smallholders' children, who had cut his leg.'

Cynweard looked like he didn't want her going out at all. But then if he was the one who found Wat's drawings, Hermitage couldn't blame him.

'You conversed with them?' the abbot sounded surprised.

'I have a smattering of Welsh and their tongue is similar in many ways. We made ourselves understood.'

'Passing by where?' the abbot pressed.

Alodia chuckled as if this was charming gossip of no significance. 'They said they were making for Wales themselves. From there they would head south and back to their homes. I gather they had had a trying time with one of the Normans. They do seem a churlish lot.'

'A trying time, yes,' the abbot confirmed. 'They did indeed.

But you saw no monk?'

'I'm afraid not.'

'Or anyone else following them?' Hermitage asked, thinking that the fake monk may have cast off his garb, in an attempt to avoid further altercations.

'I don't think so,' Alodia spoke carefully. 'There was a rough fellow who seemed to be more interested in the ditches than the road. Probably some tinker cast out from Patrington. I certainly didn't speak to him.' Speaking to tinkers was something for which she did not need her grandfather's prohibition.

'And how long ago was this? When did the Bretons and this tinker leave?' Cwen asked.

'This morning, but only two hours ago or so. I'm sure if you hurry, you could catch them up.'

'That is our intention,' the abbot was decisive. 'There is no time to linger and loiter I am afraid. Perhaps, if we get this all sorted out, I can return and catch up on those old times.'

'That would be fine,' Cynweard smiled. 'But the times we live in are bad enough. I had even heard rumour that you yourself were dead. Of course, I believed not a word of it. Even when they told me there had been a ceremony. I said, "if Abbo has died he would have invited me to his funeral". And now I am proved right.'

'Just so,' the abbot nodded.

'The Normans are a worry though. How long before they stamp their name upon the land and we all fall under them?'

'Not long at all, I suspect.' The abbot was trying desperately to take his leave from an old man who hadn't had enough people to talk to for years, by the sound of him.

'Things were better when you were lord of everything hereabouts.'

'Yes, yes, I'm sure.' The abbot was taking half steps towards the door.

'Even taking the cloth didn't change things, but now? I heard old Hrodulf at Drypool had his manor given to some Norman called Drogo. Did you ever hear the like? Drogo? What sort of name is that? Not that he stopped working the place of course. Oh no. Still has to plough the land, just give all his tithes to the Normans. And he's not a young man. If they can do that to…'

'Yes, yes,' the abbot's impatience burst out. 'We must depart and find our..,' he paused and gave Cynweard a significant look, 'monk,' he pronounced it very particularly.

At last, Cynweard got the message. 'Ah, the monk, yes.' He gave half a glance to Alodia. 'You go off and find your monk. And good luck to you.'

With Cynweard still standing on his door and waving them away, Alodia firmly clamped to his side, the abbot, Hermitage and Cwen stepped smartly away down the track.

There was no telling if Wat really had gone ahead to look for the Bretons, or whether he was simply resting on some bank nearby. The abbot strode ahead, obviously inspired by the thought that they were not far behind.

'Did you think that was odd?' Cwen asked Hermitage when they were out of the abbot's earshot.

'Oh, I don't think so,' Hermitage replied. 'It's quite natural for a grandfather to want to protect his grandchild in these trying times. Particularly one as lovely as Alodia.'

'Lovely,' Cwen's tone was a rather fierce tone for some reason. 'Right. I didn't mean about her, actually. I meant about the land.'

'What about the land?'

'That business of the world being a better place when the

abbot was in charge.'

'The abbot was the lord of the land in effect,' Hermitage explained. 'If the land belonged to the monastery then the abbot is the lord. Isn't that what this is all about?' He couldn't quite see why Cwen was confused all of a sudden.

'But the old boy said nothing changed when the abbot took the cloth. What did that mean?'

'I imagine it was just that the abbot carried on the ways of the lord before him. As far as I'm aware the monastery treated the tenants within its lands very well. Taxes and tithes were not high and everyone lived as well as could be expected.'

'Do you know who the previous lord was?'

'Oh, heavens no. That was long before my time.'

'Hm,' Cwen still seemed to be pondering something.

'I did read about the transfer of the land in some of the parchments, though.'

'And?'

'And what?' Hermitage really couldn't see what the interest was.

'Was the old lord as wonderful as dear Abbot Abbo when it came to running the place?'

'I don't think it was mentioned specifically,' Hermitage reported, wondering why it would be.

They walked on a few more paces. 'Of course,' Hermitage expanded on his researches. 'The monastery only received the land fairly recently. Just before Abbot Abbo's rule began.'

'It didn't have it before?' Cwen was very interested. 'So the previous lord wasn't the previous abbot? How did the place survive?'

'Donations and gifts from great Saxon families,' Hermitage described the normal process.

'Like Abbo's?'

'Could be, I suppose. Is there a problem?'

'I don't know,' Cwen was very thoughtful. 'How come the monastery suddenly got this huge amount of land?'

'Probably to keep it out of the hands of the Normans.' Hermitage had a rare moment of understanding. Understanding of the ways of Normans and landowners and the like. It was normally a completely blank page to him. Perhaps his time with Wat was affecting him, but some of the parchments he had read started to make sense.

'I imagine they'd think twice about taking land from the church. Taking it from ordinary people won't be a problem at all. If a Saxon lord gave his land to the church but kept some of the tithes, it would be harder for the Normans to rob him.'

'Hm,' Cwen hummed. 'There's still something nagging at the back of my head.'

'Oh, I know what that feels like.'

Cwen shrugged it away and brightened up. 'Apart from all the usual problems of course; a dead Norman, a killer monk and an undead abbot.'

Hermitage pondered that. He appreciated that the abbot had been declared dead when, in fact, he wasn't, but he wasn't convinced that undead was quite the right term.

Caput XVII: Home?

'We met Alodia,' Cwen said when they caught up with Wat. To Hermitage's ear, it sounded as if she had not enjoyed the encounter when actually they had all got along fine. 'Lovely girl, according to Hermitage,' she went on, sounding quite cross now. There really was no telling with her, sometimes.

'Ah well,' Wat was cheerful, 'if Hermitage says so, she must be lovely.'

Cwen didn't seem to take this very well at all and walked close by Wat, hissing words into his ear that Hermitage could not quite catch. For which he was quite grateful.

The day was starting to draw to its close as the outskirts of Torn came into sight.

Wat had extricated himself from Cwen's lecture which had gone on for quite some time. Hermitage was glad that she was remonstrating with him about his old trade. With both of them doing it, there was a better chance that he would not relapse. Admittedly most of Cwen's remonstrance seemed to revolve around Alodia, but perhaps using her as a clear example was the best approach. Hermitage always relied on broader concepts around the eternal soul and good against evil, which Wat never seemed to take seriously enough.

'The Bretons and our killer are going to have to stop for the night,' Wat said as he stepped along the road with the abbot and Hermitage. Cwen was still behind staring intently at Wat's back. When Hermitage turned, he saw the expression on her face was quite capable of driving Wat forward from a distance.

'If he does want to kill the Bretons he clearly can't do it on the road or doesn't want to. So the night would be his best opportunity. If they don't know he's following, they'll take their rest, and then he can pounce.'

'If he wants to pounce at all,' the abbot said. 'It could be that he simply wants to know what they're going to do. If they're not going to the authorities he could well leave them to their own devices.'

'Lot of trouble to go to.'

'If it's Normans he's after, like FitzGilbert, why would he bother with the Bretons anyway?' Hermitage asked. 'Particularly as they're leaving.'

'And if it is abbots?' the abbot said. 'If he is connected to my apparent demise and FitzGilbert's actual one, all he'll want to know is that the Bretons aren't on their way to get another abbot.'

'And if they are, and he kills the next one as well, we'll know it's abbots,' Wat said, helpfully. 'Mind you, as he dealt with the most recent abbot by sticking a knife in his chest, finishing you off by writing a letter seems a bit mild. Out of keeping, you might say.'

'Maybe he simply couldn't find the abbot,' Hermitage suggested. 'If he was off on pilgrimage at the time.'

'Knowing what the man is capable of, I think he'd have waited.'

'Until we find him and question him, this is all speculation,' the abbot said. 'Look, we are upon the town now. I think I know where we can go for lodgings. We can also ask about visitors.'

Abbo led them through the streets of Torn, and Hermitage noted several worrying indications concerning the origin of the place. There were indeed village signs all over the place, and there was no mistaking the Viking helmet.

This one even had wings and seemed to be a mark of pride as the villagers used it on every building. It may only be a small carving above a door but still, a Viking helmet with wings was not a comforting image.

Of course, there was a church, a good Saxon-looking Christian church, but Hermitage would not be surprised to find the emblem scattered over that sacred place.

And the people were a worry. They all looked friendly and not at all hostile to the new arrivals, but they were all just a bit too tall and, well, Viking looking.

One rather well-dressed individual approached, clearly on his way somewhere else, but he did give them an intense look as he drew near. He looked as if he were someone of import in the town. His stride was purposeful and a mature but a questioning face said that he would expect to know everything that went on.

'That's not Abbo, is it?' the man asked, doubting his own eyes.

The abbot just gave a short nod of the head in acknowledgement.

This brought the man to a halt and he came up to them, a broad smile on his face.

'My dear fellow,' the man called, holding his arms out to embrace the abbot. 'Or should I say Father?' he asked at the last moment, transforming his hug into a polite pat on the shoulder. 'It's me, Hendor.'

'Ah, Hendor,' the abbot replied, now smiling himself. 'It is good to see a friendly face. How do you fare?'

'How do I fare?' Hendor replied as if this was the least relevant question in the world. 'Never mind how I fare. What brings you here? We've not seen you for so long. Wait until father hears that you are in town.'

'Your father still as strong and fit as ever?' the abbot asked.

'Of course. What could keep him down? And you are not alone?' Hendor looked at the others for some introduction.

'This is Brother Hermitage,' the abbot brought Hermitage forward. 'He was once a monk with me at Kilnsea but is now in the king's service.'

'My goodness,' Hendor bowed acknowledgement.

'And this,' the abbot reduced his voice to a mumble. 'Is master Wat, he's a weaver.' He said this last bit very quickly and quietly.

'My goodness and gracious on top,' said Hendor. 'Wat the Weaver? Here? And in the company of an abbot?'

'Actually, he's in the company of Brother Hermitage, as is mistress Cwen here.'

Hendor bowed his welcome to Cwen, all the while staring at Wat.

'Then you must all come to meet father. He would not forgive you being allowed into town without his hospitality.'

'We had thought of imposing on you for accommodations.'

'Then we shall see that is done,' Hendor laughed. 'If ever there was an excuse for feast and conversation, this is it.'

'They seem terribly excited about an abbot,' Wat observed to Hermitage.

Hendor waved to a boy who was passing and gave him instruction to take word to Hendor's father that visitors were coming, significant but friendly visitors. Their old friend Abbo was returned.

'We'll send word,' he said to the abbot. 'Father is old now, and it is best to manage any sudden surprises. And, erm, shocks.' He sounded a bit more hesitant now, 'So perhaps it would be best not to raise the name of Wat the Weaver?'

'We're used to that,' Cwen snarled a bit. 'Haven't got a

sister have you?' she asked, also staring at Wat while she did so.

'A sister?' Hendor seemed puzzled by the question. 'No, no sister. You will have to suffer the company of a gaggle of old men, I'm afraid.'

'That's perfectly fine.'

They were taken straight through the middle of the town towards a large house at the top of the street. Like Winestead, this house was a whole order of comfort and quality better than the rest of the village. It was also a whole order better than Winestead. They were clearly moving up the orders of society quite quickly.

The door of this place also had an old man at it when they arrived, but he had a couple of servants at his side, one holding a tray with a flagon and mugs on it, and one simply waiting to be told to do something. This was a serious family.

As Abbot Abbo drew close, the old man bowed low and beckoned the flagon-bearer forward.

It looked as if they were all expected to take a mug and drink to something or other. They did so without a word being said and the old man raised his mug high.

'To the return of happier times,' the man called in a strong and firm voice. 'Welcome,' he held his cup towards the abbot. 'Welcome indeed, my lord.'

"My lord?" thought Hermitage. The abbot wasn't a bishop. Why would they call him "my lord"?

Caput XVIII: You Might Have Said

There had been a flurry of activity as they were taken into what was clearly a magnificent house. A servant led the way into a great hall where a table was laden with food and drink. A joint of pork, nuts, bread, fruits, all piled high for the visitors. That there was so much available was a surprise. That it had been got ready so quickly was a bigger one. The place must be crawling with servants to have moved this lot so quickly.

Hendor's father had insisted that they fill their plates and eat and drink to this happy occasion. Of course, Wat and Cwen were more than happy to do so.

When they were out of earshot of their hosts, Cwen's question was generously splattered with breadcrumbs and pork fat. 'Why do they call you my lord?' It sounded more like a demand for an explanation rather than a polite enquiry.

'Simply a remembrance of old times,' the abbot explained. 'Old master Hendor has been lord of this manor for over forty years.'

'Old Hendor?' Cwen queried. 'His name is Hendor and he called his son Hendor?'

'Of course.' The abbot couldn't see any problem with this. 'He inherited the title very young and is over sixty now.'

'That's what good food and lots of servants can do for you,' Wat butted in. 'I've always said that being poor is bad for your health.'

'My lord?' Cwen got back to the question in hand.

'It's just that old Hendor harks back to the time when my family was significant. The time before I took the habit and relinquished all claim to title.'

'And land. Land and title, I imagine?'

'I have been over all this. I gave that up many years ago. That old Hendor still lives in the past is out of my hands.'

'But more precisely, this land,' Cwen pointed out. 'The land we're in now. This actual bit.' She even pointed to the floor to make sure they were clear which particular bit they were referring to.

Hermitage joined them now. He had eaten a small piece of bread and an apple and was feeling quite full.

'What you're saying is that you were the lord of this land. Your family owned it and now it is in the hands of the monastery.'

'We held the land for our lord, but that's about it.'

'How did that happen?'

'How did it happen? The way it should happen. The land was gifted to the monastery in a legal and proper manner.'

'By you?'

'Not at all. That would not be proper. Questions could be raised about my appointment as abbot if I had given tracts of land. People might think it was an exchange.'

'Yes,' Cwen said, 'they might indeed.'

'It was a family decision.'

Hermitage was following this with interest. He had come across no details of how the monastery acquired the land, only that it had. To have this missing piece filled in was most satisfying. He then thought about a large tract of land and what people were prepared to do to get one, and new ideas bothered him.

'If I understand it then,' he began. 'The land which may be the reason behind your theoretical death and FitzGilbert's very practical one belonged to you originally.'

'Yes.' The abbot sounded weary at repeating this

irrelevance.

'And as abbot of the monastery, it came under your control once more.'

'It did.'

'And when you died, it passed to the new abbot, FitzGilbert, who obviously didn't get to keep it very long.'

'Just so.'

'So we wait for yet another abbot, or for you to be brought back to life again.' Hermitage hated to say resurrected, as it didn't sound at all appropriate.

'Is there anything else you haven't told us,' Wat hissed at the abbot.

'How would I know? There are lots of things I haven't told you. Several of which I'm not likely to, either.'

'I mean,' Wat was sounding a bit cross now. 'Anything else relating to the matter of your death?' First of all, it's nothing but a mistake. Then we find that your monastery owns an awful lot of land and that a Norman has turned up to take it. Apart from him being murdered, we also discover that the land belonged to you in the first place.'

'So?'

'So? So?' Wat was keeping his voice down so as not to draw attention, but he was getting a bit excited. 'You don't think any of this is connected? Perhaps you'd like to mention that you've had threats of death in mysterious letters that tell you to leave the monastery and never come back.'

'Hardly,' the abbot dismissed the idea.

'Good.'

'Every abbot gets letters and visits from strange people. Many of them are poor, disturbed fellows, who need the help and guidance of the church.'

'What?' This did burst from Wat in a loud shout, which

made the two Hendor's raise their heads.

'You have had letters threatening you with death?' Wat clearly could not believe this.

'It is quite normal,' Hermitage explained. 'Monasteries are frequently the most significant institutions in their area. Naturally, they attract people who believe they have some complaint to make.'

'And they threaten the abbot with death? In writing? Bit of an extreme complaint.'

'That would be unusual. But it is as the abbot says, many of these people have very fixed ideas in their heads. Ideas that they have nurtured over many years and about which they will brook no contradiction. Even in the face of the plain facts. They think that their lord is conspiring against them, or that their neighbours are watching them, or the fact that they poisoned their husband was entirely justified because he kept looking at them in a funny way.'

Wat just gaped.

'That was a very particular one,' Hermitage admitted.

'But in this case.' Wat was all fierce intent now. 'In this case, we have an abbot who used to own the land that now belongs to the monastery. The land the Norman was after.'

'It was family land,' the abbot explained again, impatiently.

'A family of which you were head,' Wat even pointed at the abbot, which was quite rude. 'And you had letters?'

'Of course, I received many letters.'

'About death and land and the monastery?'

The abbot made a face that said there were so many that he couldn't be expected to remember them all.

'Do you recall the very learned fellow in the north? Hermitage asked Abbo.

'Ah, yes,' Abbo nodded a smile.

Wat demanded an explanation with a simple look.

Hermitage did his best. 'Someone claimed that the abbot was not entitled to his position and wrote pages and pages with biblical and legal references. He must have been pretty wealthy himself, to have afforded all the parchment. They would come quite regularly, usually accompanied by a bill of sale for all the work he had done in proving his point.'

'He wanted you to pay?' Cwen asked. 'How much?'

'Six hundred thousand pounds,' said Hermitage.

They all had a bit of a laugh at that.

'We didn't pay,' Hermitage confirmed.

'Really?' Wat sounded surprised, for some reason. 'If we could focus on death threats to the abbot who soon found himself dead?'

'It was nothing.' The abbot waved the issue away. 'Some poor individual who had something against the abbot, or the monastery, or even the church in general.'

'Or you and your land?'

'This one simply said that I ought to die. More of a suggestion than a threat, really.'

'Oh, that's all right then,' Wat clearly didn't think it was all right. 'And you have no idea who it was?'

'With anonymous letters, one seldom does.' The abbot raised his dismissive eyebrows.

'I don't believe this,' Wat muttered to himself. 'You never thought that the fact you were declared dead might have something to do with the person who was suggesting, in writing, that you might like to be dead?'

'Not at all.'

'Remarkable. An abbot and an idiot in the same habit.' Wat went for a little circular walk.

'And then suddenly, guess what? You are dead. What a

coincidence. If the Norman hadn't come along what would have happened? What if no abbot is found, ever?'

'Hardly likely,' said Hermitage, feeling quite cross with Wat for his rudeness. 'And anyway, a monastery can operate perfectly well without an abbot for some time. The land simply resides with the establishment.'

'But what if the whole monastery disappeared?' Cwen suggested. 'What would happen then?'

'I hardly think it likely that an entire monastery could vanish.'

'I think the one we just came from is in a very good position to do just that. One really good wave and the whole place will float away.'

'Or the king or some bishop simply decides he doesn't want it anymore and dissolves it?' Wat added.

'Dissolution of a monastery?' Hermitage laughed at the very idea. 'It's completely unthinkable. It would never happen.'

'Hm,' Wat wasn't so sure. 'Tell us about this family decision to hand a huge amount of land over to the monastery where you ended up as abbot?'

Before Abbo could reply, old Hendor came over and there was more patting of backs and noises of mutual appreciation.

'Of course, it is a great joy to see you here,' Hendor touched the abbot's arm. 'But we have not had a visit these last twenty years at least. What brings our old friend here just now?'

'A pursuit,' said Abbo.

'A pursuit. My gracious. And who or what do you pursue?'

'A monk.'

'A monk? Haven't you got enough of them? There's one right here.' The old man indicated Hermitage as if the abbot hadn't noticed.

'We pursue a very particular monk, who may not actually be a monk at all.'

Old Hendor stared at the flagon of wine in his hand as if an explanation for this would float to its surface.

'And he himself is pursuing two Bretons, or so we think.'

'You're chasing a monk who's chasing Bretons. It all sounds most peculiar to me.' The old man clearly wanted to dismiss this confusion from his head. 'You can probably ask the Bretons who passed through a while ago. We directed them to the Inn at Preston. They might know the ones you're after.'

'There are two Bretons in Preston?' Hermitage burst out.

'Absolutely. The whole country seems to be awash with them at the moment. Never seen any before in my life and now we've got four of them. Whatever next?'

'Maybe our two are your two?' Hermitage suggested.

'Our two, your two, two in Preston and two being pursued! That's eight!' Old Hendor exclaimed in alarm. 'Is this an invasion? The Normans are bad enough, but Bretons as well?'

'Have some more wine, father,' Young Hendor stepped quickly over and filled his father's flagon. He gave the others an apologetic glance.

'There's no time for wine, the town is full of Bretons. Call out the town. To arms, to arms!'

'There are only two Bretons, father,' Hendor insisted, very loudly.

'Ha! Got the other six already eh? Well done men. Stand down. By, that was quick.'

'Father is still good with his numbers,' Hendor explained. 'It's everything else that's a problem.'

Old master Hendor settled on a chair, drinking his wine with visible satisfaction that the Breton invasion had been fought off so successfully.

'Are there really Bretons at Preston?' Hermitage asked.

'There are. They passed through a few hours ago. A noticeable presence in the town but they seem friendly enough.'

The four pursuers looked at one another and reached a decision. 'We need to go to Preston,' Hermitage said.

'We have more than enough food and drink here,' old Hendor pointed out.

'We need to talk to the Bretons, I think.'

'I have to agree with my father that this does all sound peculiar. And strange activity for an abbot, a monk and two weavers.' Young Hendor looked at them all with interest. 'Not that I can think of any activity to suit such a band. Apart from tapestry for a church perhaps. But then I don't think that's the normal line of work, eh?' He looked at Wat.

'It is now,' Wat looked at Hermitage and sounded very unhappy at the change.

'You know Wat's works then?' Hermitage asked, with some disappointment.

'Although we are away from the main centres of the country, we are on the route to the coast and see a lot of trade. The name and appearance of Wat the Weaver is no secret, and of course, his own particular works are well known.'

'Oh, dear.'

'Yes,' Hendor spoke quietly. 'As I said, I wouldn't let father know who is in his hall if I were you.'

'Ha, where have we heard that before?' Cwen's eyes stabbed at Wat.

'He would be horrified, I imagine.' Hermitage shook his

head.

'He'd be delighted,' Hendor said, confusingly. 'Always been a bit of an enthusiast himself, until mother found out, of course. He did have quite a collection. I suspect he's still got some hidden away somewhere if the noises late at night are anything to go by.'

'Your father's not someone I'm familiar with,' Wat said. 'But then sometimes I don't know where the works end up.'

'Oh, he's very discreet. Always gets someone else to buy them for him. Borrows them from a friend, that sort of thing.' Hendor snorted. Clearly, he did not share his father's interests.

'I gather the abbot here used to be your lord?' Wat said as it was only a minor point of interest in an otherwise boring conversation.

'That's right.' Hendor nodded towards Abbo. 'That was a few years back. We've been on monastery land for a while now.'

'A big thing to do, I'd have thought, hand over a large part of the country to a monastery.'

'I really wouldn't know, you'd have to ask the abbot.'

'That's what I've been trying to do,' Wat said with extravagant exasperation.

'All right,' the abbot held his hands up. 'If you need it in words even a weaver can understand, let me explain.'

'That would be good.'

'Of course, it involves the call of God, so you might not understand that bit.'

'I'll do my best.'

The abbot beckoned them all to sit. When everyone was comfortable he took a breath. 'My father, old Abbo,'

'Bit of a feature round here,' Cwen said. 'Re-using the same name over and over again.' The abbot glared.

'My father, old Abbo, died and naturally, as the eldest son, I inherited the bulk of the estates. However, for some time I had felt the call of the monastic life and my younger brother was far more suited to the life of the lord, and more interested in it as well. His sons were of a mind with me. They had other interests and didn't want the burden of wealth and land.'

'Poor things,' Cwen muttered.

'Then there was Harold.'

'King Harold?' Hermitage asked.

'He wasn't king then, but he and his family, the Godwinsons, were very difficult people. They had the ear of the king, old Edward, and between them, they were cutting the country up. Anyone who thought about giving land or money to the church got a visit from a Godwinson, frequently late at night, when they would be persuaded to change their mind.

'We had a family meeting to decide what to do. The nephews and I were of accord, our estates were simply too big and too attractive to the wrong sort of people.'

'The problems you had to put up with,' Cwen shook her head in sorrow at their condition.

Abbo ignored her. 'The Godwinsons or the Vikings or someone or other would be along sooner or later to turf us out. Easier to turf people when they're dead. So, we decided that we could reduce the size of our holding. If we became minor landholders, instead of major ones, we would have enough to live on, but we wouldn't be a target, as it were.'

'So give a large portion away, to the church,' Wat said. 'Didn't you get a Godwinson after dark?'

'We moved very quickly. The deed was done before we

even told anyone. And Kilnsea is an obscure place. No one was likely to be paying attention to its holdings.'

'I bet they weren't very happy though.'

'But I had taken the habit as well. They could not, in all conscience, deal poorly with a monk.'

'I hadn't heard about the Godwinsons having a conscience,' Wat observed.

'A neat escape,' Hermitage said. 'The king and Harold put off the land, you in the monastery and your brother and the young nephews left with enough to get by.'

'And able to blame me if anyone did come calling,' the abbot rounded off.

'And then your brother died?' Hermitage asked.

'He did,' the abbot nodded, sorrowfully. 'Soon after I was elevated to the position of abbot. In the event, our decision to bequest the monastery has turned out for the best. The nephews did not want the land and so we are all content.'

'Which brings us back to the question of what happens if you die, and there is no monastery?' Wat pressed.

'In those ridiculous circumstances, it would go back to the family.' The abbot dismissed this idea with a flick of his fingers.

'Would it, indeed?' Wat was most interested.

'Of course. We wouldn't want it reverting to the crown, that would mean Harold getting his hands on it. Or so we thought at the time.'

'So you did think about it?'

'Our advisers said we should make provision for all eventualities, no matter how bizarre.'

'And this was something else that you didn't think was relevant to the fact that you had mysteriously died without being informed?'

'I can assure you that my nephews have as little interest in the land as anyone. If they were significant landowners now, they would receive the attention of King William, who I think is probably worse than Harold.'

'He is,' Hermitage confirmed.

'Well someone is up to something,' Wat was decisive. 'An abbot who tries to hide land from the Crown ends up dead? This is no mistake. I think we need to talk to the nephews.'

'Entirely irrelevant,' the abbot huffed.

'Possibly. Unless, of course, they're dead as well.'

Caput XIX: Enough Motive?

'This isn't going to involve another great journey, is it?' Hermitage complained as they gathered their belongings together.

'You'd rather have a death in Wat's workshop then?' Cwen asked. 'So we won't have far to go.'

'I'd rather not have a death at all.'

'Well, at least you're getting ahead of them this time. I bet the king doesn't even know FitzGilbert is dead yet, and you're already investigating.'

Hermitage had half-forgotten about FitzGilbert. The dead Norman was going to be another problem.

Cwen nudged him in the ribs. 'We could put up a sign when we get home. "Tapestry woven and murders investigated, enquire within."'

Hermitage just groaned at the very idea.

'Better not mention it to Wat though, he'd probably rent you out.'

'This is all a complete waste of time.' The abbot joined them as they headed for the front door, having bid embarrassed farewells and apologies for not taking up the offer of the accommodation.

'Where's Wat?' Hermitage asked, looking around.

A few moments later the weaver came scuttling up to the door.

'What have you been up to?' Cwen narrowed her eyes.

'Nothing,' Wat protested. 'Just saying goodbye to our hosts. Least we can do I think, don't you?'

'Saying goodbye to old master Hendor, mainly?'

'We may have had a word or two.'

'But no money changed hands?'

'What are you suggesting?' Wat sounded mightily offended.

'I couldn't possibly repeat it in the company of two monks.'

'Are we ready?' The abbot sighed his impatience.

'Lead on,' Wat waved the way ahead.

'Is it far?' Hermitage tried not to let a whine of complaint creep into his voice.

'Not at all. The family seat was in Preston. Just up the road really.'

'And you really owned all this land?' Hermitage knew that the calling of the monastery was a strong one, but didn't imagine that great landowners felt it as well.

'We held it. Which is much the same thing. As long as we paid our tithes.'

'And who did you hold it for?' Wat asked.

'Earl Tostig.'

Wat whistled a whistle of worried wonder. 'Another Godwinson,' he noted. 'Now gone the way of all Godwinsons.'

'Yes, and a troublesome fellow.'

'I'll say. Good job he was farther north most of the time. That man's been banished more times than a dog from a butcher's shop.'

'Indeed. And another good reason to be rid of the land. When King Edward sat on the throne there was order in the country. Particularly when he exiled Earl Tostig for a while. Things were peaceful. Once the king had gone and the Godwinsons started arguing with one another, it was not sensible to be caught in the middle.'

'Tostig would have had you joining his army against Harold. And Harold would have sent his army to take the land from Tostig.'

'When Tostig came back from his most recent banishment, this time with Vikings at his back, the monastery had a fine vantage point. We could see his army sailing up the river and immediately called the brotherhood together for prayer.'

'That they would be defeated?' Cwen asked.

'That they would just keep going.'

Just when they thought they were away, old master Hendor reappeared with more spring in his step as he came down the path to wave goodbye. Servants were summoned to form a respectful phalanx and a woman joined Hendor at the door to wave them away.

'Who was that?' Cwen asked as she looked back.

'Well,' Hermitage was intrigued by the whole business. 'Apparently, Hendor does have a sister after all. Much younger than him. Goodness knows why he said he had no sister. Perhaps she's very shy and didn't want to join us.'

'Shy,' Cwen laughed. 'Yes, shy. That'll be it.'

The abbot led the way out of town to the west, the road well-trodden and easy.

'How long to Preston then?' Wat asked. 'About an hour?'

'Thereabouts.'

'And these nephews of yours?'

'Sons of my brother. That makes them nephews. You see?'

'Yes, I see,' Wat snapped. 'I know how a nephew works. And that makes you their uncle. The uncle who gave away half their land and is probably entitled to what's left if he wanted it.'

The abbot just shook his head and sighed.

'It might be useful to know something about them, Father,' Hermitage put in. 'Before we meet them in person.'

Abbo appraised Hermitage and smiled, 'Very well.'

'Just a minute,' Wat protested.

'What is it now?' Abbo snapped.

'When I ask about the nephews I get my head bitten off, when Hermitage asks, it's a charming subject for conversation. Every time Cwen makes a helpful suggestion you look like you want to throw her under a cart. All Hermitage has to do is open his mouth and he's little monk perfect. Sorry, Hermitage.'

Hermitage just smiled and shook his head as if it didn't matter. Actually, he didn't know what the problem was. As far as he could see the abbot had been as kind and helpful as usual. It was Wat who had been rude and abrupt.

'If you want to know, master weaver.'

'I do.'

Abbo gave him a clear and piercing look. 'Brother Hermitage is the best of us.'

'Oh, now,' Hermitage was embarrassed.

'You see? Give him a compliment and he thinks it's not deserved. Ask him to help you in some way and he does it without thinking. Tell him some tale of horror, committed by a noble of greed and depravity, and he probably won't believe it.'

'Your point?' Wat said, clearly thinking that everyone knew all this about Hermitage.

'Shouldn't we all be like that?'

'If we want to be robbed by the next greedy and depraved noble.'

'But the nobles should be like that as well. And the king and the church and the peasants and everyone. If we were all like Brother Hermitage, strife and wrongdoing would be banished from the world like Earl Tostig from Northumberland.'

'And you?'

'And me. I know my faults, at least that's my strength. I know the ways I fail, that I can be impatient and contemptuous and I try to do something about it.'

'You don't try very hard,' Cwen said.

The abbot took a breath. 'You are right. I don't. And what are your faults mistress? And yours master weaver. And how much effort have you put into correcting them? Brother Hermitage is the example to us all. And he isn't even trying. It's just the way he's made. He is naturally trusting and innocent and thinks the best of everyone.'

'A bit of a disadvantage in an investigator of murder,' Wat noted.

'I don't doubt it, but he has solved these murders?'

'He has.'

'Probably because he comes without any preconceived notions. He treats everyone the same until he finds some incontrovertible fact which he has to accept.'

'That is usually how it works,' Cwen said.

'And then I imagine he is mortified that he has found someone capable of such an act.'

'Yes. He seems more upset about the killer than the victim.'

'When we were at the monastery and Hermitage was working through the parchments, he came across one from the old rule of Benedict. One that said any visiting brother should be able to offer constructive criticism to the monastery if they found something amiss.'

'It is in the rule,' Hermitage explained, feeling most awkward that people were talking about him. And how nice they were being. Well, the abbot was.

'Can you imagine how I would receive such a suggestion?

240

Me with my natural impatience and contempt? Any other Brother would have quietly lost that particular work, but not Hermitage. He brought it to my attention, full of enthusiasm and interest. And what could I do but note that he was right? We should put measures in place to make sure visitors were invited to comment. Not that we had many visitors.'

'Good for Hermitage,' Wat said.

'And then,' Abbo went on. 'He found a further note that said if this monk offered criticism in the manner of a gossip and without humility, he should be reminded of his duties by two large brothers.'

'It says that?' Cwen snorted.

'It does,' Hermitage confirmed. 'But we didn't have two large brothers. Even our largest was still quite small.'

'You see.' The abbot held a hand out to Hermitage, as if in triumph. 'Not a thought of guile or deceit in his head. The truth and nothing but the truth.'

They walked on in silence for a few moments after this, each one deep in his own thoughts. Hermitage was thinking that the abbot really was very kind and that he would like to have another look through the parchments, see if he could find any more interesting rules.

Eventually, Cwen spoke. 'The world doesn't really work like that though.'

'That's the world's problem,' the abbot noted. 'It needs to sort itself out.'

'Unfortunately, I suspect it may sort Hermitage out first,' Wat said.

Hermitage reflected on a number of his own brothers who had tried to sort several things out over the years. He knew that he thought the best of people and tried hard not to. There was very little evidence to support his position and more to the contrary arrived almost daily. It was strange that in Wat, someone who definitely had many improvements to work on, he had found a trustworthy and honest soul. All right, maybe not honest, but trustworthy. Perhaps all his failings were put in his work, leaving the man himself above it all.

And Cwen. He suspected she had led a life that had been hard and that had hardened her to it. Nevertheless, she was kind to Hermitage. They both helped him understand all those aspects of the world that troubled him. Which was basically all the aspects of the world.

It was very nice to hear the abbot say such generous things about him, he just wasn't sure how any of it was going to help.

'So the nephews?' he asked, quite anxious that they should move on from picking Hermitage apart, even if the bits had a rosy glow about them.

'Yes,' the abbot seemed happy to move on as well. 'Ardro and Anselm.'

'Ardro, Anselm and Abbo,' Cwen noted. 'And your brother?'

'Was Audley.'

'Another family tradition?'

'Quite so. They are fine young men, well-liked and respected and quite happy to be small landholders. Small enough not to attract the attention of those higher up.'

'And who is higher up?' Wat asked. 'Now that Tostig has gone the way of all Godwinsons?'

'Someone called Drogo de la Beuvriere, apparently. The same Drogo master Cynweard referred to, I imagine.'

'Very Norman,' Cwen said. 'I wonder if he knew FitzGilbert had turned up to claim his abbot's cowl. If this

Drogo is anything like the Normans we know, he'd have seen a dead abbot as the perfect opportunity to get some land back.'

'Send a killer, you mean?' Wat asked.

'It's the sort of thing they do. The Normans have people they send to commit murder, and then they send Hermitage to investigate afterwards.'

'Ardro and Anselm will be able to give us any relevant news,' the abbot said. 'Of course, this Drogo may have sent FitzGilbert himself. Hardly likely to have him killed as well, I'd have thought.'

'Not met many Normans, have you?' Cwen observed.

Abbo ignored this and waved ahead to where the town of Preston was opening up before them.

If the towns got larger as they moved away from the coast, the dwellings of the better off, got better off. The manor of Preston was positively impressive.

It had clearly been built in older times when the best form of defence was defence. Tall, thick walls with small windows presented a face of impenetrable strength. A good quantity of high-quality stone had been used in this place, much of it stolen from Roman buildings, by the look. It was most unusual to see anything but a church made of stone. Timber and thatch were the building materials of choice, largely because there was very little choice. Whoever put this place up must have been someone of great influence and power.

There was no welcoming party here, no hosts beaming from the doorway, no feasts on display, or daughters of the house being hidden in high towers while Wat the Weaver came to visit. The place glowered down at them with a dour expression on its stony face.

The town of Preston itself was as bright and busy as any

place of size should be at this time of the evening. It had taken them the full day to make the journey this far and the local folk were returning from their toil for rest before their toil began again with the rising sun.

The place was not exactly bubbling with gaiety, but compared to the quiet and foreboding presence of the manor house, or whatever it was supposed to be, Preston was like a fair.

Hermitage thought the house might even be empty. If these nephews had land all over the place to be managed, they might be at some other part of the estate. Even so, a servant or two should be left behind. Probably with strict instructions not to let anyone in.

The abbot had paused in the roadway, taking in the sight of the place, his arms folded across his chest.

'Home again, eh?' Cwen asked as if she saw comparisons between the gloomy building and its son.

The abbot turned a hard stare on her.

'Impatient and contemptuous,' she cautioned.

'The place looks deserted,' Wat looked up at the unedifying edifice.

'Yes,' the abbot was puzzled. 'Even if Ardro and Anselm are away, there should be a steward in attendance.' He led the way up to the main entrance, a solid door set within the stone and clearly built to take any punishment thrown at it.

Hermitage had an awful thought that the nephews might really be dead. All this talk of death was worrying. First the abbot, then the Norman and now the nephews. Speculation that they could have been killed was a jest, surely. Yet here they were at the home of the landowners and it had all the life of a graveyard. Perhaps whoever was after the land had come here first? He really didn't want any more deaths on his list of investigations.

Abbo hammered at the door with his fist and made absolutely no noise whatsoever. He searched the ground for an implement that might rouse the inhabitants.

'You won't get no one there,' a voice called from the path at their back.

They turned and saw a peasant, on his way back from the fields, a collection of tools over his shoulder.

'And why's that?' the abbot asked. 'Where is everyone? Why have they left?'

Hermitage was pleased that the abbot had not reached the same conclusion; that the inside of Preston manor would be a litter of dead nephews.

The peasant took the tools from his shoulder and rested them on the ground, clearly preparing for a good long chat about the situation. He was a fit and healthy-looking young man, probably no more than twenty summers, and quite capable of defending himself if any of these new visitors turned out to be trouble. The chances of the two monks and a young woman being trouble were fairly slight.

'They haven't left,' the man explained, mysteriously. He said no more, obviously wanting the mystery of his statement to have its effect.

Hermitage's stomach shrank. So they were dead.

'Then what?' the abbot demanded, his impatience finding a new outlet.

'They don't come out no more.'

'Don't come out no more?' The abbot didn't understand this. 'What do you mean they don't come out no, I mean anymore?'

'They's in there,' the peasant explained, carefully. 'But they don't come out no more.'

Abbo was starting to shake with frustration. 'Why?' he barked.

'You'd have to ask them that,' the peasant nodded at the building.

'How can I, if they don't come out?'

'Ar,' the peasant nodded to himself. 'That's a problem and no mistake.'

'Well,' Wat stepped smartly between abbot and peasant. 'You've been very helpful. Thank you very much. We won't keep you.'

'Ar.' The peasant hoisted his tools once more and prepared to set off. Doubtless, he would have a good evening's tale of the strange folk who were trying to get into the house where the people don't come out no more. 'If you do get in?' he added.

'Yes?'

'Tell 'em I need a new plough blade.'

'We'll be sure to let them know.' Wat ushered the man away.

'Apparently,' Wat said when he rejoined the others. 'They don't come out no more.'

'This is ridiculous.' The abbot found a rock the size of his fist on the ground and strode up to the door. He hammered hard, regardless of the damage he was doing to the woodwork, which was actually very little. 'Ardro,' he called. 'Anselm? Where are you? Open up.'

There was a marked lack of activity on behalf of the door, and no answering cries came from within.

'Ardro, Anselm, answer me this instant. It is Abbo, your uncle. I need to speak with you.'

Hermitage stepped slowly over to Wat and Cwen who were watching the abbot with wry interest. 'What if they are dead?' he whispered.

'Who?' Cwen asked.

'The nephews. What if the reason they don't come out anymore is that they can't? Because they're dead?'

'I think the peasant would have mentioned it. He didn't say they were dead. And I think he would have brought it up. Be a fine topic of conversation at the tavern.'

'Maybe he doesn't know. He just thinks they've locked themselves in when actually they've been murdered.' Hermitage's fretting was making his voice shake.

'I think being investigator is turning your mind,' Cwen frowned at him.

'I know it is.'

He was distracted by a clatter at the door and looked over hopefully. The abbot was standing back looking at the ground at his feet. It seemed that something had fallen from the roof and just missed him. A lucky escape, or a case of poor aim.

They all looked up. The top of the wall was at least twenty feet above them and nothing was immediately obvious. It was clear that there was space behind the wall, much like the parapets on the new Norman castles, from behind which death could be thrown.

'Who's up there?' the abbot demanded in a booming voice. 'Show yourselves.'

There was no reply, although Hermitage thought he could hear a whispered conversation from above. A rather desperate one, by the sound of it.

'Ardro?' Abbo called. 'Is that you?'

After more whispering, and what sounded like some pushing and shoving, a single voice did call back. 'Go away,' it said, and it was accompanied by another small piece of masonry that came sailing down.

'I will not go away. You answer your uncle this minute.'

'He's dead,' the voice called back. 'We're not coming out.'

The abbot sighed and shook his head. 'Foolish child,' he shouted.

'Impatient and contemptuous,' Cwen called softly, in a sing-song sort of voice.

The abbot took a very deep breath. 'Nephew,' he sounded friendly and encouraging in a very insincere way. 'You can see that I am not dead. It has all been a mistake. A simple letter that was sent in error. Of course, I am not dead.'

'He's a spirit,' a second voice warned. 'Don't believe him.'

'Anselm,' the abbot cried, as warmly as he could, and with a sideways glance at Cwen. 'I am here with others. Brother Hermitage, from the monastery and, erm, some weavers. They would not accompany a spirit.'

There were some scrabbling noises from the roof at this and it seemed there might be a chance of someone coming down.

Instead, as they gazed upwards, a head appeared over the edge of the roof. It appeared very briefly and was immediately pulled back, but at least it was a sign of life.

'He didn't look very dead,' Cwen helpfully pointed out to Hermitage.

'He didn't look very well,' Wat noted.

Hermitage had to admit that was true. The head that appeared, while belonging to a young man of means, was unkempt, dirty and had a wild look in its eye.

More whispering from behind the battlements led to more scrambling and this time two heads appeared. The second head only served to double the overall impression of wild and unkempt and added a generous dash of just plain mad.

'I must say,' Wat considered the faces above them. 'They seem to have taken news of your death particularly badly.'

The eyes from above took time to appraise the abbot and confirm that it was him. At this, they simply let out a shriek of terror and disappeared again.

'For the sake of the Lord,' the abbot exclaimed, raising his arms above his head. 'Will you two come down and open this door. What is the matter with you?'

'Spirits,' the voices from above wailed down.

'We are not spirits.'

'We bar the way so the spirits may not enter.'

'If you don't come down this instant, I shall climb up this wall and use your heads to batter the door down.'

'There goes patience,' Cwen commented.

'We daren't,' one of the voices replied.

'I have told you I am not a spirit. I am not dead. I am standing here before you.'

'It's not just you,' Ardro or Anselm complained. 'It's all the others.'

'All the other what.'

'All the other spirits. The rest of the dead who will punish us.'

Wat gave a low whistle. 'What a pair,' he said. 'Are we sure we want to get in?'

The abbot gave him a very hard look.

'We can see they're alive,' Wat pointed upwards. 'Well, as near as they're going to get. Not sure they're capable of managing their own heads, let alone the family land.'

Hermitage thought that perhaps getting these brothers to think about something else might take their minds off, well, take their minds off their minds, which clearly weren't working properly.

'Who told you that the abbot was dead?' he called up. 'How did you get word?'

'See,' one of the voices said to the other, 'I told you he was dead.'

'No. He's not dead. I just wondered who told you that he was?'

'Dead.'

'Yes, who told you he was dead?'

'Only the people who would know,' a nephew called down. 'We have it on the very best authority.'

'A letter from the bishop?' Hermitage asked, wondering if a letter had gone to these boys as well, being the next of kin.

'Letter? No. The church, that's who told us. And they should know, shouldn't they? They deal with dead people all the time.'

'The church told you that the abbot was dead.' Repeating the words didn't help Hermitage make any sense of them. 'Any part of the church in particular? There wasn't a letter from the bishop?'

'You don't need a letter.' The voice clearly thought Hermitage was some sort of idiot.

'It was official though,' the other added.

'The church came,' the first brother howled with the memory. 'They came in the night and told us that Abbo was dead.'

'Who came?' Wat pressed. 'Was it a monk perhaps? What else did he say?' Wat asked.

'What?' the terrified brother sounded puzzled now.

'What else did he say? Did he have any other news? Being the voice of the church he probably had a lot he could tell you. Or was it just "Abbo is dead" and off he went?'

'Well, of course, there was more,' a voice protested. 'You

don't think we'd lock ourselves in here if that was all there was to it?'

'Maybe the rest of the town locked them in,' Cwen suggested, quietly, making the universal sign of the loon.

Wat ignored her. 'What else did he say then? What did he tell you that made you lock the doors?'

'Only that it's judgement day,' one announced proudly.

'You shouldn't have told them,' the other wailed. 'Now you've done it.'

'But we're safe. This is the only place that's safe.'

'Safe from judgement day?' Hermitage asked.

'That's right.' They now seemed quite proud of the fact that they'd been given advance notice of the event.

'When is it going to be?'

'Any day now. We have to stay in here while the land is ravaged.'

'And that's what the monk from the church told you?' Wat enquired.

'That's right. So you're not coming in, see.'

'I do see. And is it just this bit of land that's going to be ravaged, or all of it?'

'All of it, of course. You can't have judgement day if bits get left out.'

'And you have to stay in there until it's all over?' Cwen asked.

The voice sounded proud and worried at the same time. 'We have to stay here for eternity.'

'That's quite a long time. And is the church going to look after the land?'

'They can do what they like with it.'

Looks were exchanged between those at the bottom of the wall.

'This monk who came and told you,' Hermitage asked. 'Did you know him?'

'Hardly.'

'Hardly?' Hermitage looked to the others to see if anyone could make sense of this rubbish. No one had any ideas. Even the abbot was looking a bit worried at the state of his nephews' minds.

'They wear hoods, you fool,' the voice was contemptuous of Hermitage's lack of basic knowledge.

'A cowl,' Hermitage said, knowingly. He nodded at the others confirming that this sounded like the monk. 'Was it a brown cowl?'

'How are we supposed to know? It was nighttime.'

'Then how do you know it was even someone from the church?' Cwen demanded.

That brought about a rather awkward silence. 'Because they said so,' was the eventual reply, followed by the descent of another piece of stonework. 'Now go away. We're not getting caught outside when Judgement Day begins.'

The sound of feet and bodies moving away came from above, accompanied by a whispered but rather heated debate. It seemed that some seeds of doubt had been sewn in the nephews' heads.

'Sounds like the monk's the man.' said Hermitage, turning to face the others.

'Who probably isn't even dressed as a monk anymore,' Cwen noted.

Wat cast a look up to the house and shook his head in disappointment. 'I can't imagine any killer bothering with those two. Just say "Boo" and they hide under the table forever.'

'But he couldn't do anything to the nephews until the

abbot was officially dead. They wouldn't own the land or anything until that happened,' Hermitage explained.

'Abbot first, then Norman, then nephews,' said Cwen, understanding the process perfectly.

'But now that the abbot and the Norman are dead, it's time to come back for a couple of nephews,' Wat concluded. 'Then all encumbrances to the land are gone. Perhaps this is Drogo himself. Wiping out all opposition?'

'We need to find our monk, whoever it is and stop him,' said Hermitage, now very keen on the idea that stopping a murder was a better thing than investigating one - for everyone concerned. 'I'm not sure a Norman noble like Drogo would need any disguise to go round killing his rivals. But we won't know until we find him.

'What about this? We split up and go and ask the people of the town if they've seen a stranger. We could even go into their houses to see if anyone is hiding a monk's cowl. Of course, we'd have to knock and seek permission at every dwelling. We could call it a door to door.' Hermitage liked to have a name for everything.

'Better idea,' Wat nodded his head down the street where a number of people seemed to be heading in the same direction. 'Let's just go to the tavern.'

Caput XX: Judgement Day? Now?

'If the official word of the church is that Judgement Day is upon us, I'm an abbot,' Wat said, as they walked through the door of the tavern.

'The official word of the church is that Judgement Day is upon us,' Hermitage pointed out.

'Yes, but not today.'

They had decided that spending the night in the tavern was unavoidable as getting into the manor seemed a hopeless task. The nephews' disappearance from the roof raised a forlorn expectation that the door might be opened but this dissipated as they heard the sounds of furniture being piled up behind the entrance.

They found a table in a corner and sat quickly. Hermitage thought that perhaps some of the villagers would be able to shed light on this situation. If it turned out that everyone around here believed that Judgement Day was imminent it would at least explain the nephews. It would mean they were all damned for heresy, of course, as only the church would know that date, but it would be consistent.

If that were the case it might not be good to let them see the abbot, who was probably the only one to be officially dead.

'FitzGilbert marv,' a loud and cheerful voice exclaimed as Wat felt a huge thump on his back, almost forcing him to bang his head on the table.

He jumped up to see the two Bretons beaming at him. In fact, they were beaming at everyone. After slapping Wat on the back they grabbed the abbot's hand and shook it firmly, they waved and held their arms out to Hermitage, who was grateful to have two bodies between him and them, and then they went for Cwen.

One of them took hold of her shoulders as she sat facing them, bent down and planted a kiss on each cheek. The second stepped up to do likewise but caught the look on Cwen's face and all his joy fled. Instead, he took a step back and gave her a very formal bow.

'That's better,' she snarled, wiping her cheeks with her sleeve. 'Don't do that again.' She pointed at the first Breton who, despite not understanding a word of the language, received the message loud and clear.

'Yes, FitzGilbert Marv,' Wat agreed, nodding politely.

One of the Bretons gave a fine impression of someone who did not know why Hermitage and the others were there. He looked at them one at a time, produced a very puzzled looking face and shrugged a lot.

Wat beckoned them to sit at the table, which they did, mugs of drink in their hands. Once there, with their own supplies ordered from the landlord, Wat produced a little play with his hands.

First of all both hands walked across the tabletop on their fingers, followed by Wat pointing at the Bretons. They nodded happily, understanding that the walkers were themselves. One of them made a comment which brought howls of laughter from the other.

Hermitage thought that these certainly were very jolly Bretons. Well, they were now that FitzGilbert was dead. Who knew what they were like beforehand.

Next, Wat demonstrated a single two-fingered person, moving a lot more surreptitiously across the table, following the Bretons. He then indicated that they were all following this lone figure. Had they seen him? he asked with shrugs and frowns of his own.

No, they hadn't.

'It's a very effective way of communicating,' Hermitage observed.

'I once sold a hundred pounds worth of tapestry to a Flemish merchant without speaking a word,' Wat said. 'Mind you, I don't think you'd want to see the mimes I did for that.'

So, the Bretons did not know they were being followed. 'Can you ask them where they're going?' Hermitage asked. 'Are they intending to report the death of FitzGilbert to King William and Le Pedvin, or is it really their plan to return straight to Brittany?'

'That's a bit of a mouthful for a few gestures,' Wat complained. Nevertheless, he gave it a go and after much waving, finger waggling, putting his hands on his head like a crown and looking very regal, he seemed content with the answers.

Hermitage had figured out most of them, as this language of sign and gesture was quite clear. They had shown utter contempt for King William and had no intention of going anywhere near him. Much waving had accompanied that part of the story. Along with looks on their faces that said they had just eaten dung.

Wat also went on to explain that they were trying to find out who killed FitzGilbert. Regular use of their one word of Breton, marv, stabbing gestures and looks of shock and puzzlement made their intentions clear.

When the Bretons understood this, they gave a simple response. A shrug that said "who cares?" They were delighted that the Norman was dead and everyone else should be as well.

Trying to explain that the abbot had been declared dead

when he wasn't was beyond even Wat's powers of presentation and so they just had to give the rather vague impression that they'd quite like to know who the killer was.

When Wat managed to get one question across, it produced gales of laughter that almost knocked the Bretons off their chairs. He'd simply mimed the stabbing and then pointed to each person in the room with a quizzical face. Was there anyone who would want FitzGilbert dead?

The Bretons answer was simple. Yes. Yes, there was. In fact, there were lots. Certainly, everyone they knew, their distant relatives, friends of cousins and passers-by who had only heard the name.

When they got back to Brittany and reported that the man was dead, the rejoicing would go on for weeks. The Bretons happily got up from their chairs and leapt about the inn indicating that there would be music and dancing and eating and drinking until everyone fell down. After which they would get up and do it all again.

FitzGilbert, it seems, was horrible. And there were many ways of indicating this. He tasted as horrible as rotten fish. He smelled as awful as the rotten fish after it had been left in your bed for a week. He did horrible things, he frightened children and old ladies and he was lucky to get away with a knife in the chest.

Using his crown-on-the-head gesture, Wat asked if the king liked FitzGilbert.

No, he did not. No one liked FitzGilbert. William was a terrible man, mainly for being a Norman and not a Breton, it seemed, but even he hated FitzGilbert.

That made Hermitage feel a lot better. The king never bothered calling for investigations into the murder of people he didn't like. Usually, because he did it.

After this comprehensive denigration of FitzGilbert and all his family, the Bretons settled down again to take their ale. They grimaced and pulled faces as they drank, perhaps indicating that FitzGilbert was a bitter as ale.

'Nan sistra,' one of them complained.

Hermitage looked inquisitive.

'Sistra,' the one repeated. He made gestures in the air, followed by representations of a complicated manufacturing process that led to a drink in a mug. And smiles all around.

Hermitage considered the movements carefully. They certainly weren't harvesting grain to make their drink.

'Cider!' he announced. 'They want some cider.'

'Sistra,' the Breton repeated, happily.

The landlord replaced the mugs of ale with brimming cups of cider, which the Bretons looked at with unalloyed joy. The clear impression was that the cider was on the table now, but the Bretons would be under it before long. Staying in the company of these men would at least make sure they stayed alive, even if the consumption of cider was probably going to cause problems of its own.

'So anyone could have reason to kill FitzGilbert,' Hermitage fretted as the noises of happy drinking washed around the table.

'But only someone who was there at the time could have done it,' Cwen pointed out.

'He might have been killed just for being FitzGilbert. He doesn't seem to have been a popular fellow. Maybe it really was this Drogo or one of his men.'

'It's still a bit of a coincidence he gets killed in that monastery, just after he's turned up to be abbot,' Wat raised another mug to the Bretons. 'And you know what the Normans are like, if they stab someone in the chest there's usually a celebration and lots of shouting about it.'

Unsurprisingly, most of the occupants of the tavern were staring with open curiosity at the strange goings-on in the corner of the room. None of them seemed willing to actually approach, but several of the older men of the village did acknowledge Abbo as they sat with their ale for the evening. None of them remarked that they thought he was dead although one old fellow did give them intense scrutiny.

'Don't tell me,' Cwen called over. 'You thought he was dead.'

'Nope,' the old man grunted. 'I thought he was taller.'

'You haven't heard that he's dead then?'

'Is he?' The man stared even harder at the abbot.

'No, of course, he isn't.'

'Well I don't know, do I? Never seen a dead abbot. Don't know what they can do.'

'No one's come around telling you that he was dead. You've heard no reports.'

'I wouldn't come in the tavern if I thought it was going to be full of dead abbots.'

'So why do the men at the manor think he's dead.'

'Ha,' the man scoffed. 'Those two? They probably think he's dead because they're as mad as a pair of March hares with bats on their backs. They think it's Judgement Day and everyone's dead but them.'

'Everyone?'

'Seems to be,' he grunted. 'Anyway, got more important matters to consider than them two.' The man lifted his leather mug, which appeared to be empty. They could see it was empty because he pointedly waved it in their direction.

'Let me get you a drink,' Wat sprang up.

'Oh,' said the man, a completely fabricated look of

surprised delight spreading across his face. 'Don't mind if I do.'

Wat beckoned the man to join them while he hopped over to the landlord to get the mug refilled.

'There we go,' he said. 'Now. Ardro and Anselm. Do they really think Judgement Day is upon us?'

The man settled in for a good gossip, at Wat's expense. 'That's what they say.'

'They said that someone from the church told them,' Hermitage put in. He couldn't see how anyone could make such a fundamental mistake about something as significant as Judgement Day, even if someone dressed as a monk had told them. The Bible was very specific about the warnings and portents when the day was going to come. And there was a detailed process for the whole thing. There was such a lot to get through that made it highly unlikely the whole thing could be completed in a day anyway.

Seven seals, trumpets, spiritual figures and bowls had to be dealt with in the right order. There were all sorts of beasts and dragons to be managed; the dragon alone had to reside in the pit for a thousand years. He doubted that the nephews would be happy to wait on their roof while this was done.

Hermitage considered all this from a very practical point of view. He knew for certain that all of these events would come to pass exactly as they were described in John's Revelation. But before everything began there had to appear a lion, an ox, a man and an eagle. The last three he could imagine but he didn't even know what a lion looked like, let alone seen one around the banks of the Humber.

He wondered if it was something about this part of the country. Was it common to think that Judgement Day was coming? He couldn't recall it being an issue at the monastery, but then he did bury his head in the parchment most of the time.

Perhaps there was some heresy, or vestige of the old religion that held that everyone was already living the end of days. Grimsby had been an enclave of pagans, could the rest of the area be the same? Surely the bishop would have known and rooted it out. But then the nephews seemed to think that Judgement Day was only going to affect everyone else. They were safe. That really did require a convoluted system of belief.

And the two nephews on the roof didn't strike him as having any sort of system of belief at all. Throwing bits of your house at people and shouting at passers-by was much more consistent with plain madness.

'Judgement Day,' the man with the ale reported. 'They say that it's Judgement Day.'

'They told us that Judgement Day was coming,' Hermitage said.

'Coming? Arrived? What's the difference? None to them two. One minute the day is coming, then it's already been. Bit of a shock when they started off, I can tell you.'

'I can imagine.' Hermitage couldn't, really.

'When your lords and masters take to the roof of their house and start shouting down that you're all damned, you think you've done something wrong, you know. You've planted the wrong crops and you're all damned, that sort of thing. Normally you just shrug and wait for it to pass over. This time they seemed a bit more, what's the word?'

'Sincere?' Hermitage suggested.

'What's that mean?'

'It means that they really believed it.'

'Ar, yes. That'll do. Just the job. It wasn't like a threat, it was like they really believed it. And when they locked the place up and wouldn't come out, well, it was clear.'

'Was it?'

'Oh yes. They was mad as a mad thing.'

Well, that was a relief to Hermitage. He wasn't in a village full of wild heretics after all. Heretics who might welcome newcomers by making them damned as well. He knew of sacrifice, of course, there was quite a lot of it in the bible, but that was just animals or fruit or grain and was always for a good cause. God had stopped Isaac being sacrificed, and all that business with Jephthah's daughter was his own fault.

The Druids on the other hand did it to people for the most appalling reasons.[Or did they? You'd better read Hermitage, Wat and Some Druids to get to the bottom of that.] These villagers didn't look like druids and they clearly thought the nephews were wrong. And if there had been a sacrifice, the people would be dead for real. And they weren't. Satisfied with his reasoning, he concluded that the townsfolk were not dangerous after all. Well, not dangerous for that reason anyway.

'But why did they think Judgement Day had come?' the abbot asked. 'You're all going about your daily business. It's pretty obvious. Why would they think otherwise?' He closed his face into a frown. 'They said someone from the church told them. What have you been saying?' he sounded very, suspicious.

'We haven't said nothing,' the man protested.

'Have you been spinning them yarns again?'

'Not at all.'

'Spinning them yarns again?' Hermitage asked.

'Yes, well,' the abbot was reluctant to expand. 'It was all a long time ago. The villagers made up some nonsense about sheep and frightened Ardro and Anselm into believing it.'

'Har, har,' the peasant laughed into his beer at the memory. 'We told them that once the sheep was sheared, all the fleeces got together in the middle of the night for a wild dance before they was woven into cloth.'

'Not a member of the weavers' guild, are you?' Wat asked, not really expecting an answer.

He didn't get one.

'And if you got a cloth that hadn't danced the dance of the fleece, it would try to escape every fleeceday at midnight, so you had to lock it in a cupboard.'

'I can see that such a tale is complete nonsense,' said Hermitage, who really could. 'But it is just the sort of thing to frighten a child.'

'They was nineteen at the time,' the peasant laughed even more heartily.

Wat turned to the abbot. 'I thought you said they were fine upstanding men, quite capable of running their land.'

'Ahem, yes, of course, they are. It's just that they can be a bit, you know, gullible at times. Easily led that sort of thing. They've not much experience of the real world' He turned to the peasant and his beer. 'Easily led by rogues and mischievous wretches.'

'So, if someone told them that it was Judgement Day, they might believe it,' Hermitage speculated.

'What does the priest have to say about all this?' The abbot demanded of the beer-swiller.

'Him,' the peasant would have spat on the floor if it wasn't a waste of ale. 'He's off on pilgrimage again.'

Another one on pilgrimage thought Hermitage. It seemed to be cropping up quite frequently.

'Ar. If you count putting your feet up in your parlour and

drinking a barrel of ale. He calls it pilgrimage, but we know he's in there. Still, gets us out of church.'

'He has done nothing to put them on the right path?' The abbot did not sound happy with the priest's efforts.

'Oh, he talks to them all right. At least they let him in. But then he comes out again and nothing's changed. Back to his church, back to his ale and the rest of us just has to put up with it.' The man supped his own ale deeply. So deeply that Wat had to go and refill his mug.

All through his explanation, the man had kept a wry smile on his face, as if the whole business was amusing somehow. Hermitage supposed that being in a village where your masters locked themselves in their manor and the priest stayed in his church might be quite a pleasant place to live. He did think that the priest would be able to explain. After all, the nephews reported that it was the church that gave the news of Judgement Day.

'I will have words with this priest,' the abbot announced in his stern voice.

The locals didn't seem so happy about this and they held a muttered debate.

'That's right,' one of them called out after they'd come to some accord. 'You take him away and show him the error of his ways.'

There was a rumbling agreement with this proposal and it was accompanied by the suggestion that they could manage perfectly well without a priest for a while. If the abbot wanted to take the nephews as well, that wouldn't be a problem.

This promoted the awful thought in Hermitage's head. Obviously, he kept a lot of awful thoughts in his head but they tended to be of a general and all-encompassing nature.

The specific ones always worried him most.

He waited until the local man's face was heading to the bottom of his tankard once more, before expressing it. 'What if our killer has come for the nephews?' he asked, in a hushed tone.

'Eh?' Cwen frowned at him.

The beer drinker had emerged from his ale and was looking at them all with interest.

'More ale,' Wat announced, standing. 'And for your friends as well?' He subtly guided the man to his feet and helped him back to the table with the rest of the village.

'This is costing me a fortune,' he complained when he returned.

'About sixpence, I think.' Cwen made it quite clear that this was not a fortune to Wat's purse.

'Still,' he grumbled as he sat. He turned to Hermitage. 'You think the killer's after the nephews? Why? It could be him that told them Judgement Day is on their heads.'

'Because if it is to do with the land, they're next. First, there's a letter saying that the abbot is dead. Then FitzGilbert gets a knife with the same message. Could be that the nephews have to be done last. Judgement Day kept them quivering in their manor. Now he's coming back to finish the job.'

'I think you're getting a bit carried away,' Cwen said. 'Why's he following the Bretons if he just wants to kill nephews?'

'He isn't. It could really be a coincidence. They're coming this way and so's the killer. They're heading for Wales and home, the killer's reasons are completely different. They just converge on Preston.'

'In which case, the nephews are quite right to lock

themselves in their manor,' Wat observed.

'Even it is for the wrong reason.'

'Who cares, if it keeps a killer out?'

'So he could be here now,' Cwen pointed out in a harsh whisper.

'Almost certainly is,' Hermitage said. 'The Bretons have been here for a while, our mysterious monk was not far behind.'

Wat leaned back in his chair and casually called over to the other table, where his sixpence worth of ale was rapidly disappearing. 'Haven't seen any other strangers about, have you? Man on his own, probably skulking about a bit?'

The ale table gathered in conclave to debate the question. This did not seem to be a straightforward issue. Each man had his say, sometimes several of them went at it simultaneously. Proposals were made and rejected, alternatives offered and suggestions revised. All of this took so long that Hermitage was starting to think the place was awash with skulking strangers, they just couldn't make up their minds which one to report first.

Eventually, the man who had sat at their table, and so had been elected some sort of intermediary, delivered their carefully considered conclusion. 'No.'

'No?' Wat exclaimed. 'It took you that long to come up with no?'

'Ah, well,' the spokesman explained. 'There's old Gart, over near the mill, he tends to skulk a bit, but then he's not a stranger, see. Then there's Erik, he's a stranger, but not so much of a skulker.'

'Erik's a stranger, but you know his name?' Wat asked.

'Of course. But he's still a stranger. Only been here five years or so.'

'Six,' someone, perhaps Erik, pointed out.

'Ah yes, six.'

Wat put his head in his hands. 'No one who has arrived today, I should have said.'

'Apart from you lot and the two drunks, no.' the man confirmed with a nod to the Bretons. 'But then none of you have skulked, have you?'

Another fellow at the locals' table put his hand up.

'Yes?' Wat asked with resigned weariness.

'If this other one was skulking, we wouldn't see him anyway,' the new contributor proposed. 'Always assuming he was a good skulker.'

The rest of the table nodded and grumbled their agreement to this excellent point.

The abbot leant forward into the middle of the table and quietly said, 'And you wonder why I left?'

Wat was now shaking his head while the other table continued their debate on the relative qualities of strangeness and skulking, and what proportion of each would be required to make a skulking stranger or a stranger who skulked.

Hermitage suspected that many of the evening conversations in this place were of a similar nature. He also thought that this topic was going to keep the place going for a month.

'Perhaps we should go and keep watch on the nephews,' he said. 'Assuming the killer is after them, he may strike tonight.'

'And if he's after the Bretons?' Cwen asked. She nodded at the two men who were now resting their heads on the table, only raising them to take fresh swigs of cider, most of which ran down their chins. 'I don't think they're in any condition to defend themselves.'

'Then we have to split up. Two of us stay here and guard the Bretons and two go back to the manor.'

...

Hermitage did feel bad as he sat with the abbot at the table in the tavern while Wat and Cwen were outside, waiting for a killer to turn up out of the night.

It had all sounded quite sensible that their individual skills should be considered when assigning roles. The abbot was an old man, he accepted this and that he would be best placed in the tavern instead of trying to scale walls or run after people of ill will.

Hermitage's ability to call for help was not in doubt. His prowess at fighting off dangerous monks in the dark was felt to be less strong.

Cwen on the other hand seemed to be actually looking forward to confronting the possible murderer. Doing it in the gloom was just a bonus.

Wat was the natural choice as he was well versed in dealing with physical threat. Hermitage did think that he must be one of the few weavers in the world who had had to fight his customers, but then that was a problem of his own making.

This strong reasoning did not assuage his guilt that he had left others to the most perilous task. Unless he was wrong, of course. If the killer really was after the Bretons, he and the abbot would be the ones facing him in the dark.

He went and asked the landlord if he could have another candle.

Caput XXI: The Night of The Killer

The night of the killer, Hermitage told himself, was not a helpful title. He only hoped that he'd be able to stay awake until the events came to pass. Even then, he only half hoped it. Waking up in the morning to find that he'd been wrong about everything would be marvellous.

The tavern had emptied, eventually, the locals expressing their gratitude to Wat and inviting him to return the next night when they'd probably have a lot more they could tell him.

The landlord had cleared up and left them to it. He said that the abbot was well known to him and so could be trusted to treat the place well. Then he pointed out that the abbot was well known to him and so he'd know where to come if there was any damage.

As the townsfolk staggered back to their dwellings, Wat and Cwen wrapped themselves up and stepped out into the darkness as well. It was considered unlikely that any attempt would be made on the nephews while the town was awake, well awake and quite drunk, at least. Much more reasonable that any murderer would wait until they had the darkest quiet of night before going about their awful business.

And if this was wrong, and Wat and Cwen found the place ransacked and nephews already dead, they would come straight back and report.

Each party nominated a messenger to fetch the others if trouble did break out. For the tavern this was Hermitage. The abbot acknowledged that he was unlikely to be successful in fighting off a motivated killer, but he was even less likely to run to the manor and fetch help without several stops on the way to catch his breath.

For the manor, the question was more complicated. Cwen insisted that she was the one to stay and do battle, while Wat ran to fetch Hermitage and Abbo. Wat said that he was not going to leave Cwen to fight some hulking great murderer while he scuttled off to fetch a monk and an old abbot.

Cwen pointed out that Wat had no evidence that the murderer was either great or hulking and the debate had continued as they left for their night's duty. One of them would be back, Wat assured them and, if the murderer turned out to be great and hulking after all, it might well be both of them.

Now left alone, Hermitage was uncomfortable for so many reasons. He was never very good with taverns and would only go in one alone in the most desperate of circumstances. At least he had the abbot with him now, but that only helped a little. Then there was the discomfort from waiting for a murderer to turn up, a situation he couldn't imagine being comfortable anywhere. On top of all that, his mind had filled itself with a panoply of speculations about what happened when murderers arrived at taverns to find monks and abbots waiting for them. None of the scenarios ended happily for the monks or the abbots.

'So, Brother Hermitage.' The abbot seemed a lot less put out by their situation, and relaxed in his chair, the vestiges of the only serving of ale he had taken all night, swilling in the bottom of his mug. 'King's Investigator eh? You haven't had the opportunity to tell me, how on earth that came about? Last I heard you were on the way to the monastery at De'Ath's Dingle, which was a very strange choice if I may say so.'

Hermitage didn't like to say that it was only Godric who

made him leave Kilnsea in the first place. Perhaps he'd be able to weave it into the tale nonchalantly, as if he never intended to get the prior into trouble at all, but had done anyway.

Beginning with the ridiculous business of the great conclave, Hermitage worked his way through two kings, several weavers, Normans, Druids, Nuns, Saracens, hidden monasteries and far too many deaths and murders. All of which, when he said it, seemed to offer very little explanation as to how he came to be sitting here at this moment.[Needless to say, there's a book for every occasion. Read them all -   or just buy them all anyway.]

The abbot listened to it all with great interest, asking questions now and again, getting Hermitage to go back over some tricky point, or to explain once more how he had worked out who did it.

'I must say, Brother,' the abbot was impressed with this telling. 'You certainly seem to have found your calling.'

'Oh no,' Hermitage wailed. 'You don't think so, do you?'

'Of course.'

'I was hoping this was all just a distraction. An inconvenience because I just happened to be there at the time. I keep hoping that word will arrive that the king has found a real investigator, and I can go back to just being a monk.'

'Just being a monk never suited you, really.' The abbot had a smile on his face, which took the sting out of the comment. 'You are far too inquisitive and curious for that. And you know that the other brothers tend not to take to you very well.'

Hermitage just nodded at this.

'The idea of being a hermit, and your name arose from that. And here you are.'

'I'd still rather be a hermit,' Hermitage mumbled.

Perhaps, in his heart, he had half hoped that the encounter with the abbot would bring back those happy days at Kilnsea. The years that had drifted by since then would be reduced to the blink of an eye and everything would be as it was. He would never have been King's Investigator and his simple and straightforward view of the world would be restored. There would be the abbot, there would be parchment, and there would be devotion. He was sure that it hadn't been that simple back then, but it felt like it now.

'But you are,' the abbot was gentle.

'I am what?'

'A hermit.'

'Erm,' that dropped Hermitage through his soft cloud of reminiscence.

'You are away from the monastic community.'

'Well, yes, but I'm hardly secluded and in isolation.'

'Secluded and isolated from the religious life, though.'

'Very much so,' Hermitage acknowledged.

'Not every hermit gets to live in a cave. Some have to be hermits among others. Think of yourself as living alone amongst the failings of ordinary men.'

That didn't help at all.

'What you have done with Wat the Weaver appears to be remarkable.'

Hermitage shrugged. 'I think he saw the wrong in his works, he just needed some encouragement.'

'Excellent,' the abbot beamed. 'And you resolve murders and the like.' He made this sound like an amazing achievement.

Hermitage looked at the table. 'I still think I'd rather be in a cave,' he muttered.

'And I would rather not be dead. And all of the monks and abbots and priests and bishops I have come across would rather there was something that there is not. Duty, Brother. You always had and always will have duty. You have just been given a new one. I think you forget that your life in the monastery was not the easiest. I imagine that life with the weaver is quite comfortable, in between the murders and so forth.'

'Well, yes, I suppose so.' Hermitage had to suppose that it was very comfortable indeed.

'And what would King William have done if you had not been there to investigate for him?'

'I really don't know.'

'Lost his temper?'

'Most likely.'

And taken it out on others?'

'Very possibly.'

'Gone on a rampage?'

'Without doubt.'

'Leading to more death and destruction. You have probably saved many lives, young Brother.'

When the abbot explained all this it didn't sound so bad. But then that was probably his duty. Perhaps now that he had found the abbot again he should make efforts to visit him occasionally. Or quite regularly. Or maybe he'd like to move to Derby.

'Enough of this idle chatter though,' the abbot said, brightly. 'We have a long night ahead of us.' He leant forward onto the table. 'So plenty of time for you to update me, in detail, on your latest thinking concerning the lexicography of the post-Exodus prophets.'

Hermitage smiled his broadest smile.

. . .

At Preston Manor, the situation in the dark was much as it had been in the light, only darker. The nephews were not on the roof anymore, but neither was the place open to visitors. There was no telling from the outside whether the brothers were alive or dead.

Wat and Cwen had circled the building and found no sign of any new way in or out. They reasonably concluded that no one had got in since they were last here, not even a nephew killer.

'He could have climbed the wall,' Cwen suggested.

Wat looked up to the roof. 'Possible,' he acknowledged. 'But even then would he find a way in? If they've barricaded the doors and windows down here, they've probably done the same for the roof, naturally assuming that the angels of Judgement Day can fly.'

'Can they?'

'Don't you start,' Wat snorted. 'It's bad enough the two of them in there believing all this.'

Bored with standing looking at a manor in which nothing was happening, they found a spot at the end of the path leading to the front door and sat down, Wat clearing as much of the dust from the floor as he could manage.

'I only asked,' Cwen protested.

'Well don't.' Wat instructed. 'It's not helpful.'

There was a brooding silence, most of the brooding coming from Cwen.

'Anyway,' Wat went on. 'Of course, angels can fly. Everyone knows that.'

Cwen looked at Wat and saw a broad grin on his face. She

let out a laugh which she quickly stifled. 'Didn't notice anyone in the tavern flying about.'

'They're probably shy. Don't like doing it in front of strangers.'

'And they were drinking a lot for angels. Not much need for ale in heaven, I'd have thought.'

'Lots of advantages to being an angel though. Don't need to worry about being killed anymore. Can't get the pox, starve to death, fall in a river. Any of that.' Wat made it sound quite attractive. 'But I think I'd like a pot of ale now and again when I get there.'

'Oh, that's where you think you're going, is it?' Cwen snorted at this hopelessly optimistic expectation. 'They must have some other special powers, as well as flying though. We could ask Hermitage, he'd know.'

'He would. But they'd be good ones, I should think. Probably know what you're thinking. See the future. Talk to animals. All that. And if they're proper angels they can walk through walls.' Wat snapped his fingers that this was the solution to their dilemma. 'So what's the point locking the door?' He held a hand out towards the manor, displaying the blatant idiocy of two nephews who didn't even know basic facts like that.

'Maybe they're not proper angels,' Cwen said, still smiling.

'Ah, well, in that case, our course of action is clear.'

'Is it?'

'It is. We get Brother Hermitage to come and investigate them to find out what they are. They could be cherubim for all we know. And you know what trouble they are.'

'Ha, ha,' Cwen sniggered. 'And then we can report to the king and Le Pedvin.'

'Naturally. They won't want angels and cherubim

wandering about the place. You know the Normans prefer their people one or the other. Alive or completely dead.'

They paused and considered the impact that the Norman invaders had made and perhaps the reality of death weighed heavily on their shoulders for a moment.

'Do killers usually come to the front door?' Cwen wondered, nodding to the manor, clearly not weighed down by very much at all. 'I thought they'd be more sneak-round-the-back types.'

'Wherever they go they'll have to make a lot of noise getting into this place.' Wat nodded towards the boarded-up windows and the solid door.

'It's odd, isn't it.'

'Not if you think the angels of Judgement Day are outside your house trying to get in. I think I'd block the place up as well.'

'No, I mean sitting here, now.'

Wat looked at Cwen as if she'd just started discussing the best way to snare a ferret.

'Here we are, two weavers of skill and repute sitting outside the   manor in a place we've never been before, waiting for a murderer to turn up.'

Wat nodded at the truth of their strange situation.

'Meanwhile, a monk and an abbot are waiting in the tavern for the same thing to happen.'

'Doesn't get much stranger.'

'And the monk lives with us in a weavers' workshop.'

'You couldn't make it up.'

'Well, it's not all strictly true,' Cwen was thoughtful.

'Really?'

'Yes, you're just the weaver of repute, I'm the one with the skill.'

Wat nudged her, quite hard.

'And I've met the king, and dealt with deaths and investigations. If you'd told me that this is what I'd end up doing, I'd have knocked you flat.'

'I can believe that.'

Cwen nudged him back. 'I suppose it's not a bad life, really. Apart from the murders and the Normans and the threats of death and all.'

'Could be worse.'

'Could be.' Cwen leaned her weight against Wat's shoulder. 'Mind you. Anyone in their right mind would be safe in bed about now.'

'Can't be in our right minds then.' Wat pressed his weight back to her.

'At least we're not as dead as some of the dead people.'

'The one with a knife in his chest or the one with a letter?'

'I think I'd prefer the letter,' Cwen nodded that she had given this serious thought.

'Perhaps it's the way around here that you get a letter first. And if you're an abbot you get your letter from a bishop. Ordinary people probably just get a priest. Bit tricky that, as most priests I know can't write.'

'Know a lot of priests then?' Cwen snorted.

'More than is decent,' Wat admitted.

'The abbot gets a letter and the Norman gets a knife,' Cwen pointed out. 'They'd probably like that. Suit their nature, like Vikings being burned on their ships. To each their own.'

'What would Saxons get then?' Wat considered the issue.

'A letter sounds about right,' Cwen snorted. 'Old King Edward had the place organised right and proper. Laws and rules for everything - until the Godwins sent it all to pot.

Can't imagine he'd want people just dying all over the place without it being arranged in advance. Dear Master Wat, it is with pleasure that we inform you that you are now dead. Death will attend upon you on Thursday at vespers so please make sure you've packed. Ha ha.

'Letter would be nice though, wouldn't it. Let you know it's coming and give you time to sort everything out. Get all those things done that you've promised yourself.'

'Oh,' Wat gave a mock shiver. 'Not so sure about that. I'd like it to be a surprise. Just when I'm in the middle of one of those things I've promised myself.'

'I'm not sure Death would want to interrupt some of the things you've probably promised yourself.'

'I don't know what you mean,' Wat sounded offended.

'We both make the tapestries,' Cwen noted. 'Or rather, we used to make them.'

'But you wouldn't want to do what's in any of them, surely?'

'Oh God, no.' Cwen sounded pretty appalled.

'What then? What would you want to do before your day arrives?'

'Well,' Cwen was reluctant to say. 'You first.'

'Visit the Holy Land,' Wat said as if it was obvious.

Cwen looked at him with open shock. 'You? The Holy Land? Would they take you?'

'They take all sorts. Holy Land, you see.'

'On a pilgrimage?'

'Oh, heavens no. Just to look.'

'Not sure you're allowed to just look.'

'Ah, but if I've got my letter, they'd have to let me.' Wat nodded to himself that this was assured. 'And you?' he asked.

'Me?' Cwen sounded even more tentative now.

'Yes. What would you do between getting your letter and the man with the scythe turning up?'

'There is one thing I've said I'd do,' she looked at the floor.

'Aha.'

'But of course, I'm so much younger than you that I'll probably think of a lot more.'

'Of course. But what's this one?'

'I did think of it a long time ago. Long before I met you. Even when I was little.'

'Yes?' Wat pressed. 'And what is it?'

'Mumble mutter,' said Cwen.

'Pardon?'

'Visit the Holy Land,' she blurted out.

'Oh.'

'But I thought of it first,' she insisted.

'Absolutely.'

'I want to see what Jerusalem actually looks like,' Cwen sounded wistful, which she didn't do very often.

'Me too,' Wat nodded gently, without looking at her.

They considered the manor again, and the fact that there were no killers knocking on the door.

The silence stretched until it reached right around the building.

'We could go together,' Wat whispered.

Cwen breathed. 'That'd be nice.'

. . .

'The night of no killer at all,' Hermitage complained.

'Beg pardon?' Wat asked.

They had returned to the tavern with the dawn to find Hermitage and the abbot engaged in a lively conversation about the common confusion between Micaiah and Micah. No one had spotted any killers. Or anyone at all, come to that.

'Disappointed not to have a killer monk coming to call?' Cwen asked.

'Of course not.' Hermitage wondered why she seemed quite lively and cheerful, considering they'd all been up all night. 'But it means we're no further forward. If our monk-person didn't go for the nephews or the Bretons, I really don't know what's going on.'

Wat stifled a cough he must have picked up in the cold.

'There was a light in the church when we came by,' Cwen reported. 'Perhaps now is the time to go and ask this priest?'

'He sounds like a lazy and idle fellow,' the abbot complained. 'Pilgrimage in his own parlour with ale. I can't imagine what he is doing up at this time.'

'Vigils probably, Father,' Hermitage said.

'He does not strike me as the sort of man to be up all night observing Vigils. More likely fell asleep with a candle alight. Profligate wastrel.'

'It sounds like you know him,' Wat observed.

'Not at all. The priest when I was here was old Father Kerk. A wise and knowledgeable man who first set my feet on the path. He died very soon after my last visit here, so this is doubtless some new fellow. If the reports of the villagers are true, he is not a worthy replacement.'

'Going to see him would be a nice chance to check then,' Cwen said. 'You know, impatient and contemptuous,' she encouraged with a broad smile. 'We could see if his bit of the Church has anything to do with Judgement Day.'

Hermitage looked on in some wonder. A change had definitely come over Cwen. He cast his mind back to when she and Wat had returned to the tavern. Surely his memory was playing tricks on him, but he could have sworn they were holding hands.

'There seems nothing else to do,' he admitted, trying to concentrate on the matter in hand. 'Unless we can actually spot our mysterious monk, or killer, or whatever he may be wandering around the place.'

'Very well,' the abbot agreed.

Wat gave him a look that said this wasn't actually his decision.

'I suppose I should have paid my respects before now,' Abbo looked resigned to the visit.

'Respects to a profligate wastrel?' Cwen asked.

'Hardly. Respects to my forebears. I shudder to think that the family tomb is now in the charge of this priest.' He used the word priest as a serious insult. 'He's probably putting his candles on it.'

Wat and Cwen raised eyebrows at this but Hermitage's eyes had frozen. 'Your family tomb is in the church?' he asked, very quietly. 'Actually in the church itself.'

'Of course,' the abbot replied. 'The manor is here, that is our church. Where else would we be?'

'Out in the churchyard, I'd have thought.' Hermitage was enthused by this new information.

'Normally, yes,' the abbot acknowledged. 'But my grandfather had some quite improper ideas, as well as a great fear of being put in the earth. He had heard of saints and holy men being interred indoors and thought it suitable for him as well. It became a family tradition and it is where I will go, come the time. It's not something I like to talk about, really.'

'Approaching death a bit of a worry?' Cwen enquired.

'No,' the abbot snapped back. 'Being buried indoors is disgusting and in a church is disgraceful.'

'Does it matter?' Wat asked. He looked at Hermitage with a weight of expectation and nodded Cwen to look as well.

As they both gazed at him, he looked back with an intent, but rather surprised look on his face. 'Aha,' said Brother Hermitage.

Caput XXII: Family Plot

'So?' Cwen demanded for about the fifth time as they made their way to the church.

'I can't say,' Hermitage gave the same reply.

'Can't, or won't?'

'I can't. I could be wrong. It's too peculiar. I'm sure that once we get there we'll find that it's nothing to do with anything.'

'But you said Aha, Hermitage,' Wat insisted. 'You can't just say Aha and leave it at that. It's not fair. How much longer are you going to drag this out for?'[Not much longer now.]

The abbot was just looking at them all as if they were slightly mad.

'Hermitage knows what this is all about. He's worked it out,' Wat explained.

'I don't know how he can have done that. We know no more now than we did days ago.'

'That's true, but he's put it all together. All those bits that we don't see joining up, he's added them together and it all makes sense. Well, it makes sense to him.'

'The letter saying that I'm dead?'

Hermitage was not answering anything. The ideas in his head were so truly bizarre that he dare not say anything to anyone. It would be awful if they all laughed at him when he turned out to be completely wrong. And the nephews turned out to be completely dead as well.

'And the Norman,' Cwen said. 'It'll cover that as well.'

'And the land and your prior and probably More the boatman.'

'Not sure there's any explanation for him,' Cwen huffed.

'We just need to go to the church, see the priest and discover what we can,' Hermitage tried to caution them. 'It could be nothing at all, in which case my aha was presumptuous.'

'Never known a presumptuous one before,' Cwen muttered as they walked along.

The light of dawn was full now and any illumination from the inside of the church was invisible. Doubtless, the priest had extinguished the candles with the arrival of the sun.

The church itself followed the pattern of all such buildings, being mainly a tower. As the church in Grimsby had provided early warning and defence from Viking incursion, so this place, only a short distance inland, must have served the same purpose.

This though, was clearly a church of more wealth as projecting chancels sprang from the east and west walls of the tower, which itself would hold the nave. Most of the fundamental construction was timber and the roof was thatch, but stonework had been added here and there to give the place a very solid and permanent appearance.

On to one end of the eastern chancel, a simple timber and thatch building leaned; leaned rather precariously by the look of it. To describe such a place as the priest's parlour was doing it a great favour. It was more hovel than home, displayed a notable lack of care in its construction and showed no signs of any subsequent maintenance at all. It appeared that the owner would simply wait for it to fall down, after which they would build a new one, rather badly, probably.

A graveyard outside, busy with simple memorials, indicated many years of good Christian practice. No more building hills out on the fields and putting the family in there. The old pagan barrows were still seen here and there, Hermitage thought that the people of Grimsby probably still used them, but here there was order and propriety.

Apart from people who buried their family inside the church of course. Hermitage had heard of such things, he couldn't deny it, but it was usually reserved for saints and kings and the like. Anyone who could pay, or threaten the church sufficiently to receive the privilege. That an ordinary family should take it upon themselves was, well, rather offensive. Even if it was the abbot's family. Where would such behaviour end? You wouldn't be able to walk through a church without stepping on graves or bumping into tombs.

They had come to the entrance to the churchyard now and the abbot led the way up to the door of the building. At least this time the place was open and there was no Father Birinus in there, fighting off the pagans.

The interior was as bare and functional as it should be. The morning light was struggling to make it to the floor as the only windows were high in the tower, the gloom making it hard to discern any details as their eyes adjusted.

There were other indications that the place was not in the very best condition though, the main one being the smell. There was straw under their feet, but it was now ready to be spread on the fields as muck. It was clear that the church had not had a good clean for many weeks. It hadn't even had a rather bad clean and had probably been used as the dumping ground for other people's filth.

'Phew,' Cwen said, in a manner not really appropriate for a holy building. 'What a stink.'

'Perhaps the place has been deserted,' Hermitage suggested, generously.

'What do you want?' a voice barked at them out of the darkness and nearly jumped Hermitage out of his habit. It was the darkness to the east that had spoken, so this was probably the priest. He had obviously not deserted the place, unlike his sense of smell.

Hermitage was about to introduce himself and start to explain the reason for their visit when the abbot interrupted.

'What do we want?' he barked back. 'We enter the house of God and are asked what we want. Bring yourself forward this instant.'

There was a clattering in the dark as the sound of a surprised priest tripping over something reached their ears.

The priest emerged and looked at them angrily. He then saw the abbot and stopped. Then he gaped and swallowed and made some noises that might have been intended as words but didn't come out that way.

'Well?' The abbot continued his tirade. 'And just look at you. And at the state of this house of God.'

The priest did look at himself and the others did the same. It was not an inspiring sight. Whatever the priest had been drinking last night, and it could well be ale, a lot of it had been mopped up by his habit which hung, stained and not a little stiff, across a huge chest. And the chest was only huge because it had to fit on top of a stomach that was even bigger.

This was not a priest of pious poverty.

The abbot now paced up to the man, who blinked in the face of obvious authority. Hermitage thought that the priest would have no reason to know who the abbot was, but he just behaved like an abbot. He somehow carried abbot-ness in front of him like a banner. And if you didn't quake before it, he'd probably hit you with it.

'I had heard reports from the townsfolk,' the abbot went

on, very disparagingly, 'but I couldn't believe all that of a priest. Now I see they were being kind. You are a disgrace.'

The priest cowered before the onslaught, but then seemed to recall that this was his church. 'Just a minute,' he protested. 'Who the devil are you?'

'The devil? Outrageous.'

'You can't come in here shouting at me like that.'

'I certainly can, and I think when the bishop hears of the state of his church at Preston he will do a lot more than shout at you.'

'Who are you people?' the priest demanded, now looking a little worried. 'Do you know what time it is?'

'We know very well what time it is. And I also see the state this fine church has fallen into. When Father Kerk was here it was a place of sanctity and praise. Now it looks like a cowshed.'

'Well I am its priest and you are not, so you can all get out.' He did sound rather resigned to the fact that this was not going to work.

'And I am Abbot Abbo of Kilnsea,' the abbot announced. 'Previously of this parish.' He said parish as if he was now thoroughly ashamed of the fact.

The priest's mouth just dropped open, which was not a pretty sight. The inside of the mouth had been given less care than the interior of his church. If there were teeth in there, they didn't look like teeth anymore. And the smell that came out when he breathed at least made the odour of dung in the church like rose petals strewn upon a tinkling brook.

'You're dead,' he said, in a very hushed tone.

'Really?' The abbot drew close and stared the man in the eye. Hermitage thought that this was very courageous. He wouldn't want to go anywhere near this priest.

'But, but,' the priest looked around and into the gloom as if someone else would come to his aid. 'Everyone said you were dead.'

'Which is why we are here,' the abbot said with quiet intensity.

'Ah,' the priest was devoutly worried, which gave Hermitage some encouragement that his bizarre idea might not be wrong after all.

The abbot looked over to Hermitage with the clear instruction that he could take over now.

There was nothing for it, they were here now. He couldn't get everyone to leave again and come back when he was absolutely sure. He wasn't even clear how he could be absolutely sure until he made his accusations. Courage in hand, Hermitage, he told himself. At least the abbot looked supportive. A bit too expectant for comfort but supportive.

'I'm told the tomb of the abbot's family is here,' he said. 'In the church.' He couldn't help an element of distaste creeping into his voice, but it had been the abbot's grandfather's idea.

'Erm,' said the priest, which encouraged Hermitage further.

'What's the tomb got to do with it, Hermitage?' Cwen asked.

'It's in the church,' Hermitage explained. 'Not in the church grounds.'

'Thanks,' Cwen gave a blank shrug. 'That doesn't explain anything.'

'Can we see it?' Hermitage asked, politely.

'It's over here.' The abbot indicated the direction, ignoring the priest completely.

Their eyes had become used to the gloom now and the interior features of the church were more clear. There weren't many of them. A font stood by the door, dry and unused. Various simple carvings could be seen in the walls, a cross here and a very crude representation of what might be Adam and Eve beneath a tree over there.

The abbot led them to a spot where the west chancel opened up from the main tower. He directed their attention to the ground where a black slab of stone lay in contrast to the grey flagstones around it. It was about six feet long and looked very tomb-like.

Hermitage immediately got down on his knees to examine it in detail, carelessly brushing some of the revolting straw out of his way.

'Hermitage!' Cwen called out in disgust.

'I don't see what the tomb has to do with anything,' the abbot said. 'It has been here since my grandfather's time.' He looked to Wat and Cwen for some explanation.

'I want to check something,' Hermitage said. 'If I can just find what I'm looking for.'

Wat moved over and squatted at Hermitage's side. There was no way he was going to put his fine leggings on the floor.

'When was it last opened?' Hermitage asked.

'Last opened?' The abbot was completely nonplussed by the question. 'What do you mean, opened?'

'Well, I assume there is a space underneath?'

'Of course.'

'Room for everyone?' Hermitage did feel a bit ashamed to be asking impertinent and vaguely sacrilegious questions like this.

'Well, yes.' The abbot gave it some thought now. 'I suppose the last occasion was my brother and the next will be me.'

Hermitage brushed some more straw away and pointed to the edge of the tomb for Wat's benefit.

The weaver looked and raised his eyebrows.

'Hm.' Hermitage stood again.

'Some explanation perhaps, Brother?' the abbot asked.

Hermitage drew his breath and nodded to himself. He thought that he had all he needed. Or at least all he could reasonably gather.

'The abbot was declared dead when he wasn't,' he began.

'Er, yes,' Cwen said, clearly thinking that they all knew this perfectly well.

'And the Norman, FitzGilbert wasn't dead and then he was.'

'With you so far.'

'Which got me thinking. There's death all around us, some of it genuine, some not.'

The priest had started to sidle away towards the door. 'Where are you going?' The abbot snapped. The priest stopped sidling.

'If people who are really alive are reported as dead, perhaps people who are really dead are actually alive.'

'People who are dead, aren't?' The abbot looked thoroughly confused.

'Exactly. There's so much confusion about, who can tell who is dead and who's alive? Just because you have a letter from the bishop doesn't make you dead.'

'If it was the bishop,' said Wat.

'Exactly. And then, when the abbot said that the family tomb was in the church, well.'

'Well, what?' Cwen was starting to sound impatient.

'We had to come and look. And now it makes sense.' He gestured towards the slab on the ground. 'This tomb has been opened recently. Very recently. There are fresh marks of tools around its edge.'

'Opened recently?' the abbot asked, as he looked at the priest. 'Who has been interred here?' he demanded.

'No one,' said Hermitage. 'But someone has come out.'

'Come out?'

'Haven't they?' Hermitage asked the priest, who did not seem inclined to answer.

'What has been going on?' The abbot was now at full authority. 'Who has been desecrating this place?'

'Your brother,' Hermitage said.

That stopped the abbot in mid-flow. 'My brother is dead,' he stated the fact.

'Is he?'

'Yes, of course, he is. I buried him.'

'You put him in the tomb, it appears. And if it had been in the churchyard then he would almost certainly be dead. All the earth on top would make escape impossible. But in the church, with a simple slab, it would be relatively easy to get out. Particularly if he had help.' He looked to the priest, who looked away.

'Dead men do not climb out of their tombs,' the abbot insisted, sounding as if he was losing patience, even with his beloved Brother Hermitage.

Cwen frowned at this. 'I thought rising from tombs was considered quite a good thing.'

'Only if you are the Son of God,' the abbot snapped back at her.

'Mortal man does not rise from the tomb,' Hermitage explained, more considerately. 'Apart from Lazarus, obviously, but that was our Lord's miracle. But if the mortal man isn't really dead in the first place?'

The abbot was clearly getting quite angry now. 'What do you want to do then? Open the family tomb and look at his dead body?'

'Why do you think the brother is alive, Hermitage?' Wat asked, holding his palms out to assuage the abbot's anger.

'So many things.' Hermitage counted them off. 'The tomb is one. It is the sort of thing someone could get out of if they wanted to. But that's only relevant if everything else fits.

'Second is the land. Of course, the Normans want land, that's understood, but they sent FitzGilbert to get it only after the abbot was dead. If they were behind it they'd have just turned up with swords, as usual. Even if it did belong to the church.

'Then there's FitzGilbert himself. Who killed him? Someone who wanted to make sure that he didn't get the land. Our mysterious monk who escaped from the monastery in the morning and who we are fairly sure is not a monk, judging from his behaviour.

'The letter from the bishop could well be false, so we need someone capable of producing a convincing work with parchment and quill, someone well educated, probably of good family. Finally, there were the attacks last night.'

'There weren't any attacks last night,' Cwen sounded completely lost.

'Exactly. The killer monk or not monk obviously did not want to attack the Bretons. They were an irrelevance. It was true that he just happened to be going in the same direction as them. This direction, to Preston.

'Then he didn't attack the nephews either, who actually hold the land. Why would someone who has just stabbed a Norman warrior in the chest not deal with two rather nervous and frightened young men? Because he's their father.'

'This is nonsense,' the abbot waved his arms about. 'Complete nonsense. I buried my brother, he is dead. Why on earth would he pretend to be dead when he isn't and why would he go to all this trouble?'

'Because he didn't want you to give the land away in the first place.' Wat nodded at Hermitage's explanation. 'You said that he was the only one capable of running the estates but you gave the land away to the monastery. And as you said yourself, you are impatient and contemptuous. I bet he never got a word in edgewise. Then you became abbot of the monastery that had the land. What an opportunity. With you dead, the land would come back to the family.'

'But he didn't want to actually kill you,' said Hermitage. 'He probably holds that a crime too far. Stabbing Normans is all well and fine.'

'Well, it is,' Cwen confirmed.

'But stabbing your own brother?'

'I buried him,' the abbot repeated. 'I don't bury people who aren't dead.'

'Did you see his body?' Hermitage asked.

'Well, no. I had word at the monastery that he had died and so I returned for the funeral.'

'Must have been several days before you got back then?'

'Probably two weeks.' The abbot looked thoughtful. 'We put his coffin in the tomb.'

'No telling if he was in it,' Cwen said. 'Or that he was actually dead inside. And it could have been the same empty one they used for you. If they bothered at all. I assume our priest here would have carried out your ceremony.'

'Quite probably,' the abbot snarled towards the priest.

'Tell me, who did word of your brother's death come from?' Hermitage asked.

The abbot's eyes narrowed and his head turned. 'Supposedly Father Kerk.' He pointed at the priest, who tried to shrink, which he was never going to be able to manage. 'But the quality of the writing was very poor, which I put down to great age and infirmity.'

'So it could have been another,' Hermitage struggled for the word - there must be one. 'A fabrication,' he came up with, triumphantly. 'A fabrication by a priest who stands to see his parish extended considerably if the monastery land comes back within his remit.'

'Hm. But why in heaven's name go to the bother of pretending to be dead?' This was clearly an idea beyond the abbot's imagination. 'If he wanted the land he should have simply said so.'

'Of course, he could be a bit mad as well,' Cwen suggested. 'There seems to be a bit of it in the family.'

'Faking your own death does seem a bit extreme,' Hermitage admitted.

'A bit extreme?' The abbot gawked at the understatement. 'It's more than a bit extreme, it's ridiculous. Why do it?'

'Because if he was dead he could vanish?' Hermitage suggested. 'No one would suspect a dead man of making up false stories of the abbot's death. The murder of FitzGilbert must have been an unexpected necessity, but being dead, he couldn't be accused of that either.'

'If your death was confirmed and the land went back to the brother, who's the first person the bishop or the Normans would come looking for?' Wat asked. 'Answer, the brother. As it is, the land would go to the nephews. Nephews who seem a bit, what can we say, distracted at the moment? I don't think they could organise a goose, let alone quill and parchment. No one is going to suspect them.'

'Which could also explain why the nephews think Judgement Day is coming and have locked themselves in the manor,' Cwen said. 'If you saw your father emerging from his own tomb, I think you'd hide under the bed as well. And our friend the priest probably helped their fears along a bit.'

The abbot at least gave all this careful thought. He also gave the priest some careful glares. 'Where is he then? If he is still alive, where is he? If it was him we followed with the Bretons, he must be here somewhere.'

Hermitage shrugged. 'In the tomb, I suspect.'

'What?' The abbot seemed to have run out of expressions of surprise. This was simply one too many. He looked like he really needed to sit down.

'I imagine that was what the light in the church was. The priest and your brother meeting up again and exchanging news. Come the daylight he returns to his tomb. If there's plenty of room down there he would avoid being seen. Even staying in the church he might be spotted by someone.'

'There are already two generations of dead bodies in there,' the abbot pointed out. 'Real ones. Who, in their right mind would spend time in a tomb?'

'I thought we'd decided he wasn't in his right mind,' Cwen commented.

'I expect he had a plan to begin with,' Wat said. 'When everything is sorted and the land has come back to the family, lo and behold he turns up again. Get the priest to deny he was ever dead in the first place. If a letter works to make people dead, I imagine they can be brought back to life again.'

The abbot considered everyone in the room. He left his eyes on each of them for an uncomfortable length of time. Even the priest received the gaze, but he was the one who looked away.

Reaching a decision he took a deep breath. 'Open the tomb,' he said.

Caput XXIII: Into The Tomb

'You can't do that,' the priest protested. 'It's blasphemy, it's sacrilege.' He tried to take a commanding stance. 'You will open that tomb over my dead body.'

'That'll be handy,' Cwen glanced from priest to tomb.

The abbot held him with his glare. 'We are not putting that man in my tomb,' he protested. 'Dead or alive.' He pierced the priest with a question. 'Are you telling me, are you swearing on the Holy name that you have not seen my brother?'

The priest squirmed a bit. 'Never,' he announced. 'As you well know, he was dead before I got here.'

'How long before you got here?' Wat asked, in a very suspicious voice. 'Exactly?'

'I don't know,' the priest flustered. 'I don't keep count of every day.'

'This Father Kerk was here when you buried your brother?' Wat asked the abbot.

'Just so. It was one of his last acts. I think the shock of seeing a young man he had known from a babe put in his grave was too much for him. He died very soon after.'

'And the very next day this one turns up,' he gestured at the priest.

'It wasn't the very next day,' the rotund fellow protested.

'I thought you weren't counting,' Cwen narrowed her eyes at the priest. 'I bet they've been planning this for a while,' she said. 'In fact, how do we know he's even a priest? After all, the monk isn't a monk.'

Hermitage directed them back to the practical question.

'There are clear marks that the tomb has been opened,'

Abbo moved over to the tomb and bent to look at the marks Hermitage pointed out. The edges of the slab forming the tomb, and of the flagstones around it, were gouged and chipped with the clear indications of a tool of some sort being forced into the gap.

'Maybe with this,' Cwen said.

They turned and saw that she was holding up a short metal bar, probably some part of a plough, but a strange thing to see in a church.

Hermitage beckoned that she should bring it over and, taking it from her hand, he fitted it neatly between two grooves, freshly carved in the ground.

The abbot gave a short nod and Hermitage pushed the bar into the crack between tomb and ground along its shortest side and pulled back on the top of the lever. Which immediately snapped back as it slipped from its purchase and hit the ground with a clang before bouncing up and very nearly having Hermitage's eye out.

'Oh, for goodness sake,' Wat said. 'Give it here.' He waved Cwen to join him and the two clerics stood back while a neatly dressed weaver and a slip of a girl used a heavy implement to prise open a tomb in a church floor.

They had much more success in getting a gap between tomb and floor and used the metal bar to wedge the tomb lid open by an inch or two.

'Come on Hermitage, you can manage this bit,' Wat called.

Hermitage joined him and Cwen stood back slightly as they got their fingers under the rim of the tomb lid and heaved. It didn't take much heaving at all as it did seem that the slab was used to being moved. They hoisted it open.

'Do you mind?' a voice called from below.

If Hermitage hadn't suspected for some time that there was someone down there, he would have jumped out of his skin.

'Brother?' The abbot boomed through the echoing church.

'Eek,' said the tomb. 'You're dead.'

'So you would have us believe. Come out here this instant.'

'No.'

'No?'

'I'm not coming out. You don't know it's me.'

The abbot looked very puzzled by this.

Hermitage touched his elbow. 'Perhaps Cwen's right. Spending too long in the family tomb when you're still alive is not good for the wits.'

'I can see where the nephews get it from,' Cwen mumbled.

'Do you want us to leave you there?'

'I've got an idea,' Cwen was bright and loud. 'We close the lid again and put something heavy on top, that way the dead stay where they're supposed to be.'

'And we could put the priest in there with him,' Wat added.

'I'm coming out,' the voice from the tomb shouted, quickly.

They waited, and a few moments later a pair of very pale and thin arms crawled over the edge of the tomb to be followed, even more slowly by a head in a very similar condition.

'Audley.' In one word the abbot expressed recognition, remorse, infuriation and a strong indication of forthcoming punishment.

'Abbo,' the body from the tomb replied as if they'd just met at a social gathering they didn't think the other was invited to.

'Remarkable,' the abbot shook his head. 'I still don't know

how Brother Hermitage did it, but he did.' He patted Hermitage on the shoulder. 'Through all of the trials and tribulations we have suffered, he saw the truth of it all. And that truth was hiding in my own tomb.'

Hermitage smiled at the praise, praise that was genuine and came from someone he respected. He nodded a humble acknowledgement of his meagre efforts.

Brother Audley, on the other hand, was giving him a very hard look. Coming from a man who stuck knives in people while they were asleep this was a lot less comforting.

'Audley, what have you done?' The abbot shook his head in sadness.

'Tried to restore the family to its rightful state,' Audley bit back. 'Get back what was ours before someone decided to give it all away.' It was clear who the someone was.

'Instead of leaving it so that the whole lot could simply be taken by Tostig, or Harold, or William?'

'Swearing fealty's not in your nature is it?' Audley complained. 'Someone with lots of men and weapons comes along? You swear fealty. Pay tithes, do whatever they want. The Godwinsons were changing sides like a man in a bed full of fleas, we could do the same.'

'It's not right.'

'Right! There you go, always doing what's right instead of what's necessary.'

'Stabbing a Norman?' The abbot shouted. 'Murdering a man while he rested in a monastery. Is that what's necessary?'

'Could be,' Audley didn't sound quite so sure about this one.

'What on earth possessed you to do that?' The abbot was back to his full impatient and contemptuous self. 'Making up my death, frightening the boys, I can understand that.' He paused for a moment. 'No, I can't. But it's a whole different world to go round actually stabbing people in their beds.'

'He believed you were dead,' Audley complained.

'I'm not surprised,' the abbot shouted. 'You're the one who's been telling everyone that I was.'

'Yes,' Audley argued back. 'But the Normans weren't supposed to believe it.'

'Perhaps you should have made that clear in the letter?' The abbot was reaching peaks of volume now. 'Dear everyone, except the Normans, Abbot Abbo is dead so please can we have our land back?'

'How was I to know they'd think you were dead and that they could come and take the land?'

'Common sense?' Abbo suggested. 'After all, you're the one who claims to know how to deal with kings and lords.'

'He just turned up. What else was I supposed to do?'

'What else were you supposed to do?' The abbot now added incredulity to his vocal range. 'Not stab someone in their bed would be a good start.'

'How did you know the Norman was coming anyway?' Cwen asked.

'More the boatman told me.' Audley seemed pleased to talk to someone else for a change.

'Ha,' Wat said as if this explained everything. 'The man who will do anything for money and who brought the letter in the first place.'

'He's been keeping an eye on the monastery for me. Making sure things were going to plan.'

'I wouldn't trust to More to stand the right way up in a puddle.'

Audley ignored him. 'And when he sent word that the abbot had reappeared, I knew I had to act.'

'Bribing a boatman, making up a letter from a bishop, murdering a Norman?' the abbot was aghast. 'I don't know which sin is worst.'

'The bribery, probably,' Cwen shrugged.

'And who did you think was going to replace me? You wrote that another abbot would be along. Was that going to be you as well?'

'Of course not,' Audley protested at this ridiculous suggestion. 'Can't understand anyone who actually wants to be an abbot at all. They'd have got along fine without one and after a few months they'd sort themselves out.'

'Sort themselves out?'

'Of course. Didn't want a new abbot appointed straight away. He'd get the land. I hinted that maybe Godric the prior could do it. He seemed quite keen.'

The abbot growled at this. 'But then I turned up again. Perhaps you were going to really kill me this time?'

'I wouldn't do that.'

'So why didn't you just give up?'

'Because things were going so well.'

'Going so well!?' Abbo was truly outraged at this. 'If you think this is things going well, I dread to think what a disaster would look like. Have you seen the state of your sons? I assume that they stumbled upon you rising from the grave?'

'Might have been in church at the wrong moment,' Audley admitted, although he made it sound as if it was the nephews' fault.

'I have no idea where we are going to even start putting all this right,' Abbo complained. 'And goodness knows what's going to happen when the Normans find out about FitzGilbert.'

Audley did look a bit shamefaced about this, which was

decent of him.

'First of all, we need to get your boys to open the house. Convincing them that Judgement Day is not upon us is going to be tricky.' He pointed once more at the priest. 'I think we need you to come and make confession. Probably to the whole town. Both of you.'

Audley and the priest exchanged looks. Pretty hopeless and resigned ones.

Hermitage was looking on with interest as Abbo took charge and gazed upon a subjugated priest and brother when he felt a tug on his sleeve. He looked around to see Wat pulling at him and nodding his head towards the door, where Cwen was already heading. The door that she held open, indicating that this was a way out of any more trouble.

Completely ignored by the arguing brothers, Hermitage, Wat and Cwen gathered in the doorway.

'Best leave them to it, I think,' Wat said, quietly.

'Not our problem anymore. If it ever was,' Cwen grumbled.

'I can't just sneak out,' Hermitage protested. 'I must make my goodbyes properly. There may be some other assistance I can render to the abbot.'

'You stay and render then.' Cwen said. 'We'll be off, and you can catch up.'

'It's terribly rude.' Hermitage really did not want to leave the abbot at all. He now saw that life back in the monastery, in any monastery, was really not for him. That was always assuming that the abbot would go back there anyway and not return to his family estates, just to make sure the right thing was done.

He did persuade himself that this spell with the abbot had been marvellous, but a longer stay might see a lot of the marvel wear off. Life at Kilnsea had had its moments, but it had had a lot of other moments as well, ones best forgotten completely. And if the abbot stayed here, he could see there was very little help he could be.

At least he knew where the abbot was and they could maintain correspondence.

'Tell him you've been called away on another investigation.'

'FitzGilbert?' Cwen suggested, which gave Hermitage the shivers.

'I don't think anyone cares he's dead,' Wat saw the look of sad disappointment on Hermitage's face and relaxed. 'Just say a quick goodbye then. Quick I mean.'

Wat and Cwen waited while Hermitage scuttled back to the abbot, who was now engaged in a heated discussion about which pasture only had Lammas rights.

'I'll, erm, I'll be off then?' he said to the arguing brothers.

'What?' the abbot barked. 'Oh, sorry Hermitage, yes, yes, right.'

'Nothing else I can help with?' Hermitage asked, disappointed at being dismissed so lightly.

'You've helped quite enough,' Audley complained.

'At least he found you out,' the abbot piled in.

Hermitage spoke before they could start again. 'It was nice to do an investigation where there are more people alive at the end than there were at the beginning. Makes a change.'

'One dead Norman,' the abbot pointed out.

'But you and your brother are alive again.'

'Yes,' the abbot growled towards Audley. 'We are, aren't we. Sorry Hermitage,' he ignored his brother and turned to his Brother. He took Hermitage by the shoulders and gave him a broad smile. 'Whatever the outcome, you have solved the problem I brought to you, and in a quite remarkable way. You have done well young Hermitage and I am sure will continue to do so.' He released the shoulders and gave Hermitage a hearty hug.

'Go well, Brother Hermitage, and remember,' he glanced over to Wat and Cwen by the door. 'You are a hermit among heathens. It's a unique role, but one entirely suited to you, I think.'

'Thank you, Father,' Hermitage nodded and closed his eyes to hold back a small tear that was forming. He turned to the door and waved back before he got there.

'Don't be a stranger,' the abbot called after him.

'Absolutely,' Audley endorsed the sentiment, loudly. 'But if you're not going to be a stranger, for God's sake do it somewhere else.'

Finis

Printed in Great Britain
by Amazon